Praise for *American Studies*

"This engrossing novel encompasses more than half a century of gay life in America, focusing on the sometimes brutal and uneasy compromises gay men are often forced to make with the heterosexual world."

—Jameson Currier, *The Washington Post*

"A funny, moving, and beautifully written novel, but most important, it is a brave book. Merlis dares to celebrate those who are often dismissed as the poor, benighted queens of the fifties, many of whom ended up destroyed in the McCarthy witch-hunts. Merlis reminds us of the dignity which surrounded their silence, of the bravery that accompanied their self-control, and the humor that made it possible to survive. *American Studies* is a novel to remember because it dares us not to forget."

—David Bergman, editor, *Men on Men 5*

"Merlis's portrayal of the bureaucratic and psychosexual brutalities which are such a familiar part of gay experience . . . makes this a crucial piece of art, the paragon of politically meaningful writing. . . . The power of this novel is in Merlis's writerly skill (his fiercely perfect timing, his flawless, always-believable diction), in his comprehension of American cultural history, and ultimately in his human wisdom. . . . With this novel, gay literature enters maturity."

—Christopher Davis, *The James White Review*

"I was dazzled and deeply moved by *American Studies*. A wickedly brilliant portrayal of life in the closet that gays were forced to live before Stonewall. It is the most persuasive argument for gay liberation I have ever read."

—Edward Field, author of *A Full Heart*

"*American Studies*, a moving and finely crafted first novel, offers a unique perspective on the horrors of the McCarthy years and reads like a cautionary signpost in the current landscape of American social politics. . . . A work of discreet, almost gracious, anger. *American Studies* is not a polemic, but it most certainly is an unforgettable reminder that an American's civil rights cannot and must not depend on the tolerance of any other citizen."
—Hadley Hury, *Memphis Flyer*

"An intelligent, compassionate, and moving novel"
—Dale Peck, author of *Martin and John*

"A riveting new voice. That voice takes bits of human spirit and holds them under the light like pieces of fabric."
—Diane Scharper, *The Baltimore Sun*

"I was surprised over and over by the turns that Merlis's seasoned voice accomplishes in this wise, sexy, funny, level novel that finally takes on as its ambitious subject the Civil War between gay men and straight men in America."
—Brad Gooch, author of *City Poet*

PENGUIN BOOKS

AMERICAN STUDIES

Mark Merlis grew up in Baltimore and attended Wesleyan and Brown universities. He currently lives in New Jersey and works at the Library of Congress.

AMERICAN STUDIES

MARK MERLIS

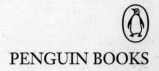

PENGUIN BOOKS

PENGUIN BOOKS
Published by the Penguin Group
Penguin Books USA Inc., 375 Hudson Street,
New York, New York 10014, U.S.A.
Penguin Books Ltd, 27 Wrights Lane, London W8 5TZ, England
Penguin Books Australia Ltd, Ringwood, Victoria, Australia
Penguin Books Canada Ltd, 10 Alcorn Avenue,
Toronto, Ontario, Canada M4V 3B2
Penguin Books (N.Z.) Ltd, 182–190 Wairau Road, Auckland 10, New Zealand

Penguin Books Ltd, Registered Offices: Harmondsworth, Middlesex, England

First published in the United States of America
by Houghton Mifflin Company, 1994
Reprinted by arrangement with Houghton Mifflin Company
Published in Penguin Books 1996

10 9 8 7 6 5 4 3 2

THE LIBRARY OF CONGRESS HAS CATALOGUED THE HARDCOVER AS FOLLOWS:
Merlis, Mark.
American studies/Mark Merlis.
p. cm.
ISBN 0-395-68992-9 (hc.)
ISBN 0 14 02.5090 5 (pbk.)
1. Gay men—United States—Fiction.   2. Anti-communist movements—United
States—Fiction.   3. College teachers—United States—Fiction.   I. Title.
PS3563.E7422A47   1994
813'.54—dc20   94–6593

Printed in the United States of America
Set in Janson Text
Designed by Melodie Wertelet

For Bob,
for Hastings,
and for Bob and Suzy

Only that historian will have the gift of fanning the spark of hope in the past who is firmly convinced that *even the dead* will not be safe from the enemy if he wins.

— WALTER BENJAMIN

AMERICAN STUDIES

ONE

THE BOY IN THE NEXT BED lies sprawled atop the sheets, his gown riding up on his heroic thighs, an inch or so short of indecency. I would stare, but he is on my blind side and it hurts a little to turn my head. They have tapped me like a sugar maple: a vial taped to my forehead, over the bandaged eye, is collecting some fluid I apparently don't require. Sap, sapience. When my head is empty it will cease to ache.

I don't have my glasses, anyway. Howard's supposed to bring them, if he ever shows up. So the boy is more a presence than a body, a concept whose details I am left to sketch in. I draw his contours from the memory of all boys. Merely to know he is there fills me with excitement and shame. I could be in study hall, eyes locked on my geometry text, while to either side boys glow like suns I must not look upon. I long to touch myself. What would he think? He must want to also.

He may lose his thumb. It is bandaged to the size of a baseball, like that of a do-it-yourselfer in the comics, and he spends much of the day just looking at it, cradling it mournfully in his intact hand. He tried to tell me his story, last night or this morning, a complex tale of confusion and malpractice, but he lost his way. After a while he went back to the television, which he controls, having got here first. I didn't attempt to tell my story in return. Just an especially unrewarding encounter with rough trade. While the tale is not without its entertaining features — I was quite the raconteur in the ER — it might alarm the child. He might be a little less free about baring his upper thigh.

Oh, as if he couldn't tell what I am, anyway. But maybe he can't. What with the tubes and the bandages, my flame is shaded if not extinguished.

It is Thursday morning. We are watching cartoons, though I can scarcely make them out. The boy says, audibly, "Uh-oh," as an audacious mouse skirts peril. His muscles dance as he laughs at a feline pratfall. Born in another time, he might have watched Falstaff with equal pleasure; the groundlings were no finer than he. Instead we have offered him, by way of drama, Tom and Jerry. The tendrils of his soul curve toward the blue light, knowing no other. My tendrils would curve toward him, but for the damn tubes.

Howard comes in, carrying a shopping bag. He is wearing a tight, thin sweater that shows off his maidenly bosom, and slacks that might have fit him twenty years ago. He looks like a sausage about to burst its casing. He is also — I know this thought is ignoble — so plainly a member of the sisterhood that I fear he has blown my cover. I glance at my roommate, but he pretends to be watching television.

Howard, meanwhile, fails to suppress a shudder at the way I look: I am a visible exemplar of the price of indiscretion, and compared to Howard I am choosy.

The boy gets up to go to the bathroom, but he has put his robe on before getting out of bed, a novel precaution that suggests he has not failed to draw his conclusions about Howard.

"Mercy," Howard says. "Nicest thing I've seen in a gown since —"

"He'll hear you."

"What if he does? I've never understood why straight boys couldn't handle a little innocent adoration. As if looks could rape."

He takes advantage of the boy's absence by giving me a peck on the top of my head, the least repulsive part of me just now.

"You'd think they'd like a bit of attention," he goes on. "The only way I get attention any more is by waving money."

"That's what I did. I could have done without the attention."

"Poor dear, you must tell me all about it."

"What's there to tell? Except I thought I was going to die."

"But you didn't," he says, summing up so I'll skip the details. Now he feels that he must kiss me on the top of my head again, to indicate that the outcome is satisfactory. "Are you — did they tell you if you're going to be able to see out of that eye?"

"They're pretty sure, yeah. I can't even see out of the good one now. Did you bring my glasses?"

"Oh." He fishes in the shopping bag, brings them forth. The horn-rimmed ones that make me look like a senescent schoolboy. I try to put them on, but they won't fit over the bandage. "Oh," he says again. "You'll just have to wait."

"I can't wait. I can't read or anything. I can't even watch TV."

"Well, what can we do? We could break them in half, I suppose. I mean, you could hold half over your good eye."

"Yes, do that."

"But you'll ruin them."

"I'm going to be here for days. I can't stay like this."

"All right." He gives them a timid jerk, as if he thought they would just snap like a pretzel. They do not. He tries twisting them from various angles; he sticks out his tongue.

The boy comes out of the bathroom and looks on. Howard says to him, "We're trying to break these glasses in half. So he can get half of them on." He holds them out to the boy; the boy raises the hand with the bandaged thumb, to show he can't help. He sits on the edge of his bed and watches as Howard goes on ineffectually toying with the frame.

Howard looks to be embarking on a classic snit. Any second now and he'll put the glasses down and stomp on them. "Just forget it," I say. "It's only a few days."

The boy gets up, goes to the wardrobe, and fetches from his duffel bag a Bic lighter. He lights it with his good hand and gestures to Howard to hold the glasses to it.

"Aren't you the cleverest thing," Howard says. They huddle together over the lighter as Howard holds the nose-piece to the flame. It takes a very long time before it begins to soften, but soften it does. Howard keeps his eyes fixed on their little project. He doesn't dare look up at the boy, any more than I would. Now he is bending the frame back and forth at the nosepiece, as one bends a coat hanger; now it is broken. And with it the working intimacy of Howard and the boy: the boy pulls back sharply, as if recoiling from Howard once the job is done.

Howard brings me the glasses and rummages some more in his shopping bag. "Now that you've destroyed a two-hundred-dollar pair of bifocals, I guess you'll want to read something."

"God, yes, I'm bored out of my mind. What did you bring?" I peer through my spectacles — spectacle — hold-ing it up like a dandy's lorgnon. I can see, among other things, the boy much better now. Howard hands me a couple of books. Heavy ones, too big to read in bed. "*Daniel Deronda*, for God's sake? And what's this?" Tom's book. *The Invincible City*. He's brought me Tom's book.

"I'm sorry, I just picked the first ones that caught my eye. I couldn't stay there very long."

"What do you mean, they wouldn't let you?"

"I couldn't — it doesn't look good."

"You mean, to be seen there?"

"The apartment doesn't look good."

"The apartment?"

He nods. An odd time to bring up my deficiencies as a decorator. It takes me a moment to realize that he is talking about my blood.

"I've always meant to read *Daniel Deronda*," he says.

"Here, borrow mine."

"What will you do? Can you read the other one?"

"I've never been able to read the other one."

"Well, I'll try to find something down in the gift shop. What would you like, couple of Harlequin romances and a *Muscle and Fitness*?"

"Shh."

"You going to need anything else?"

"Clothes, at some point. In case they ever let me out of here."

"What happened to yours? Oh." He pictures, probably, more blood: Jackie's pink suit.

"They cut them off me. Snip. And toiletries and things, I need all that kind of stuff. Can you stand going back to my place?"

"I suppose. Maybe I should try to get someone in to clean. You know, on top of everything else, the police dusted the place for fingerprints. There's this black greasy powder everywhere." He folds up his shopping bag and picks up his coat. "I called your office for you."

"Oh, you did, good." Then I'm a bit alarmed, reticence not being one of Howard's virtues. "What did you tell them?"

"I didn't know what to tell them. I just said you'd been hurt and you were in the hospital."

"Did you tell them which hospital?"

"I kind of had to. I mean, it would have sounded funny."

"But you didn't tell them anything about my . . . how I got hurt."

"Well, I thought of just making something up, but then I was afraid they'd get in touch with you before I could fill you in."

"I hope you told them I was in a coma and couldn't have any visitors."

"Well, to be honest, they didn't sound like they were rushing out to get flowers or anything. They didn't even ask for your room number. Just when you might be back. Oh, and whether you wanted the time charged to sick or annual. They said you had a lot of use-or-lose hours and you might want to just charge it to the annual."

"That's very considerate of them. Anyway, I guess I have some time to figure out what . . . how to characterize my little incident."

"Don't get fancy, now. Sometimes your stories just get too elaborate."

"I don't make up stories." I lower my voice: "There wasn't anything in the papers, you didn't see anything?"

"Uh-uh, I checked. I always look for my friends in the papers."

"I know what page, too."

"Well, that's where we show up these days. You can always tell one of us: survived by a sister and three nieces. Anyway, you weren't there."

* * *

6

In the ER, a cop went over the story with me again. "You never saw this guy before?"

"No."

"You just . . . met him in this bar." The phrase charged with meaning but without apparent reproach. Mine was not a fresh story.

"Yeah."

"You think — I mean, you must have got a good look at him — you think you could identify him? I mean a picture, maybe he's got a prior, maybe he's in one of the books."

"I'm not sure. I had my glasses off most of the time." And, he must have imagined, everything else.

"Could you come in and just try, look at a few of the books, for me? You know, this same guy is going to go do this to other people."

"Okay," I said. He nodded, perhaps believing me, and went on filling out his report form. After a while I said, "You think this is going to be in the papers?"

"Huh?"

"I'm worried about . . . do you people give this kind of story to the papers?"

"Oh, jeez, no. You're not dead, right? They don't put things like this in the papers." He looked up from his form. "You don't need to worry about that, mister. This happens every day."

It's funny, I guess, that I could have moved so quickly from fearing for my life back to my usual fear, that my life will be uncovered. A senseless worry: I am so poorly camouflaged it would scarcely matter if it went right on the front page: REEVE ASSAULTED BY HOMOSEXUAL PICK-UP. Heaven knows they wouldn't fire me, though I suppose the biddies in the office — the optimistic ones who think I'm still eligible, if a mite over the hill — would be a little let down. So what is it I want to hide, if not my predilection?

7

The scene itself, I think. I just don't want anyone picturing the actual scene.

I remember reading about poor Walter, last year, when they found him trussed and naked on his bed. He'd been strangled. My grief, such as it was (I hadn't talked to Walter in years), was quite overwhelmed by the vision of him on his bed, like a huge, pale fish, eyes bulging. I let the paper drop and tried to imagine how he felt, those last minutes. What it was like to be in someone's power, wondering what he might do next. Now I know: it is just like wondering if it's going to rain. Your room becomes the world ever so quickly, and your assailant a thunderhead that will or will not burst and over which you have no control, no more than over the weather.

After Howard goes, I spend some time discreetly ogling the boy through my new appliance. He loses nothing from greater specificity. Tom's book is still in my hand. Finally I let myself look at the back of the dust jacket.

The photo is badly reproduced, but still plain enough: the formal portrait Tom sat for when *The Invincible City* came out. There's one spot on the picture that has obviously been retouched. But what lay beneath this little patch of clumsy airbrushing I cannot guess. I remember no blemish there. This photograph replaces memory. Whenever I look at it, I think that Tom was somehow marked. That I was the only one who never noticed. The real face I don't remember at all, obliterated for me by the sight of the smashed pumpkin head in the morgue.

He looks like a general. The book came out in 1949, so he is fifty-five in this picture, but barely touched with gray. The hair is close-cut and stiff, and the eyes with their long lashes are the eyes of a general, soft and overcoming softness. His effeminacy, like MacArthur's or Eisenhower's, is just below the surface, a secret he defies you to uncover.

Between this martial picture and the hard, cadenced prose, a young reader (if anyone still reads him) must get the idea that Tom was a model of manliness and reason. The sort of chap who could order the bombing of Dresden or who could inspect the line of English poets as if reviewing his troops.

I wonder sometimes if Tom's enemies didn't hit him all the harder — harder than the times demanded — because they felt deceived, because under that manly surface was something entirely different. Something that could also, by definition, have resided under their even less persuasive masculine armor. And I wonder, too, if he caved in so quickly because he had no strength beneath that shell, strong as he had always seemed to me. Once they found their way in, he was as defenseless as a tortoise in dishabille.

Those of us who walk about unarmored, who have no camouflage, are tougher, maybe. Here I am, after all, having flitted my way through the terror that took Tom away, having swished through every subsequent pogrom, straight through to the other night. I look around, and the people who are still standing, who haven't yet shown up on that page in the papers we all turn to first, are the ones like Howard and me, who never fooled anybody. It is little enough to crow about, just making it to sixty-two. But I think it is better to be alive than dead.

Lunch comes. Salisbury steak, they must call it, with a little globe of instant whipped potato and some nameless leaves in a green puddle. No gravy, no salt. But there is white bread and some imperfectly congealed butterscotch pudding. I feel like a child, picking my way through a meal remarkably like my mother's cooking so I can get to dessert. This morning they wanted me to check off my meals for tomorrow, but without my bifocals I couldn't make out my unappetizing options. I told the lady just to check anything, so long as she would never, never again bring me the scrambled eggs I had for breakfast.

The boy sits up, at the edge of the bed, to eat. He is facing away from me, toward the window. The ties of his gown have come loose, leaving only gossamer white wings of cotton at his shoulders, exposing nearly all of his back, which is of transcendent beauty. As he eats, the muscles are stirred to great turbulences; they are complicated and shimmering as water coursing over rapids. When he is still, they cast their warm shadows in a pattern like a cloak of golden feathers.

Apart from his thumb, there isn't anything wrong with him. He is here while they make up their mind what to do about it. Here for observation, as they say, which means a bunch of doctors and doctorlings passing through at dawn and then, probably, nothing else till the next day. I am making up for their negligence, observing him assiduously as I try to swallow bits of my meat patty.

His great perfect back doesn't belong here. It is useless here, he might as well be baggy old me, in this democracy of the sick-in-bed. I know he is here for just a little while, but it seems, looking at him, as though he is trapped for good, wings not thumb clipped, stranded here until every one of the muscles he carries with such casual entitlement atrophies and he is just another old carcass. Like me, a step away from the autopsy table.

The doctors said Tom didn't feel a thing. But doctors always say that. As far as they're concerned, anyone who doesn't spend his final weeks in intensive care, undergoing torture and running up bills, dies instantaneously. I am sure it was quick enough. I had to go and look at him, identify that blasted head as his. There was so little of him there, I might have been a paleontologist, conjuring up an ancestor from a jawbone and a toe. No, he didn't have time for lengthy ruminations.

Still, when I consider the millions of thoughts — *an appointment tomorrow, what is this guy's name again, where the hell are my glasses* — that used to fly through my head in the instant before climax, the volumes I thought at the moment when the boy first struck me the other night, how can I suppose that Tom thought nothing at all? No matter how fast he went?

I have pondered this so many times, these forty years. It is almost a parlor game for me, something I mull over on long train rides or when I wait in line at the bank machine. I believe I have it nearly worked out.

Tom pulls the trigger, the muzzle of the gun in his mouth. The bullet passes through the brain, which feels nothing, then exits through the superficial nerves of the scalp. The impulses from the scalp, and maybe from the roof of his mouth, are traveling down to the spinal cord and back up again, while at the same moment the bullet is throwing great globs of gray matter out onto the floor. I don't know which travel faster, nerve impulses or bullets. But with these distances there's no point comparing, everything is virtually simultaneous. Even as his skull explodes, the message is coming back up his spinal cord: "Hey, something just made a big hole in the top of your head!"

I imagine — perhaps I'm wrong — I imagine the parts of his brain that weren't hit directly go on working for a few moments. So it seems to me there are two possibilities, depending on which part of the brain is intact and which part is mussing up the bare floor of that last apartment where he didn't stay long enough to unroll the rug.

The first possibility is that the part that feels pain is gone. The messages from the nerves find no one at home. And the part that's left, the part that decided to pull the trigger, is saying, "Lord, I know I pulled that trigger. Why am I not feeling anything?"

The converse possibility is that the part that decided to pull the trigger is out on the floor. That part is Tom, his will and being and memory. What is left behind is a chaotic congregation of motor and sensory centers, with no Tom to call them all to order. The messages from the nerves are duly received and logged in. Two messages from the roof of the mouth and the scalp, entry and exit, nothing in between. Elsewhere, the sound of the gun is registered. The optic nerves file their report: everything is red. The inner ears sound the alarm that he is falling, confident that he will correct the problem.

Some kernel of consciousness, not Tom any more but Everyman, manages in the last moments to piece all these messages together. Something went in one side and out the other. It checks its hypothesis with whatever other parts of the brain are still functioning, and they come up with a consensus. Someone has shot us. God in Heaven, who has done this to us?

There came a point, the other night, when I was persuaded that the boy was going to kill me. No, I wasn't sure, I thought he probably would or, more precisely, *might very well*. Might very well.

I wasn't ready, exactly. I didn't want him to, I was not content that he should do it. But I was not resisting it. I was kneeling on the floor, naked and bleeding, my wrists bound, as he stormed around the apartment with the carving knife, demanding to know where I had hidden the cash. I was not resisting. Oh, I am sure some part of me would have tried to fend him off if he had actually stood before me and raised his hand for the coup. I don't mean that the animal in me had given up. But I, *ego*, had withdrawn to the heights, watching with an interest only lightly tinged with melancholy, and even that giving way to an abashed near-eagerness: so this is it.

We could have been anywhere. My room had disappeared, and it was just the two of us. As in Homer the battle recedes from view and you are left with two men acting out their moira in the dust. They may still wear their epithets like heraldic bearings: bureaucrat-Reeve, hundred-dollar-trade. But under that useless armor of names they are just bodies. They complete their episode, and the winner strips the loser and drags him around in the dust, as if a dead body could be humiliated. So I was strangely calm, just a body.

He went out into the living room, banging around, upsetting books and opening drawers. I was shivering. The window behind me was open, I never felt anything so cold as the draft from that window. I wanted it to be over so I wouldn't be cold any more. After a while it was quiet, no sound but the breeze stirring the blinds behind me. I never actually heard the door close. After some time I just sensed that he could no longer be there. I crept forth into the hall like a child who has been sent to his room and wants to know if the punishment is over.

It was over. I didn't feel that at once. When I went into the bathroom for my clothes and saw what he had done to my face, I thought the worst was ahead. That the worst would be riding the elevator down to the lobby and having to show my face to the woman behind the front desk. I didn't know how badly I was hurt. I thought I would have to get her to call a cab, and then I'd have to sit in the lobby while she stared at me — knowing what had happened, she had seen us come in, probably watched us on her closed-circuit monitor as we rode up in the elevator. I thought the punishment was ahead, having to sit there and become a story for her to tell.

I think it is better to be alive than dead. But my tormentor lingered only a few minutes in the living room before departing. I felt for only a few minutes that I had lost my name and become just a body to be discovered in the morning. And even in those minutes I was nearly ready for it. If I had lived as Tom did, so many months being stripped of his titles and his armor, just a body, I might eventually have said, Hurry, finish it.

My roommate has a visitor. His girlfriend, evidently, sitting by his bed. I don't know when she came in. I've just been staring at Tom's book. My spectacle has slipped onto the covers. I pick it up to look at her. I think she was here last night, but I was still groggy from the surgery and anyway I didn't have my glasses then. She is a tiny and rather plump redhead, her hair very long and straight, as from the sixties. Her dress seems to be from the same era, very short, but more austere than provocative. Perhaps this is all in fashion again. I don't spend much time scrutinizing hemlines.

She is aware of my inspection. "Hi, hon," she says. "You got an eye on me, huh?"

"Just one."

She laughs, but grows serious at once. "Yeah, what's with the other one? Is it going to be okay?"

"They say it's fine. It's the socket that got hurt."

"Jeez, how'd that happen?"

The moment of truth. I really meant to think it through this morning, before I got all wrapped up in Tom. Now I have nothing worked out. "I got mugged," I say.

"Wow, that's awful."

The boy looks over quizzically. Has he heard something

to the contrary? Did I say anything to Howard, or have the nurses been talking? The expression fades and he turns back toward his girl.

She goes on talking to me, though. "This one's here for his thumb. Well, you can see that. But they had him here a whole week. They come in and unwrap it and then they wrap it up again and that's all."

"Uh-huh," I say.

"You know what this costs, just so he can lie around here? This kind of money, we could have a suite someplace, with champagne and stuff."

"Well, I hope you can afford it."

She laughs again, a laugh of all-embracing good nature. "Don't look at me," she says. "I don't got to worry about his bills. Not for a while yet." So they must be engaged, or in one of those semiengaged states children have concocted these days.

"But it must be thousands," I say. The boy is wide-eyed. I entertain, just for an instant, the ludicrous notion of helping with his bill and winning his heart. We go to recuperate together in a suite someplace, with champagne and stuff. We watch television. I teach him to talk.

"Oh, it's no problem. He'll get workers' comp. It's just such a waste." What a practical girl: he will do well to stick with her. Someone had better mind him. "Anyway, they're going to decide tomorrow, one way or another." This is said so lightly as to seem almost cruel. The boy shrugs, trying to act stoical for her. She gets up from the visitor's chair and sits on the edge of his bed. She strokes the back of his neck. He accepts this with no expression. "If they're not going to do anything, we can go home." Then she whispers something to him, and he smirks.

I am stung with jealousy. No, it isn't a sting any more, not the way it would have been when I was younger. Just a little empty feeling. When I was a kid, I was continually tormented by the happiness of others. Back in my rooms at college I would hear, beneath my window, a car door slamming and a burst of talk and laughter. Or I would see a couple — any permutation — walking down the street and exchanging their tiresome secret smiles. And, until not very long ago, I would say, Why not me? Why am I alone left out? Even when everything was going fine.

I could be on a streetcar on a spring evening, on the very day of getting a promotion at work, headed for a celebration dinner with a fresh lover. Then I would glance at the man standing next to me and — maybe just because he was handsome — imagine I could smell his contentment wafting over at me. Picture the finer dinner and more charming lover he was headed for. Only now, when for me the summit of happiness is an effortless emptying of my bladder, am I able to tolerate — almost to be thankful for — the sights and sounds and smells that betoken the existence of happiness in the world. Thankful but a little empty feeling.

She turns back to me with a sudden look of concern. "You getting workers' comp, too?"

"No, I —" I am about to remind her that mine wasn't an on-the-job injury when I realize that she's only worried about my bill. "I can handle it."

"Oh, you got money. That's okay. Some day we'll have money, if I can get this one out of here."

She gives this one a quick kiss and jumps up. "I gotta get moving. Oh, my name's Janice," she says to me. "I hope your socket gets better."

"Me too."

She is scarcely out of the room when the boy turns up the volume on the TV.

* . * . *

He couldn't believe there wasn't any money. I was on my knees, with the belt tight around my wrists, he had every drawer in the bedroom open and now he was coming back from the kitchen with a knife and he was going to have to kill me if I wouldn't tell him where all the money was.

Where had he been all his life? As blood dripped from my head onto my bound hands and I averted my one eye from the carving knife that was starting to look like my future, I tried to explain the world where people keep their money in banks and use little plastic cards to take it out, a bit at a time. There was the hundred he was supposed to get and maybe another twenty or so in my wallet and that was it.

No, bullshit, this apartment, my fancy watch and all, I had to have money around someplace.

I was going to die over a silly cultural misunderstanding. I begged him to take anything he saw before him. Jesus, if I felt better I'd help him cart it away, but what he saw was all he was going to get.

It's easy enough to guess, now, that he probably believed me already. He hadn't just landed here, like some captured aboriginal escaping from the anthro lab and wandering baffled through the big city. He knew about bank cards. He was just keeping it up to make sure, to be certain I wasn't the kind of eccentric who actually did keep money around the house. Or maybe it didn't matter if he believed me or not: maybe he understood his miscalculation, and was mad enough to kill me just for all the wasted effort. Coming all the way to my apartment, too late now to score again, and getting only the contractual amount. When he stalked out into the living room, leaving me there on the floor blubbering, maybe he had to master himself, maybe he just had to stop looking at the pathetic red and white blob I had become to keep himself from finishing me off out of simple disgust.

These alternatives appear in hindsight. At the time, all I could think was that I had to make him understand. It was a scene from one of those movies in which the hero, armed only with the implausible truth, dashes himself hopelessly against a wall of disbelief. Don't you see, the pods; or there aren't really witches. I don't have any money.

I was rich for three weeks in 1952. Tom, provident fellow, left a will. Not an agitated testament of his last days, but a clean humdrum legal instrument, written some years before his death. He endowed a fellowship, named for his father. Odd joke — an arrow shot at a dead target by a dead archer. The stipend was specified, stupidly; what might have supported a frugal student for a year in the fifties wouldn't cover his recreational drugs today. Students probably get more excited about a good night at poker than about winning the Slater.

There were some other gifts: to the maid who left him when he was thrown out of Winthrop House, to various good causes, many of them on the attorney general's list. And the remainder, including the entire income from his trust: the residual estate, as they call it, he left to me.

To me, of all people. Well, I can guess his reasons. He didn't want to leave it to his family, of course. And he couldn't give it all to charity; that would have been to declare that he had passed a whole life without ever making a human connection. So he just picked the first name that came to mind. My name. He might have picked more carefully if he had had some tangible property. But a trust is such an airy thing. He bequeathed it as casually as a monarch gives away a million acres in a New World he has never laid eyes on.

In his last weeks we had stopped speaking. He could have revised the will, must even have considered doing so — it was left in plain sight on the desk in his new apartment, not filed away with everything else in his cage of unopened cartons. He had laid hands on it, had sat down and looked at it. And he had, to the last, stuck with me.

I enjoyed, then, in those slow August weeks after his death, the usual consolations of the executor. These are twofold: first, you have a great deal to do and, second, you get to paw through the decedent's private papers. One of the reasons I have never seriously thought of doing myself in — not even on the day when I realized that my looks were irrevocably gone and I was damned to permanent toadhood — is that I cannot bear the idea of someone rummaging through my droppings as I did through Tom's.

Well! I fairly moved in with him, night after night in his last sad digs on Marsden Street. There were a million things to read. Prep school literary magazines, with Tom's deeply closeted love poems, manner of Housman. Letters from Pauline, his abandoned fiancée, with the breathless dashes modern maidens have learned how to fill in. And letters, sealed and never mailed, from Tom to his boys — letters as coy and full of dashes as Pauline's. There must have been other letters he actually got up the nerve to send, for there was an entire carton of replies. Brief, adequately cordial notes, stolidly declining to notice Tom's dashes or get his hints. How industriously Tom cultivated those Dink Stovers and Frank Merriwells, for so little return.

More. All the manuscripts, of course. The scholarly work, most of which I'd seen. Short stories, which I hadn't seen: manly tales of fishing and the like, destined for the *Saturday Evening Post*. Could he actually have printed any of them? Under some other name. How many names did he have?

And the journals. Intermittent — on a year, off a decade — and uninformative. Weather, meetings, bad parties. Little book reports. Predictions, mostly political, all inaccurate. Only occasionally a titillating ambiguity. *X stopped by*, or *Y is warming*. The journal for '43 and '44 I took back to my place, meaning to read through it a second time, minutely. He couldn't have gone through that entire year, our year, without mentioning me once. Not even as *X*.

It was, I think, while I was sitting in my rooms engaged in this hunt for my third-person self that the knock came.

I opened my door and saw Tom. The apparition spoke, in Tom's voice. "Mr. Reeve?" I stepped back, and the ghost glided into my living room. It didn't walk like Tom — it had none of Tom's military bearing — and it was, now that I looked, puffier than Tom. Its voice, as it spoke further, was Tom's high simper, yes, but with none of the insinuation behind it. "Mr. Reeve, I've just gotten in from Chicago. We were out of the country, you see, my wife and I. So we didn't hear anything about my brother until we got back."

"Uh-huh."

"We were — I assume I can be frank with you, Mr. Reeve — we were just a little surprised that there hadn't been any attempt at all to contact us. And now I find — really, I'd almost think there had to be a mistake, it's so, well — they tell me that you're actually in the middle of settling his affairs. All of this going on with us not knowing a thing about it." He smiled and shook his head in mock bafflement.

"I have been going through your brother's papers," I said. "Looking, among other things, for some clue as to your whereabouts. The attorney was going to advertise, I think. You know how slow lawyers are." This was improvisation. I can't say I had forgotten Tom had a brother, but I had no more thought of hunting for him than of trying to find the jar with Tom's appendix in it. Tom had, over the years, mentioned his appendix rather more often. I went on: "Actually, I was surprised — considering the write-up Tom got everywhere, the *Times* and all — I was surprised not to have heard from you."

"That's how I found out, yes. People coming up to me after I got back and asking if that was my brother, they hadn't known I had a famous brother. To tell you the truth, I didn't know myself. I mean that Tom had made such a success in his little field."

"Some little success, yes."

He stuck his hands in his pockets. "I shouldn't have been so awfully hard to find. I am a Slater."

When he said that, I imagined Slaters giving off a unique scent, so that they could be traced anywhere. Or answering, perhaps, to a special whistle. But I suppose he meant that he was in the *Social Register*. Tom, of course, was dropped by the *Register*'s spinster watchdog in 1920, after he ditched Pauline.

"Anyway," I said. "You're here now."

"I have a three-thirty train."

"Then you'll — I can take you where he is. We haven't got the marker up yet."

"No, that can wait." Forever, I gathered. "I understand that everything is still in his apartment."

"Most everything," I said. Everything but the journal I had brought back to study and that lay open on my desk, the one without my name in it. God knows what I ever did with it.

"Yes. Well, I thought I might go on over and start getting things in order. Just make a start, you know."

"Everything is in order."

"Of course, yes, I've been told how much you were doing. And I want you to know how sincerely the family appreciates it. I didn't mean — what I was saying before, about finding me, I understand that you've had a lot to handle. I didn't mean to suggest that you'd been negligent."

All of this came streaming out in a narrow monotone, as from a ticker tape. Then, cheerily: "So, I understand you have a key to Tom's apartment." I said nothing. "If you could just let me have it."

"I'm . . . you know, I'm Tom's executor."

"There was a will," he said, matter-of-factly. His impassivity was like Tom's: perhaps it was a Slater trait, or perhaps it was beaten into them at St. Martin's.

He sat down and took from his breast pocket a platinum cigarette case. I heard myself asking where he'd got it. "A wedding, long time ago. I was an usher. Tom, too, I think. He must have one — must have had — just like it."

"I haven't been able to find it."

"No? You have a light somewhere?" He started opening boxes on the coffee table. As if he owned, not only all of Tom's things, but all of mine as well. When Tom behaved that way, one could chalk it up to absentmindedness or democratic unceremoniousness. Watching his brother, I wondered if this was another Slater trait. Or perhaps a habit of the rich generally, just to go on casually appropriating things until someone protested.

I lit his cigarette, found him an ashtray. I wanted to smoke, too, but I didn't want to be chummy.

"So," he said. "You're the executor. And a beneficiary?"

"The only one," I said. "Except for charities and so on."

"What about the Wonamaddock?"

"Stays in the trust for twenty years. Then it breaks. I think that's how it works, his lifetime and then twenty years after —"

"Yes, that's how trusts work." He stood up, waddled to the window. "You haven't gone to probate?"

"No. There's — I understand there has to be some waiting period."

"In case any kin turn up."

"Yes." Kin. I realized then that I didn't even know this man's name. Tom had never spoken it, nor written it in a journal, nor for all I know thought of it, not in thirty years. The kinsman stayed at the window, his back to me. "Well, that makes things simpler. I mean, we can reach an understanding, you and I, before the estate files. There won't have to be a whole lot of publicity."

"What kind of understanding?"

"You'd sign over your interest to — my children, say, Tom's nieces. And then there'd be some sort of cash settlement."

"I don't know what you're talking about," I said. This wasn't bravado: I really was very slow to get the point. His calmness, on the other hand — that was bravado. He lit a second cigarette from his first.

"Tom was . . . funny, wasn't he?" One doesn't hear "funny" spoken quite that way any more. So many more explicit words have come into use that anyone now resorting to funny, even with the twist he gave it, would fail to make himself understood.

Even then I pretended not to get it. "How do you mean?" I said.

He looked at me reproachfully, as if it were rude of me to make him say it. "Tom never married."

"That's not so unusual. A lot of the faculty here —"

"A lot of the faculty here are pansies."

I should have let him stick with funny. Really, of all the names for us, I like pansies least.

He turned from the window, finally. He was, amazingly, blushing. Perhaps he had a premonition of how it would be to go into court and call his brother that name. Much could have been made of that, I suppose, but I was too numb. In times of peril, my adrenaline quite ceases to flow. I am not subject to the fight-or-flight syndrome. My response is like the rabbit's: I freeze. And when I regain control of my muscles I drift into the familiar make-me-a-settlement-offer syndrome. One of the great steps in human evolution. It didn't work the other night.

Nor forty years ago. While I was immobilized, he recovered. "You seduced my brother," he said. Not accusingly, just sketching out his case. "You preyed on his neurotic, deviant tendencies. Otherwise it would never have occurred to him to alienate his estate from his loving family."

"Well, maybe you should just go ahead and make that case," I said, in an anesthetic haze. "They have newspapers in Chicago?"

"They do. Indeed they do. And they have prisons here." Spoken like Tom — Tom's rhythm, exactly.

Even in those dark ages, of course, the threat was less than plausible. But I had no difficulty imagining less extreme consequences. Loss of job, for example, that prospect was especially daunting in my prebureaucratic days.

"Now, I believe five thousand is a fair sum," he said.

"Five?" The trust paid that much in a quarter.

"Oh, ten, then." He held out his hand, as if the matter had been cordially concluded.

"Why do you need any of it, for God's sake? Why can't you just let your brother have his way, with the little bit he got? You don't need it. You must have —"

"A lot." I was almost relieved to be cut off in mid-whine. "A lot," he said again. His frown suggested that it was tedious to contemplate a fortune so enormous. "You're right. We don't need any of it. I might just give it all away."

I may have asked the obvious question, but I don't hear it, remembering. He answered anyway, with a cold, sad sincerity. "There are just some things no decent man can permit."

He shook his head and averted his eyes from me: how

degraded I must have been, how far fallen from the light, if it was necessary for him to explain something so elementary. He went on. "I do think you might — after we've gone over everything — if you wanted any of the furniture. Or books, say, Tom must have had books, you might be interested in those. It's really — for me, it's hardly worth the trouble of going through a sale."

"I don't want any of it," I bleated.

"Ten," he said, offering his hand once again. Numbly I shook it, and he was gone, along with my inheritance. The catalogue for the book auction came in the mail that fall. I suppose Tom's brother had it sent, as a kind of lesson. The greater part of Tom's fortune was in that wall of cardboard cartons.

The phone rings. It takes me an instant to realize what it is, and it has rung again before I have arranged my tubes and whatnot so I can reach and get it. I remember calling old Cochran after his bypass. The phone would ring several times before he'd pick it up, and I'd wonder if my innocent call had precipitated some cardiac crisis.

"Hello, Mr. Reeve?" It is my boss's secretary. Lydia, enormous Lydia. "How are you feeling?"

"Pretty lousy." I let my voice lapse into feebleness, like a child wanting to be let off school. It is so easy, letting go: I could just slide into it forever.

"I'm awfully sorry about your accident." She sounds as though she really is. "How did it happen?"

"I got mugged." If I keep saying this, I'll believe it.

"Oh dear, where?"

"On the street." Even as I say it, I worry about being contradicted somehow. Is there some way they can find out?

"Of course on the street," she says, betraying a limited imagination. "Where, near your place?"

"Yes, right near." Is there some form I'll have to bring to excuse my absence? A note from my doctor: Reeve couldn't come to school because he was beaten by a trick.

"I just don't know how you live downtown like that. I'd be scared all the time." I can't imagine why. To attack Lydia would require the bravado of that boy in China last spring, the one who stood up in front of all the tanks in the square.

"I guess I should have been."

"What time was it?"

"Pretty late." No, I won't need a form, I'm using up annual leave. I don't need a certificate for that.

"Well, you shouldn't go out late."

"No, I won't do that any more."

"Mr. Pollen wants to talk to you. Let me put you on hold for a minute."

That is what I have been thinking. I won't do that any more. An inevitable resolution: I am not such an awfully slow learner. Obviously I'm not going to bring hustlers home to beat me up any more. But of course this entails a bigger never more I haven't really thought about. Never more anybody, never more touching or smelling or waking up with anyone beside me.

Never again, I used to say when I was a kid. I'm not going to do that any more. I'm going to study and go to college and get out of Winslow and nobody's going to fuck me any more and I'm going to stop wanting it even and I'll get married and it won't ever happen again. That was always a lie, thank God, yet time has brought me to the same conclusion. Never again: the world where these things happened no longer exists, the world of my youth, the world of three days ago, both as distant and fabulous as Arcadia. Not my fragile vows but the years have beached me on this blasted shore I used to pray, so long ago, I'd get to.

So the resolution should be easy enough to keep. A little bargain I have struck with the deity I consult only in adversity. We negotiated right there in the ER. I was lying there on the gurney like Isaac on the altar, shaking as Isaac must have done, and swearing: if He would give me my life, I would give up everything. Wouldn't live any more. And here I am.

Pollen's voice. "Reeve, is that you? Tell him I haven't looked at it yet, if he was in such a big hurry he should have had it up here sooner." This evidently not directed at me. "Reeve, how's the boy?"

Succulent, mysterious, vacant. He means me. "I'm doing okay."

"What happened?"

"I was mugged," I repeat. There, that is my official line.

"What, on the street?"

"Yeah." Having told the story three times now I can nearly picture it: the old man stumbling home, a sudden whack, unsolicited. Not his fault. He slips to the pavement without even crying out. A poor old man on the ground, irreproachably mugged. "Just came from nowhere."

"Were you hurt bad?"

"Uh-huh. They had to operate. I was afraid I was going to lose an eye."

"Jesus. But it's okay?"

"They say it'll be fine."

"Great. So how long you in for?"

"I don't know, a couple more days here, and then I'll probably have to stay at home a while."

"Uh-huh. Were you working on anything?" A reasonable question, in light of my negligible output, but he amends it: "I mean, is there anything that can't wait till you get back?"

"I don't think so."

"Well, you take care of yourself, okay? You rest up and come back as soon as you can."

"I'll do that."

"And listen, you really ought to think about getting out of the city."

"Yeah, I should," I say. "But the commute, you know I don't even drive."

"Well, your time's almost up," he says heartily. I am startled until I realize he means at work. "You ought to be thinking about where you want to retire."

"Oh, I'm not even thinking about retiring." I hope I have spoiled his day.

He pauses, about to urge me to think of it, his tongue checked by the thought of my age discrimination complaint. Hearings, paperwork. He's a political appointee, he doesn't need any hassles on the way to the next bullet point on his résumé. "Well, nobody's pushing you. I don't know what we'd do without you."

"I'd better hurry back so you don't find out."

"That's right." He essays a laugh. "Anyway, I'm glad to hear you're okay."

"Thanks."

"You take care now."

So ends the longest discourse we've ever had. I have served the government for just under thirty years. That is the normal term; Pollen and I must both have the magic day circled on our desk calendars. I could stop soon. I could stop working, Adam's curse lifted, back to the garden. Where, with no job to go to every morning, I would spend my days sipping distillates of the grape, the juniper, the homely potato.

With Tom gone, of course, I never finished my degree. I guess I am what they call now — they didn't back then —

an ABD. There should be some special honorific, I think, for people who manage to stay all-but-dissertation for forty years. It's rather like being an elderly crown prince, an Edward VII or Akihito, whose predecessor takes too long to die. Anyway, I taught high school for a few years, leaving a permanent lacuna in the education of several hundred youths, and then slipped into the civil service when no one was looking.

My thirty years, 1959–89, span nine presidentiads. This means that I have lived through eight redraftings of the organizational chart. In the first one or two my name moved vertically, toward the empyrean of the supergrades. More recently my motion has been horizontal.

Each redrafting was accompanied by some slogan meant to signify that we had reached the last stage of the dialectic and the State was about to wither away, taking old Reeve and his position number (07921088) with it. The New Frontier was one past which I was to be exiled, the Great Society would be the greater for my absence, the New Federalism promised a leaner, trimmer government purged of frills such as Reeve. Each time, as the beneficent dust settled again, old 07921088 was still hanging on.

Ever more peripherally, it is true, relegated to the very margin of the chart, that edge past which less wary pilots would sail straight off the earth. Assigned to Special Projects or Long-Range Planning, cloudy regions from which no bureaucrat returns.

We at the edges of the map are a safe distance from the great storms, the quadrennial whirlwinds that stir the dust at the center and hurl a few of our colleagues out to join us in Thule. True, we look around us and see crudely limned monsters, and we must wonder: am I one of those? A creature that never was, dreamt up merely to relieve the awful blankness at the edges of the paper? Sorriest are those who do not see where the wind has cast them or who do not understand that they will never be called back. They work. My office mate sends memoranda to the center, like messages in a bottle, with no more hope of response.

Tom, you could have lived at the margin. I remember you joking about it, just after the catastrophe. How you could go to Smith, there was an opening. "But God," you said. "Nothing but women and an occasional fey Spanish teacher." Or you could have gone into exile, with your trust fund and your books, off to Paris, comfortably ruined. You could have made your bargain somehow and stayed alive. As I have: all you have to do is swear off everything you call life.

$\mathcal{T}$wo

THE NURSE COMES IN, bearing two little glasses of juice. "Happy hour," she says.

"I wish it were," I say.

"You're telling me. I got another four hours on this shift. Before you drink that I need to get your temperature." She has a sort of electronic thermometer; it takes only moments.

The nurse — her nametag says Sharon — says, offhandedly, "Did they tell you you shouldn't drink anything for a while? I mean, when you get home."

"No." This is quite contrary to my plans.

"Well, it isn't a good idea," Sharon says. Something less than an absolute prohibition; I will pretend I didn't hear. I raise my glass to the boy in a toast. He ignores me.

I still have Tom's last book in my lap, with the little curriculum vitae, the racecourse of his life, on the dust jacket. It is an unfinished oval. It shows him born but not dead. It shows him still at work: "Wigglesworth Professor of Rhetoric, 1935–" It says he is master of Winthrop House; no mention of his fall or his exile on Marsden Street. But the circles are easy enough to close; he closed them all himself. One has merely to add, at the end of the orderly roll call of his achievements — St. Martin's '12, Yale '16, AEF '17–'19, Yale A.M., Ph.D., and so on — blew his brains out '52. Period. Except of course that period is the end of quite a different race from the one he started. And I know so little of that other course he ran. When, exactly, did he join the "study group," as he insisted on calling it? Whose were the names he could not utter? What were they doing to him, at the end?

Perhaps these essential data are missing because they aren't part of his vita at all, but merely a part of the history of the age. Tom Slater at Yale or writing *The Invincible City*, that is Tom himself, a particular Tom. Tom joining the Party, leaving it, taking the Fifth, killing himself — that is a general instance of his times, just another familiar case.

Not even so very familiar. If he had been someone important — a screenwriter, say, a second banana, a radio announcer — people might have heard of him, Exhibit B or C in the Terror. Show business has taught us all we know of those years, and it commemorates only its own martyrs. Maybe their stories really are more appealing: a simple entertainer, only wanting to make folks happy, done in because he goodheartedly worried about the Spanish Loyalists. The kind of story one can listen to again and again, congratulating oneself for being, forty years later, on the side of the good guys.

Tom's name barely rings a bell. A few people remember having to read him in college. T. F. Slater, uh-huh. Right, *The Invincible City*, I remember that. Blue cover. And there used to be other students for whom *The Invincible City* was practically the Talmud, back before it went out of style, and who had no idea that Tom Slater shot himself. Tom wasn't a poet, after all. Poets who kill themselves are remembered for that first, for the work second, if at all. But a critic —

who cares how he lived or died? T. F. Slater: the name could be an acronym for some committee, the book could have been turned out by a collating machine.

For me it is different, it speaks Tom as clearly as any poem could have done. Perhaps it is because I hear his voice that I cannot read him — no matter how many times I open this book, I cannot read it. But of course it is to hear his voice that I open it up at all.

I don't suppose anyone actually reads it now, any more than I do. Teachers who themselves never quite got through it assign it anyway. Students buy it, look at Tom's picture, put it on their shelves. Like other unopened college texts it follows them, forever virgin, as they graduate from dorm to condo. They keep it on display, on the half shelf of books in the rosewood entertainment center or the étagère. The glossy midnight blue of the dust jacket looks well on a shelf, sets off the matched set of Bulwer-Lytton nicely, and the title is impressive enough to anyone so vulgar as to read the titles on other people's shelves. *The Invincible City:* it could be about any number of interesting subjects.

I myself can still be seduced by that title. I hold up my lorgnon to the good eye and begin, in the middle, somewhere past the farthest I've ever got.

. . . the gift of espying under every visage an inferior facsimile of his own majestic consciousness. Emerson looked on the race of men as on an endless gallery of distorting mirrors. Hence his unending disappointment, as his vaunted individuals prove, one by one, to have sensibilities of their own. From this his *volte-face* on Whitman, from this his . . .

I can hear him say it, in his high, insinuating voice. I cannot read it. Oh, it was all stunningly new, forty years ago.

But now, when everything in it is practically received wisdom: opening it is like sitting down to read Freud, someone else I never got very far in. Tom's book is boring in the same way, because it seems to us now that he was merely repeating, not discovering, the things he had to say, so much a part of our world have they become. You feel that you're listening to a moderately bright and deeply bored teacher reciting the standard views about nineteenth-century America. You have to make yourself remember that he thought it was a book about the revolution.

Of all the things Howard could have brought, why this? He didn't pick it up by chance; there must be a dozen half-read books lying around the living room, he could have grabbed any of them. But he went to the shelves, to S for Slater — I still keep my books alphabetically, as Tom taught me, one of the few lessons that lasted — and picked it out deliberately. Perhaps he thought it would be a comfort to contemplate a greater calamity than my own. I suppose I've told him the story often enough, but how could I have known that dizzy old Howard was actually listening? And why should he think that Tom's, of all stories, would cheer me up?

The day they found him, toward the end of July in '52, I got up awfully late. I'd been to the shabby little bar I used to go to — the Garland, that was it — the night before and struck out. By early afternoon my hangover was gone, the heat had broken, and I thought I might go over to Lowell Park to enjoy the weather and perhaps make a new friend. I wore my Hawaiian print shirt and some old khaki trousers I wouldn't mind getting soiled. I was waiting for the streetcar when Fuzzy Walgreen came along. From the classics department, Fuzzy the Pindar man.

I think he was C. L. Walgreen. At least I'm sure of the

C. Fuzzy was a prep school name, I guess, one that had followed him and to which he deigned to answer all his life, presumably because it was better than whatever awful given name was masked by the C. Clement? Chauncey? Other boys had worse nicknames, ones that signaled their bed-wetting or their nightmares or their effeminacy. Fuzzy referred to nothing, or at least nothing very bad: perhaps his myopia, perhaps some more general lack of acuity. It was cheerfully neutral, a sign that he must once briefly have been liked.

I saw him from some distance. He shuffled toward me erratically, barely avoiding obstacles: he would come within inches of a mailbox or a lamppost and then veer away from it, like one of those windup toys that waddle along and change direction every time they bump into something. So it took him forever to approach. I could see my streetcar, an orange blob a few blocks away. At the rate Fuzzy was proceeding, there was a good chance it would overtake him. I could jump on and be whisked away to adventure before Fuzzy ever got to me. But no, he had espied me and was coming more directly now, as if I were just the man he'd been looking for. Soon he was upon me.

Fuzzy was nearly colorless — not an albino, exactly, but so pale you could see the blue veins in his forehead, and his hair a shock of spun platinum. He had a constant sickly smile that was the consequence of a life spent squinting while breathing through the mouth. "Have you heard?" he said.

"Heard what?"

His involuntary grin seemed to broaden. "Mr. Slater shot himself." I grinned back at him, it was so absurd. "A neighbor heard it and the police were summoned. They had to force their way in, and there he was."

My streetcar came and I got on it. On the steps I turned

to look at Fuzzy. I remember looking down at him. He was in a dark suit of heavy worsted, as though he carried winter around with him, as though he were its emissary invading that sunny afternoon. The motorman was still waiting to see if he was going to get on. He raised his pale face to look at me through his thick spectacles. "Nó one can have thóught he would do thát," he said. In pæons, — ◡◡◡ — ◡◡◡ —, the relentless measure of his Pindar.

Perhaps it was just the way the streetcar lurched forward that made me feel the planet had gone off its orbit. Even after I had found a seat, everything around me seemed out of balance. Men's hats were askew, the buildings on either side leaned every which way. Fuzzy, when I looked back, was following us in a crazy zigzag — not fast, not as though he wanted to catch up, just resuming the path he had been on before he had accosted me. Looking for someone else who hadn't heard.

Once in Lowell Park, I headed straight for the dell and within a minute or two found myself heading into the bushes with a man I wouldn't have looked twice at, any other day. I was on my knees before him when I buried my face between his thighs and started to cry. He tried to step back as I held on to his legs. Finally he freed himself, pulled up his trousers, and ran; he must have thought I was loony, or at least unusually conflicted. I fell forward and went on crying, my face pillowed in dry leaves.

In a minute I sat up and wiped my eyes and tried to consider the obvious question. What do I do? Without Tom supporting and pushing me, telling me what to read next and where to get my ties and, often as not, paying for them: what to do? I stood, recovering with amazing speed once I focused on myself. There was a movement in the bushes, and presently there appeared a husky young man in grease-stained trousers, a mechanic maybe, with the most remarkable dark eyes. He was not put off by my tears, already evaporating; such a hot day, they were indistinguishable from sweat. So I never quite got around to answering that question.

Dinner is here. I have apparently checked off broiled fish, of a fishiness so pervasive that it could be the very type, the Platonic ideal, of fish. The bit of juice I can squeeze from a quarter lemon sinks ineffectually into the fishy mass of it. I pick at the little parsleyed potatoes that accompany it, trying to get down a bit of grown-up food before moving on to the beige peach cobbler.

At least I have my little mealtime recreation, as the boy sits up on the edge of his bed to eat, and I can look at his back, down to the V of muscle at its base and the shadowy concavity below. I am afraid he must feel how hard I am staring. My fork, with its little bit of potato, hovers in midair as my whole being anchors to the base of his spine.

I have always been partial to backs. I don't mean backsides, whose virtues are more generally appreciated, but backs, whose owners never see them and whose baroque, superabundant complexity is squandered, given away freely to those who will look. Here I have gone and excited myself. The potato falls off onto the cover.

After dinner, we go back to watching television, "Wheel of Fortune." I rather enjoy trying to guess the mystery phrases from the scattered letters. It's like hangman, but without the awful urgency as your body assumes its parts, one by one, on the gallows, ready to swing.

The boy is evidently more interested in the floozy who turns the letters. He has been touching himself absentmindedly through much of the show. I reach for a drink of water. He remembers me, glances over, and withdraws his hand from under the covers. For a long while we both look only at the screen. I find myself feeling that it connects us, that the lines of our vision meet at the vortex of the screen and we are comrades. But soon enough my shame takes over and I conjure instead a beam of disdain angling at me. It is his TV, I am an intruder, reading over his shoulder. He changes the channel as if to sever the unwanted intimacy. I reach for Tom's book and pretend to read, turning my back on the boy. But I am aware of him as the dark side of the moon must feel the pull of the unseen earth.

We lie, each of us enisled in his circle of light, the dark space between us only a few feet wide. I have seldom been yoked to beauty in this unnatural and tormenting way, a step apart and — not just unable to touch, but having to pretend I don't even notice. Tom must have known this half the nights of his youth, at St. Martin's, at college, in the army. Life must have seemed to him an unending tease, the soft breath of the boy in the next bed whispering no, no, over and over, every night from the time he was twelve.

He would say sometimes, when I wasn't understanding him, that I had never known the company of men. And I would laugh, thinking I had known the company of more men from a lot more angles than he ever would. Then he would go on about St. Martin's and Yale and the AEF — the last two mere extensions of the first — and how that was all an experience I'd never had.

As for the American Expeditionary Forces, I knew damn well he'd spent the war in the trenches of the Hôtel du Rhin, translating memoranda; God knows what he did at Yale. But perhaps there was something in it. Even when I met him, he still played a fierce game of racquets. And sometimes he and a straight lecturer in physical geography would go off to fish or some such rough thing, up at the lodge Tom and some others shared at Hamilton Lake. "Don't know what all the talk's about," the man would say. "I never saw him do anything funny." (But neither did I.)

Was that all Tom was taunting me with? Roughing it? Or the way he had solemnly built a body for himself just before we got into the Great War, with Indian clubs and medicine balls and the other homely apparatus of those days? Or was the company of men to be found somewhere in that tormenting distance from one bed to the next?

Tom was one of the very last boys to wear the lace dresses and unshorn locks of Victorian babyhood. On the mantel in his bedroom were photos of his androgynous infancy, then others, a little later, of him in a sailor suit, holding the hand of his Gibson Girl mother or sitting in a pony cart. Then on into Edwardian ladhood, then St. Martin's and college, the AEF, all those photos crowded onto the mantel and dozens more in albums. All of his life documented, his history looking over his shoulder every time he got into bed alone or ensemble.

We were too poor for many photographs, or perhaps my parents were simply indifferent; in any case, I have made it to the present day largely unrecorded. There must have been school pictures, but I was never given the money to buy a copy. The picture for my college application I took in a booth at the bus station in Charlow. There were two pictures, I think, but I had my eyes closed in one and threw it away. Thus I have no idea of what I looked like as a child or a young man. So many hours I spent before the mirror in those years, and all I can picture of myself is what I looked like shaving the other morning. (What I look like now I have read in Howard's face; I have managed so far not to corroborate him by looking in the mirror when I go to pee.) My memories, that is, are all from the inside out, while

Tom's were both aroused and governed by that museum of the superficial with which he had surrounded himself.

His eyes looked out from the earliest of those pictures with an imperious curiosity. He stood in his pony cart as if at the center of the world, and what entered his field of vision was his, to be studied, or eaten, or dismissed. His reign was short enough. Like other upstarts, he was forced to abdicate and packed off to St. Martin's, where all was sweat and democracy, muscular Christianity and cold showers.

I wonder if all St. Martin's boys spoke of the place with the same odd mixture of nostalgia and horror. The cold showers came up so often I sometimes thought I'd been through them myself, the showers and the hazing and the endless, numbing drill in geometry or Latin. He was so certain that he had suffered, I began to believe he really had. That the grand circle of New York and Newport and St. Martin's had closed on him as little Winslow did on me. Maybe childhood was rotten wherever it was lived.

I would have taken the pony cart. Oh, and the rest of that lost imperium he dreamt of, where servants came and went and his parents appeared at bedtime like corseted visions. Momma above all, with her great white iron bosom, sailing into the nursery like one of Dewey's fleet into Manila Bay. Or hovering over his bed, as she tucked him in, like a cumulus cloud.

While of course I have never actually read Freud and so am prepared to dismiss him as readily as any other right-thinking faggot, Tom's is too perfect a case to be denied. He called his mother Mamma to the day he died, and I think he loved her more than he would ever love God or the revolution or literature, more than he would ever love a man. Poor Pauline, the woman he almost married after the Great War — the stooge on his one foray into heterosimulation — was probably so much like his mother that she might have been grown from a cutting. If a marriage could only have been consummated by tucking Tom in and giving him a kiss, she could have been the younger Mrs. Slater.

But Tom was from his mother's arms untimely ripped, trotted off to boarding school at twelve. To the world of Dink Stover and football, petted boys hardening themselves to a daunting and precocious manliness. Under the eyes of the all-seeing Founder, the young animals lurched from Latin to grub to the playing fields, all day shoving, leaning, tackling, poking, rubbing against one another anyhow, endless friction of boy against boy, showering and shitting together, sleeping two to a room under the eaves. Never a minute without another boy, or a dozen, right there. Boys in mobs, boys in cliques, boys in twos murmuring after lights out. Boys fighting, wrestling, tumbling to the ground together. Boys in love, gruff, laconic, passionate.

He had the early crush or two, of course, some distant sixth-former with wide shoulders who happened to smile down on him one day. But he didn't outgrow it, not like the other boys. At the age when I was spreading my cheeks for every horny Canuck in Winslow, Tom was choking down sentiments, shivering at an arm thrown casually around his shoulder, averting his eyes in changing rooms. And saying to himself, nights when the tension was so great that he thought he might throw himself into his roommate's bed as if over a precipice: those nights he would tell himself that he was only homesick. And he was, except that he was also home, at home in that world of boys as he would never be again.

What he might have done, if he could have crossed the abyss to the boy in the next bed, he never figured out. Thirty years later, when I met him, he still hadn't got much beyond the sexless, puerile hugging and the boyish endearments in antique slang: "Gee, it's swell being with you" and "Say, you've got a peach of a build."

In our brief period of intimacy I seldom saw him hard, never saw him come. Once a month or so he might go into the bathroom and jerk off, with the taps running so I wouldn't hear. He was of the generation that thought a man had to come every so often, or he would poison himself somehow. So he would take care of it, as a matter of hygiene, and return abashed to bed. I could have helped, of course, but he never asked. And I think I knew a move from me would finish us; though we were finished soon enough. So I lay in bed and waited, listening above the gushing faucets for some sound. No more able to reach for him than he for whatever chum he had pined for years ago. That lonesomeness of his was catching. Perhaps its awful isolation was American manhood itself, every man in his cell.

I had found my way out the cellblock door even before puberty, at about the age when it slammed shut on Tom. Not that my freedom was so very wide-ranging. The day I left Winslow I didn't know that men blew one another or that people ever kissed with their mouths open. My body was an appliance whose user's manual was printed in some foreign tongue. Boys and men made use of it; the brief, hard instruction I had from them was the sum of my early sexual education. I thought they had shown me the limit of possibility. And I would have settled for it. I would, if no one had taught me better, have been willing to call that clumsy humping love. Tom's was simply the complementary ignorance. We might have taught each other, instead of just gliding futilely past.

Leaving Winslow. I had ridden that bus for years, just to visit an aunt in Charlow, eleven miles away. The bus was always marked Boston; God knows how many little towns it stopped in before reaching that impossibly distant terminus. I would get off in Charlow and wait a couple of minutes before going on to my aunt's. I would stand in front of the confectionery that doubled as the bus station and look at the people who were going on, past Charlow, to Boston or to the ends of the earth. I thought they were brave, staying on that bus and going as far as it would take them. They were so calm — sleeping, some of them, and those who were awake giving just one bored glance at Charlow, before returning to their crossword puzzle or their *Collier's*. They were as different from me as argonauts.

At sixteen, in 1943, I joined them. Got on the bus at the little Winslow station, rode by the familiar landscape of foreclosed farms and discarded tires, suppressed an involuntary, habitual stirring as the driver called out Charlow. It felt funny, sitting, looking out the window at the confectionery while the driver went inside. He came out, adjusted his seat, unwrapped a stick of gum. All this seemed to take hours, while on the other side — when I had stood on the sidewalk watching — it had always seemed as though the bus just spat me out and whizzed away. The driver adjusted his seat once again and sat for a few more hours, chewing his gum, as if nerving himself for the great journey. Then he reached for the lever and shut the door.

I was going on, to college and my life. I was supposed to come back, of course, at Thanksgiving if I could afford it, otherwise at Christmas. But I watched that door shut, and I settled back into my seat and casually opened my book. As if Charlow were just another stop to me, a brief annoying delay. I expected, then, that I would be back. But my body knew better; I could feel that world closing behind me.

I was mistaken. I wore Winslow on my back every day. No one pretended in those days that we were one great community of scholars. Now, when all students strive to look poor, a genuinely poor boy from Winslow might escape notice. But then, when one dressed as formally for class as one does now for Wall Street, it was plain who got his clothes from Brooks or Tripler and who was still wearing the suit from Sears that had fit all right when he was fourteen.

Among my fellow waiters at dinner every night, there might have been a few who felt able to joke with the rich boys at the tables. An athlete or two, admitted to the meritocracy of brawn and able to pretend that they just happened to be holding that dish of carrots. But not I: I knew I was a waiter. There formed quite quickly within the freshman class a special fraternity, the boys to whom it was made clear every day — we made it clear to one another, if any of us forgot — that we were here by sufferance.

We were made to feel it even in the classroom, even by the professors. They knew who we were, the scholarship boys, and they gave us the As we earned. But we were not asked to tea, and in class we were called on with a yes, not by name. Our teachers were, I suppose, the last generation of gentleman scholars. Most of them, like Tom, with private fortunes to supplement their derisory salaries. Maybe they thought it would always be that way: that their successors would be drawn from among the young gentlemen in the room. So they were busy trying to find some rich boy to whom they might conceivably hand on the torch, while the hands that were actually reaching for it were passed over.

I had no reason to suppose that the famous Mr. Slater, who was apparently teaching a section of Great Books for his own amusement (surely it wasn't for our edification), felt any differently. If Frank Merriwell, the strain of intellection visible on his scrubbed brow, observed that this Homer fellow didn't take his gods very seriously — well, Mr. Slater would take Mr. Merriwell very seriously indeed. While my own remarks — I can't recall any, only in comparison to Merriwell's did they seem so brilliant — were met with an "Er . . . yes," as the professor's eyes remained fixed on the captain of the freshman crew.

When he did take notice of me, finally, he swooped down like one of that Homer fellow's gods, swooped down and just scooped me up.

Anyone who has ever been a student will recall what *See me* means, standing alone at the end of a paper otherwise unmarked. It stands with *From the President of the United States, Greetings* at the head of the list of unwelcome brief salutations. Under *See me*, Professor Slater had written *Winthrop Wed.–Thurs. 2–5.* I went to Winthrop Thursday at about ten to five. I meant to allow him as little time as possible to make all the nasty remarks he couldn't bring himself to write.

I think I made up my mind about what I was going to do with my life the moment I walked through that door and saw how the master of Winthrop House lived. I didn't want to teach, I didn't want to be a scholar, I just wanted that apartment. Typical fairy, all my ambition hinging on a bit of interior decoration. But it wasn't that: his rooms looked even a little shabby to me. Old furniture, worn-out rug, portraits of dry old men peering out through layers of varnish — I had no idea people valued such things. Mr. Slater made me sit down on the sofa facing his own enormous club chair while he went over and stirred the fire a little — first fire of the autumn, probably, did he lay it on for me? When he came back then and offered me a cigarette from that platinum case, I thought you couldn't get any farther from Winslow than I was right then. His seduction was complete at that moment; there was no need of the pale ribaldries that followed. He had already taken me into his body.

I can't remember if he said anything very specific about my paper. Mild praise, I guess — he couldn't lie about such things even when he was putting the make on you. But then, as if he had turned a switch, he started laying it on. "What your paper has," he said. "What any true critic, and you will be one, must have, is the voice of experience."

"Uh-huh."

"I mean it. I can tell, even from your extempore remarks in the classroom, that you have seen a good deal more of life than the other . . . men."

"Maybe," I said, modestly, though no sixteen-year-old could have argued with so sound an analysis.

"I really feel less as though I'm talking to a student and more as though I'm talking to — oh, not a colleague, so much, my colleagues are all dry as dust, but a —" His hesitation before using the word was, I think, actual. "A comrade, almost, if that isn't too presumptuous." Then, as if he were only playing with the word, he murmured: "A camerado."

How we did talk in those days. Signals. Words like camerado, out of Whitman. Or — less literary, but in those days quite obscure enough — gay. "It was an awfully gay party," we'd say. And outsiders really didn't know. Or so we told ourselves.

Well: allusions to Whitman were quite lost on me. But, as a dog will, I caught the tone.

"You know, these rooms," he went on. "That you like so much." He had seen that. "These rooms, this life, can be much more lonely than you imagine."

I had no idea what was going on. He must have thought he was being daring; I am sure that in his approaches to more ambiguous candidates he was more subtle. And here he was — rather insultingly, in retrospect — dropping the most obvious of hints on the most obvious of receptors, and getting no response. Partly because no one had ever felt it necessary to hint to me before. And partly because, though he was nearing the point at which even I could hardly escape his meaning, I refused to believe it. He was thirty years older than I was, rich and learned and famous. I couldn't believe it.

He waited for an answer to the question I wouldn't hear. After a minute, during which he must have been trying to make himself go farther, he gave me a look just like the one he had the last time I saw him. Perhaps it is that time I am remembering, after all. As if he were looking at me from a distance past traversing and yet could see every cell of me, all the way inside me, even as I got farther and farther away.

Then he composed himself, and went on. "As I was saying, these rooms can be lonely sometimes. So I often have a crowd in for sherry. Perhaps you might like to come some week." He began to guide me to the door. "Tuesdays at five. Just a few of us, if you're ever free. Good-bye." I was in the hall, looking at the nameplate on the door. Thomas Frick Slater, it said. Master.

I took him seriously and actually did appear for sherry, not the next week I think, but the week after. I had to work in the kitchen that afternoon and didn't get there till five-thirty or so. I heard talk and laughter from behind the master's door, and I thought perhaps I might just walk in. But I knocked, and there was quiet. After a moment Mr. Slater opened the door.

"Mercy, a new face," he said flatly. He turned away as soon as he had let me in. The other ephebes, crew types, mostly, nodded at me. One or two even said hi in the tone they used when speaking to me in the refectory, democratically languid. Everyone but me was strapping and hand-some. Half of them in uniform, Navy V-12s or whatever. They'd be gone soon enough, most of them, and Mr. Sla-ter's sherry hour would suffer a decided aesthetic drought until the war ended and he could repopulate it with veter-ans.

I was handed a sherry at once, though I could see some of the others had been given whiskey, a precious commodity that year. I sat at some distance from the rest — there was a circle, with Mr. Slater's place open (his cigarette still smol-dering in the ashtray), and no one made any motion to broaden it for me. I sipped my sherry and waited.

What did they all think of me, in my Sears, Roebuck serge? A tiny creature then, with the wrong tie and the bottle-glass spectacles that would keep me out of uniform when the time came. I stared deep into my sherry, afraid to look at them. Not just because I was so out of place in this circle of athletic heartiness. But because they might detect, from the very way I looked at them, that I was funny.

I was so busy trying to look unfunny that I didn't at first notice that Mr. Slater had resumed his seat and begun some disquisition or other. No one was looking at me.

What was the topic that day? The second front, maybe, he often came back to that. Or the Pacific war: how it was all a distraction from the war against fascism and we were just bailing out the British Empire. Or — a favorite, he loved twitting his halfbacks and shortstops with this — how we had become indistinguishable from the Germans. How Roosevelt had surrounded himself with sleek lawyers and Republican bond salesmen, affecting to volunteer for a dol-lar a year, when in fact they were sent to him by their masters with the mission of helping to build national so-cialism.

"Already," Tom would say, "the workers belong to the

48

state and not the state to the workers. One can see it everywhere: the patriotic suppression of strikes, the ostensibly anti-inflationary wage limits, now this extraordinary proposal for a worker draft, stay on the job or go to jail, choose your prison. The distinction between Washington and Berlin is practically invisible already."

His little circle of students, sparkling in their cadets' uniforms, would practically shiver. Confused, not quite following it all, but also thrilled. One of them, with the heavy-lidded handsomeness of the man in the Chesterfield ad, might dutifully protest. All these measures were necessary, we had to win the war after all.

"Necessary, absolutely," Tom would say. "Everything that happens in history is necessary. And it is necessary just now that the industrialists should consolidate their power. So we are given the little drama of the war effort, staged for our edification by the muses of Wall Street."

"A drama? You think they're just making everything up?"

"Look at my glass. It has whiskey in it. I spent the whole of last term without any whiskey because they told the distillers to make industrial alcohol. Now there is whiskey again. What has changed, have we won the war? Have we any less need for industrial alcohol? It is all just an exercise in social control, a rehearsal for the postwar world in which the scientific managers will run everything."

"But that's just what I'm talking about, sir . . ." Only because he was so handsome could the Chesterfield man be bold. Is it possible he really didn't know it? Could any of them not have known why Mr. Slater tolerated them? "What I mean is that, when I'm out there fighting, I'll be glad to know there's enough, gee, industrial alcohol or whatever else we need to get the job done."

"Perhaps you're right," Mr. Slater would say. He knew when to stop, could tell when his fresh-faced auditors were starting to get uneasy, starting to wonder if he had crossed the line from academic chatter to sedition. "That's the most important thing after all, to get the job done."

Whatever the topic was that evening, Mr. Slater wound down a little while after I got there. It was near dinner time, and Mr. Slater's crew drifted off to see what the cooks had managed to rustle up without any meat. A few were still talking with him about Saturday's Yale game, a match of 4-Fs in which I could probably have participated. (Tom's pets, all in some officer training program or other, were forbidden to play, lest they mar themselves before they could be slaughtered on the beaches.) While he joked with them, Mr. Slater casually refilled my sherry. So I lingered when the last of them had gone.

"I'm sorry I was so late getting here. I had to work."

"You should never apologize for studying."

"No, I mean in the kitchen. At the refectory."

"Then you have even less call to apologize. You mustn't be ashamed of having to work. Most of the . . . boys here have been rather sheltered. I think perhaps you're more grown up than any of them."

I knew he was flattering me again, but I wanted to play the role he had cast me in, ambassador from the actual. "It's hard sometimes, sir."

"Yes, I'm sure it is." He put a hand on my shoulder, then self-consciously removed it. He meant to give the air of a big brother, I think. Instead, I was suddenly convinced of what I hadn't let myself believe in our earlier conversation. He went on: "Glad to see you here today. As I say, a new face for our little circle."

"Yes, sir, I enjoyed it, and I hope you'll let me —"

He didn't even hear me. He had started on his lumbering course and would not be diverted from it. "And a very handsome new face, if I may say so." He refilled my sherry.

Young as I was, I knew that he was proud of his adept seduction, and that I ought to let him finish it. But I was afraid that, if he went on much longer, I would be — turned off, we'd say now. A useful locution, I wonder how we got along without it for so long. So I hurried him on, shifted my stance in such a way that he just naturally found himself putting his hand back on my shoulder.

I learned, over the years, that most of Tom's affairs were ended by the calendar — Christmas holidays, graduations — without ever having been consummated. Tom could wait forever for the auspicious moment: he never learned how rapidly that moment arrives, if it is to come at all. He not only failed to strike while the iron was hot, but — after spending a whole semester trying to decide whether his chosen ingot was hot for him or just naturally glowed — would watch the cooling with some relief, and would be positively exuberant when the unseized opportunity left town.

"Very nearly made a fool of myself," he would say to me. I would eat my chowder and refrain from saying that he really had made a fool of himself, that the sensible thing was to do as I did, go directly for the goodies instead of stand debating until the help comes and wheels the buffet cart away. I am sure he would have had some crushing answer to this Auntie Mame sentiment. Besides, he must once or twice have made his way to the goodies before they were carted off and — given his limited repertory — experienced only anticlimaxes. Of course it is a common enough thing for a man to find his greatest pleasure in the hunt. But perhaps for Tom the prize at the end was, not merely a letdown, but a horrible negation of everything that had led up to it.

I think I must have been a sort of experiment for him,

his first and only genuine, readily identifiable fairy. When he might ordinarily have spent months building some sort of pure communion, only to see it spoiled in an hour, he found himself hurtling to bed with me before he even knew my first name. Nothing happened, of course, not what I understood to be lovemaking. My offertory twitchings of my fanny that first night went unanswered, like the memoranda my office mate writes. I must have been insulted at first. But somehow I understood almost at once that he could not imagine what I meant him to do. I didn't press him: I didn't know how.

He hugged me for a long while, until, drunk on three glasses of sherry, I fell asleep. By my next visit we had already fallen into the routine that would continue through our time together — half a year, I guess, or a little more. I would come over after waiting dinner in the refectory. We would talk in the living room — he would talk while I had a glass of the whiskey to which he had promoted me. Then we would go into his room and put on our pajamas. We would hold each other as he talked me to sleep and I breathed in his smell of soap and tobacco.

He was the one who broke it off. I was just turning seventeen: our conjugal life was, in a word, insufficient. And I had happily begun to discover other — outlets, Tom might have called them. Down at the station hotel, mostly, where I was able to make my contribution to the war effort by offering some passing solace to our fighting boys.

I would still, most nights, come back to his bed and let him hold me. It still felt right for some reason, it would feel right if I could back up into his arms this minute. But it didn't feel right to him. He knew what I was doing. He rarely spoke of it, and never openly disapproved. What could he say? He knew what he wasn't giving me, couldn't. And wasn't my body under the covers just as warm as it had ever been, no matter where else I'd taken it that night? A perfectly comfortable arrangement: it seemed to me we could go on forever.

Perhaps my inconstancies were too constant a reminder of his own incapacity. Perhaps one night he smelled someone on me, or thought he could. Or maybe he meant it when he said — the night when he let me finish my whiskey but told me I couldn't come to bed — that it was dangerous, he was taking too great a risk.

"Who's going to know about it?" I said. "It's not as though I'm going to tell anybody."

"Are you certain? If they should corner you?"

"Who in the world would do that?" I said. "Anyway, I didn't go to your fancy prep school, but I'm not a snitch."

"Of course you aren't. I could never have . . . become friends with a 'snitch.' It's one thing I can always tell. I do at least try to be careful."

"Well, I guess we have to."

"At any rate, you must forgive me, but I'm afraid I'm too tired for any company just tonight."

I forgave him all too readily and headed for East Station. The next night, and the next, I joined him for whiskey as always, expecting that he would relent. I don't know if he really didn't want to, or if he just couldn't say the words, couldn't pick up once more what had now lost the innocence of habit. We never shared a bed again.

$\mathcal{T}$HREE

THE BOY TURNS DOWN the volume. I look over. He is lying on top of the covers, arms at his sides. As I watch he raises his unbandaged hand, holds it in the air for a moment as if deciding what to do with it, then slowly brings it over to his crotch. He is looking intensely at the screen, but his eyes flicker in my direction for just an instant, to see if I have noticed. The hand stays motionless, just casually resting there.

There must be something in this book I can focus on. I page idly through the chapter on the Transcendentalists. All those dreary people Tom made me read. Theodore Parker, Bronson Alcott, prattling on about the immanent God. I dutifully tried to read every one of them, thinking this was the ticket to Tom's world, to a life in those beautiful rooms.

After our abortive romance, Tom kept me under his wing. Guided me through school, found me a summer job at the university press so I wouldn't have to go back to Winslow. Gave me a little pocket money sometimes. Took me to dinner and, once or twice, to New York to see the opera, a passion that did not prove catching. Pushed me on into graduate school, got me the job as resident adviser at

Winthrop House. I could sit in my little rooms there, a corridor or two away from Tom's grander suite, and pretend I was Tom in miniature.

Younger boys would come to my rooms for their resident advice. One would tell me about his homesickness, a malady I had never suffered. Another, more elliptically, about his feelings for his roommates and his terror about what he might be turning into. Not what he was: no one ever thought he already *was* that awful thing. But that he was in the midst of a metamorphosis, like a werewolf when he first looks down at the backs of his hands and watches the hair inexplicably thickening. Couldn't the transformation somehow be arrested? I tried to answer as Tom would have, yes of course, you're just cooped up, why don't you ask a girl up for the Yale game, it will all be fine.

I imagine that for other young men those years right after the war were exciting ones. A time when it really seemed possible that the great changes were coming. And others, poor as I was but struggling along somehow, could believe they were the makers of that new world. While I — I was comfortable. I read what Tom told me to read, wore what he told me to wear. Some days feeling trapped, other days guilty, knowing that I had been rescued and ought to be more grateful. But wouldn't I have made a life somehow? I have; the world didn't really careen from its orbit when Tom left it.

For those few years, though, everything was Tom's. He would have a party, and I would sit in a corner drinking his whiskey. Sometimes, excited by the company — some visiting luminary like Auden — I would talk too much. Tom would give me a stern look: hadn't you better be studying? And I would dutifully go off to my room and read Spenser or whatever deadly thing was supposed to prepare me for the profession I never entered.

Once when we ran out of ice, I was sent outside to fill the guests' glasses with fresh snow. It had to be fresh — in those coal-burning years snow turned black faster than winter days do. I remember, Tom was playing Mozart, just picking out the treble with his right hand while Bill Moody improvised a raggedy walking bass. Tom was so serious, eyes pinned to the music, while Moody clowned. When they broke off, Tom looked up at me and then down, deliberately, at his empty glass. I went out into the snow again without argument, like a kept boy.

My roommate has allowed his gown to ride up — or has arranged it — so that he is entirely exposed, or would be but for the hand that still rests at his crotch. While his hand is large, it is insufficient to protect his modesty. I read, over and over, a sentence about Theodore Parker. Perhaps the boy has missed or forgotten whatever clues to my character Howard might have offered this afternoon, and is just naively lying there. We're just two men in a room, what could be more natural, why should he cover himself? This hypothesis would be more plausible if he weren't actively fondling it now, though he is watching a cop show with no evident erotic content. But the contrary hypothesis, that he is actually offering himself to a battered and betubed old man, is inadmissible. Leaving open only a third theory, that this isn't happening at all, that one of the various unidentifiable pills they have made me swallow all day is giving me hallucinations. Dangerous ones, the kind that, acted upon, could get my other eye smashed in.

If it is a hallucination, it is one of remarkable consistency and duration. I cannot see his face without moving my head, and I don't dare do that. His cock is now markedly larger than the hand that clutches it. His other hand, with the bandaged thumb, has pushed his gown up beyond my line of vision. With his second and third fingers he ruffles the light hair on his breastbone. I feel weightless. He is, arguably in all innocence, adopting the classic postures of the videos. The cheap ones that show one man at a time, with you the costar hopelessly shut out by the screen.

I am not supposed to want any more. That was supposed to have ended the other night. This morning, when I was still entirely inside myself, cataloguing all the places I hurt, before I sat up and discovered this tormentor in the next bed, I had worked it all out. Everything was going to be peaceful from now on. I was going to be old.

I always just naturally assumed that, as I embarked on my golden years, I would abandon the hunt and buy a schnauzer. I think, really, that I expected some elementary fairness in Creation — that no God could be so plumb inconsiderate as to ravage the body and leave the desire intact. But, as an amputee itches in his phantom limb, so I go on needing what my body cannot deliver.

Forty years ago, I would have said it all boiled down to simple friction. All the rest — tasting beauty, touching souls — was mere embellishment. Now I wonder if Tom wasn't right all along: the acts were the embellishment. The holding and looking and touching were indispensable and will go on being so if I should live to lie bedsored and damp in a Medicaid nursing home.

That prospect no longer seems so distant. Perhaps the time has arrived when I will never feel again, not for any amount of money, the simple rightness of first light and a sleeping urchin cradled in my arms. Still, the only thing worse than not getting it any more would be not wanting it any more. Pathetic old man, couldn't you leave these things for the young? Are you really unable to find consolations befitting your age and condition, as wiser men have done? Listen: if we were short of blubber I would leave it for the little Esquimettes and sail forth unwhimperingly on my ice floe. But of beauty this world will never know a dearth, not till the last old fart has shut his eyes to it. And I will cry for my share while I have breath.

A commercial comes, louder even than the final shootout on the cop show. It startles the boy awake from his reverie of Janice. Or, under the less plausible hypothesis, it reminds him that time has gone by and I have not taken the bait. In any case, he prissily pulls down his gown and even gets under the covers. I still have not looked over at his face. It pleases me to imagine that it might register disappointment, that he really wanted me to cross between the beds.

A kept boy: is that the term for what I was? Kept is nearly right, getting my sustenance in return for small humiliations. Except of course that I was never called upon for the specific services ordinarily required in such arrangements. Protégé would fit, but I don't think Tom deluded himself (as I did, wanting those rooms, that life) that I was really going to follow in his footsteps. I aped him, when I bothered, so perfunctorily that he began to dish out his wisdom with a hint of self-mockery.

Comrade, the word he used at our very first meeting, is closer. Not that we were alike: while of course we did have the one obvious predilection in common, I had come from a different world from his and was already plunging merrily into one he would never enter. Perhaps I was a window on that world for him, or a scout, an advance party he couldn't catch up to. He followed my adventures in that realm with a distant respect, as I followed his in the more elevated realm I never got to. It made me his equal in a way, whatever his other accomplishments. Comrade is close enough.

One night during those years, Tom took me along to a dinner party at the Reynoldses'. I hated it when he took me to small parties, where people stared at me all night, as if I were the smoke betokening the fire they'd always suspected in him (a fire I had never managed to light). We had something from a chafing dish, cooked at the table. That was the year of chafing dishes, every meal spiced with the faint sickening smell of the gas. As we headed back to the living room for coffee, I excused myself, had to hit the books. Tom gave me a look — he knew damn well what subject I was going to study — but could not stop my escape.

I went to the Garland, of course. He knew the name, and exactly where it was, that door he could never pass through. How he must have imagined it, the real physical locus of everything impossible for him. A world he could have got to just by calling a cab, if he could have brought himself to utter the address. What did he picture? Roman revels, or something a bit more *fin de siècle*, flickering gaslights and decadent poets feasting with panthers and uttering bons mots?

The Garland was, as gay bars used to be, nearly invisible. On an alley between Chestnut and Dorset, a tiny neon sign, just a martini glass and, superfluously, COCKTAILS. The door was a blank slab, and there were no windows. One had to be an initiate to find it at all. Sometimes a venturesome sailor would stumble in, scary but irresistible. He would be surrounded at once, offered drinks, queried about his home town and his adventures and whether he'd been getting his share lately. As in one of Tom's favorite bits of Melville:

> About the Shark, phlegmatical one,
> Pale sot of the Maldive sea,
> The sleek little pilot-fish, azure and slim,
> How alert in attendance be.

Baffled but charmed, the wayfarer would accept the free drinks and would usually stagger off with one of his benefactors. What sort of prize he turned out to be we would hear later on: the sailor had passed out, or he had turned nasty, or — this most rarely — he had given himself up utterly. Once only, in my time, someone got killed.

Strangers aside, we were an incestuous lot, like an isolated tribe that can never catch a bride from the next tribe over. We would look around at one another grimly, sorting the familiar faces into their bins: the ones we'd had, the ones we wouldn't stoop to so early in the evening, the ones who would never stoop to us. Then we would all turn and watch the door. Not only in the hope that fresh seafood would step through, but also because there was always a chance the owner hadn't made his payoff this month and the cops would appear.

In sum, the Garland was not the inn of pure libido Tom must have imagined.

"Well," Tom said the next day, "as you made an early night of it, I assume you are prepared to explicate Mr. Jones Very."

"It was all I could do to explicate my way to your office."

"You didn't sleep well?"

"I didn't sleep much," I said.

"Ah." His back was to me; he was searching through the V section of his orderly shelves, so I couldn't see his expression. "An assignation."

"Yup." I must have been grinning when he turned around.

He returned to his desk and leafed through Jones Very. He cleared his throat and I waited as he formed some question that would go straight to the heart of my ignorance and sloth.

"What was he like?" he asked.

As many times as I had teasingly alluded to my tricks, he had never shown any curiosity before. Nor disapproval: he would simply let the subject drop, as if gentlemen didn't talk about such things.

I wasn't sure what he wanted to hear and chose to deflect him. "Just a townie. I guess Italian."

"You guess?"

"He looked kind of Italian. His name was Joe, that could be Italian or not."

"You didn't exchange your full names."

"Nobody does. It's like your — cell used to be, probably."

Automatically: "It wasn't a cell."

"Your study group. Anyway, he was . . . fun." Wrong word: I meant to make light of the subject and close it, but he must have thought I was rubbing it in. For Tom, after all, none of Amor's darts was labeled Fun.

He frowned, made a show of looking through the book a little longer. Then he closed it and began the real quiz. "I want to understand. You meet someone, you talk."

"You look first, or you don't look. You kind of look sideways."

"I see. And this indirection ends when one of you —"

"Says hi."

"Says hi. Having, I take it, lost some obscure test of wills."

"I don't know who wins or loses. It's hard to say hi."

"And then?"

"What do you mean?" I was apprehensive. There had to be some point to all this: he was leading me somewhere, and once we got there he was going to make a fool of me.

"Do you move directly to the business, or —"

"You just talk. Little nothings. Where are you from, are you a student, have you ever been to the Garland before, do you live by yourself."

"Very well, of course you exchange these banalities. But

there remains the getting down to business, some further step."

"No, all that *is* getting down to business. *Have you ever been to the Garland*, that means are you wise or did you just wander in by mistake. *Do you live by yourself* means is there some place we can go."

"A code," he said, nodding vigorously. Now we were apparently getting somewhere.

"Not a real mysterious one."

"Nonetheless, a mystery into which I evidently required initiation."

"Well, now you're initiated," I said. Maybe a little patronizingly; I so seldom knew anything he didn't.

"On the contrary, I am still very much in the dark. It would seem that this mere exchange of formulas could hardly be sufficient. That is, one might say, Yes I have been to the Garland, and, Yes I live by myself, but those responses might be merely accurate, not signals of assent. Somehow the fundamental question must be put."

"Oh, I guess. But it isn't — you know — it's 'Would you like to go someplace quieter?' Something like that."

"At this point it is still possible to receive a no."

"Once in a while. If you haven't read the guy right."

"But you are an adept reader?"

"Good enough."

"Then you leave. And then —"

"How many steps are we going to go through?"

"Just the one, the one step. You keep putting it off. The . . ." It took him a moment to find the word. "Contract."

"The what?"

"You do things. One of you does something and the other . . . has it done."

"Yes . . ."

"How . . . is . . . that . . . decided?"

"I don't know. You just kind of . . . fit together, or some-times you don't. That's all. It's not as though you sit down and write up an antenuptial agreement."

I was bracing for the next question when, abruptly, he reopened Jones Very and said, "Perhaps you would care to discuss the resemblances between Mr. Very and, oh, George Herbert?"

Having read the introduction if nothing else — an intro-duction by Tom himself that dwelt at some length on those resemblances — I did indeed care to discuss that very point. He knew it. He was giving me a breather after the inquisi-tion.

I wasn't surprised at how rapidly he had lost interest. That he had been interested at all had surprised me. Only later — I don't mean later that day, but years later — did I understand that he hadn't lost interest at all: he had lost hope. It wasn't an inquisition, but a tutorial. I was to tell him exactly how to act out his desires, whatever they were. How to cross the abyss between the two beds.

He would stalk a boy for months, reach the point when even he could tell it was now or never, and, without the contract, he couldn't go on. Yes, if Tom reached a hand out now, the boy might let himself be touched. But then what? Would it be permissible to kiss? Would he object if Tom . . . ?

Shame held him back, as if he were afraid the boy had drawn a line in the dust of his body, past which he would not let Tom cross. Tom never considered the corollary, that the boy must already have opened himself as far as that line, wherever it was. That, having drawn it, he had even pictured Tom hurling himself against it. There was no pride to be salvaged by stopping short of it. And if, incredibly, the boy had actually disclosed the boundary, uttered the contract as

Tom wanted him to: you may kiss me, but you may not . . . .
What would Tom have said then? Oh, of course not, I don't
even want to . . . . How could you think I wanted to?

I wish I had understood enough to explain it to him.
That there is no substitute for the negotiations of the flesh,
the bidding of the fingers, the counteroffer of the lips. The
decisive ringing down of the hammer when you have made
the winning bid and the prize is yours to carry off. There is
no substitute but money.

But of course no amount of money could have bought
him what he needed. Not money or the homely arts of
seduction he could have learned if he'd wanted to, the code
words he could have picked up as easily as any of his other
languages. He was looking for a ticket to the impossible city
that lived only in his book.

We talked about that place one winter afternoon, maybe
in '47 or '48. Tom was still at work on the book: I am sure
of this because I remember being in his little workroom, a
graduate student's carrel at the library where he did nothing
but write. I'd been walking through the stacks, on my way
to a men's room just off 3A, classics. It was far enough from
the more popular subject matter that boys with a literal need
for its facilities seldom wandered in, leaving it free for those
of us with a more classical bent. Anyway, I was almost there
when I found myself passing Tom's carrel. The door was
ajar, and I decided to stop for a moment.

There was a uniform blue-white light in the room, I can
still see it on his face. I remember: the room had a dormer
window and the snow entirely covered it, but in a thin
enough layer that the light shone through. He mustn't have
been working that day, or he would have had a lamp on
instead of just sitting there in that cold dim glow. Besides,
if he'd been working he wouldn't have let me in. Perhaps he

was just finishing up. Late '47 then, a few weeks before he closed that workroom, a year before he was hurled out of the study group.

I asked when I could read the book.

"You don't have to," he said. "I'm not the sort of despot who makes his students read his own books."

This was untrue. I countered with my own falsehood. "I really want to. I mean, you've been working on it the whole time I've known you. I'm not even sure what it's about."

To my regret, this remark happened to catch him on a day when he was ready to talk about it. He started to try to explain the book, the message he thought was in it and that no one else ever quite drew from it, the revolution as the triumph of comradeship. I may have been visibly squirming, thinking of the comradeship I was missing just down the hall. He leaned forward and touched my knee in the innocent, avuncular way he often practiced on his boys. "It all started with a letter, actually. I was sitting in the Faculty Club. In '42, it must have been. You hadn't come yet. A letter from a former student."

I hadn't come yet, but I can picture him in the Faculty Club every day, opening his morning mail as he ate one of those ghastly huge breakfasts he had every day of his life, probably even the last one, eggs and potatoes and bacon and toast. So there he would have been, with Fuzzy Walgreen across from him; they always breakfasted together. Tom would have worked through his business mail and then eagerly turned to the flimsy Victory envelope, no stamp, that meant a letter from one of his boys.

I must have read a thousand of them when I was going through Tom's papers. All alike: *Dear Professor. Out here in the jungle I am often reminded of ivied halls. Thank you for the book. We don't get much time to read poetry out here. Well, got to go now.* Occasionally one struck a darker note. *Did you hear about Chip Eaton? Awful tough break. I was going to write to his parents maybe. But I bet they'd really like to hear from you. Say, do you think we're going to beat Yale this year?*

It must have been one of those he opened in '42. They were plentiful enough. It was a dark time in the war. Hardly a week went by, probably, without Tom's hearing of another of his favorites beached and gutted on some sunny atoll. His losses were stunningly disproportionate. Something about his boys made them especially good candidates for slaughter. Excess enthusiasm maybe, or just stupidity. Maybe they landed on the beaches standing up, as though it were all a football game.

So perhaps it wasn't just one letter but the cumulation of massacres that broke through to him finally. In his carrel he said, very solemnly, "I put down that letter and I made myself conjure up that boy on the beach. I had been so fond of him for a little while. A shortstop. I saw him stretched out on that beach in his baseball uniform, sparkling white. His face buried in the sand. And I understood, quite suddenly, that my mourning was not unmixed with gratification." He looked up at the snow-covered window. "I didn't want him dead, nothing so monstrous as that. But I was content that he should be dead. It seemed to round things off nicely, that my boys should come to an end after leaving me."

I didn't understand how serious he was. "Very Housman," I said.

"Perhaps. I should have said Melville. The Handsome Sailor strung up on the yardarm."

"Oh, *Billy Budd*," I said, having read into it just far enough to know that Billy Budd was the Handsome Sailor. I never got to the part where he was strung up. Years later I saw the movie.

He ignored me and recited:

Pendant pearl from the yard-arm-end
Like the ear-drop I gave to Bristol Molly.

"Imagine him, Melville," Tom continued. "Silent all those years, never having what he wanted. Any more than I have."

I was so young and self-centered, I took that as directed at me. I was starting to answer that I had been ready enough. But he went on, "Finally an old man, recovering all his powers, gathering them up just so he can rise and kill Billy Budd."

I said, "Hm," trying to act as if I were taking it in.

"Before Billy can turn and stammer out s-s-sissy and go on back to his Bristol Molly."

"I'm not sure if I think that's what it's about," I said. Risking that he would turn and quiz me on the book, when I just wanted him to be a little clearer.

"That is what they are all about: Emerson, Hawthorne, Melville, all of them except Whitman. Idealists slashing away at the beauty they can't hold on to, wanting it dead or transcendent, anything but material, there in front of them but out of their reach. Emerson, do you really read Emerson? Always trying to get inside people and failing and then saying you're not an angel, you're a penis, no wonder I couldn't get inside you."

I couldn't recall this in Emerson. He was clutching my knee almost fiercely. "What I'm after, what the book is about, is the revolution built on love and not bloodletting. A world where I can watch a Billy Budd walk away and not want to obliterate him just because I can't get inside his skin."

He let go of my knee, sat back, and murmured the lines from Whitman that gave him his title:

I dream'd in a dream I saw a city invincible to the attacks
   of the whole of the rest of the earth,
I dream'd that was the new city of Friends,
Nothing was greater there than the quality of robust love,
   it led the rest,
It was seen every hour in the actions of the men of that city,
And in all their looks and words.

"This doesn't sound very political."

"Only fascists think politics is just about killing." That wasn't so, of course; his friends in the study group thought the same thing. I wonder if Tom wasn't just starting to worry that the ramparts of the next war, the class war, might be decked with the bodies of some very comely bourgeois. Perhaps that is what impelled him into his deviationist vision of a commune built on love. He who had never had it.

"I need to go to the men's room," I said.

If he ever got close to his city it was in the final year of his life. Not with me, of course: I was emphatically not the Handsome Sailor. But perhaps with — what was his name, that last boy? Jimmy, I think. They all rather run together, Tom's boys. I can scarcely remember his face.

I first became aware of him — I would hardly say noticed, those boys were so nearly routine — one day when I stopped in at Tom's office, for lunch or perhaps just to gossip. The boy was, or pretended to be, just on his way out, and Tom shook his head with a stoical expression, as if the boy were sailing next day for the front. I stayed in the doorway a moment and watched the boy walking down the hall. I thought then — here, after all, is a clear memory of him — that the boy looked better going than coming. That was odd, right there, since Tom generally picked his boys for their forward aspects.

"What do you think?" Tom said.

"Passable" would have been an accurate answer. The butt aside, he wasn't to my taste. I mean, I understood in the abstract that he was a great beauty, golden hair and the rest, but even forty years ago I preferred less polished gems. "Very nice," I said.

"Is that, if you will pardon my insistence, all?"

"That's more than you'll say for him by the end of the term."

"An understandable generalization, but inapplicable to the instant case."

"Of course. This one's different."

"He does what he likes. That is a difference."

"And that's good?"

"I mean that he doesn't simply accommodate me. Do you understand? I have been accommodated, now and then, but I've never been surprised."

"Oh. He gives you little surprises, does he?"

It took only one martial glare to tell me that this, my usual tone with him on such matters, would not do.

"I mean that —" He stopped himself. I can't remember another occasion when Tom was at a loss for words. And I think — unless it is my memory filling in the color — I think he blushed. It was no small thing, seeing a blush on Tom Slater. "He wants me," Tom said.

It seems to me now that I remember how they met, that the encounter in the office wasn't our first. It was during a reception in — what would it have been, fall of '51? But it could as easily have been another boy. Tom's finds did run together. They all looked as though they ate Wheaties.

I was in graduate school, in the resident adviser's job Tom had got me in Winthrop House. I had my meals there when I didn't eat out with Tom, and I was occasionally obliged to show up at a reception, or maybe a sherry hour. Of course I hated these events, though it was entertaining to watch Tom presiding over that little world that meant so much to him. So I must have tried, as always, to back out of that particular reception. But Tom would accept no excuses: his little wards were entitled to rub elbows with me.

The last of the veterans were gone that fall. For the first time since I had come to school in '43 you could look around a room and see nothing but real college boys. Nineteen or twenty, most of them, and almost all of them virgins. Imagine: most of the class of 1953 had never stuck it anywhere. I would meet my section, we would sit around a table while someone read his ghastly paper, and the room would be as thick with sex as the baths. Two hundred boys together, as at that reception, and you felt as though you were straddling the San Andreas Fault: energy enough to shake the world, and each of them forced to hold steady his little glass of sherry and make small talk with Mr. Reynolds from mathematics or Fuzzy Walgreen, the Pindar man.

Tom insisted that we have a little receiving line, he and I and a handful of professorial conscripts. Two hundred boys filed by, offering me their damp hands. An absurd ceremony. But I was enjoying watching Tom.

He was appallingly hearty, and quite fair: he gave scarcely more time to the boys he knew and liked than to all the corpulent, pimply newcomers. But in the second or two he had with each he could give a look so searching — even with the smile still in place — that some of the boys would be rather flustered by the time they got to me. I would then compound their uneasiness by holding their hands a bit too long and, once or twice, giving a little wink.

This game was interrupted by a backup in the line. I looked over, and there was Tom shaking a boy's hand again and again, the while giving a speech about how welcome he was to Winthrop House and how he should feel free to drop by Tom's rooms any time, any time he had a problem or just felt like talking, that's what Tom was there for. Finally he passed the boy on to me and returned to his indiscriminate heartiness. By the time Jimmy reached me, if it was Jimmy, he was blushing, not unhappily.

When I was in high school they would sometimes call out a list of names in assembly. Blais, Johnson, Laurent, Reeve, St. Denis should report to the principal's office. As I was never a discipline problem, it always meant I'd been picked for something. A little field trip, a competition, some project. The real answer was always a letdown, but I never learned. I would walk down the hall to the principal's office, a bit aloof from my fellow-elect, feeling certain that something miraculous was about to happen, something that would set me free.

That is how it must have felt for Jimmy that day. For any of Tom's boys, when they found themselves the center of his deep attentiveness, hot as a spotlight. They had been picked for something. They might have sensed, but could not have articulated, the erotic undercurrent of it all. They would have felt it only as an unidentifiable excitement, an opening in their lives. As the term went on, they would understand a little better — or they would hear, from some predecessor in the line of Tom's infatuations — what exactly they had been chosen for. Tom would never force them to say no outright, could never even have put the question. But each of them would, eventually, utter his no: no just to the whole uncertain drift of things, and then escape from Tom's line of vision.

What I was seeing on that one occasion was the start of it. I held the boy's hand almost as long as Tom had, looked at his cropped golden hair and his fresh face. His eyes when they met mine had a little pride in them, that he had been picked from among the hundreds. I tried to make out what Tom might have seen. Perhaps I thought I could find what he had seen in me.

He wants me, Tom said, that day in his office when I observed Jimmy's retreating butt. He wants me: the blush sweeping over his face as he found the words and realized that he had at last felt something simple enough to be put in words of one syllable. At almost sixty, almost my age now, after a life of missed connections and his chaste pajama parties with me, he had come out at the start of things and picked his way across the desert between the beds. How did he ever utter his yes, how did he ever hear the yes that was offered to him? And what in the world ever drew a yes out of Jimmy, the last of his Wheaties eaters?

My roommate has found a baseball game. The unceasing rhubarb-rhubarb of the crowd and the melancholy babbling of the play-by-play must be like a manly lullaby to him. I wait listlessly for close-ups of the players, with their meaty hips and thighs and their bland expressions under their silly caps. Then the beer commercials, men together, fishing, having a brew.

Let it be in the fishing lodge at Hamilton Lake, Tom and Jimmy sitting by the fire in their khakis and flannels, drinking Tom's whiskey. Their eyes meet, a resounding no passing between them. The boy knows he shouldn't have come. How could he ever have thought that he could go on basking in Tom's seriousness without ever facing him? And Tom is so sure that nothing will happen, he can almost persuade himself that he doesn't want it. No, let there be only the sublime, a weekend of ice-cold water and chastity.

Having avoided each other's eyes all through a day of futile fishing, they now stare freely as lovers might, locked together in their mutual refusal. The room disappears as it did when the boy attacked me the other night, leaving just two bodies facing each other in the dust. Until at last Jimmy — in a world pared down to whiskey and flannel against his chest and Tom's eyes — mutters *what the hell*. Just to have it over with, break the stare.

So the night is easy enough to imagine: two men with a little whiskey in them crawling into the same rough bed. The morning is the hard part. Tom is up before the boy, getting things packed, certain they cannot stay another night. He knows they will not speak of it. Jimmy will get up and profess the classic amnesia. They will have breakfast, then into the car and out of Eden forever.

He has already made the bacon and is frying potatoes when he hears the boy, creak of the bed and then of the floorboards. Jimmy is at the doorway, naked, just to torment. Tom does not look up. Shit it's cold, Jimmy says. Then you'd better get dressed, Tom says, colder than the morning.

Jimmy doesn't move. After a moment Tom turns back toward him, thinking: go ahead and look at him in the light. Jimmy scratches the little sunburst of hair on his chest, looks back at Tom. He grins. Why don't you come back to bed, he says. War passes out of the world.

$\mathcal{F}$OUR

THE NIGHT NURSE comes in. He looks to be forty or so, with a narrow Grecian beard and a thicket of black hair showing at the neck of his tunic. "Hi-how-are-you-I'm-Michael," he says to me, but before I can answer he moves to the bedside of my roommate. They speak softly. Michael says something to make the boy laugh. Then he comes back to me.

"I've got to rub some ointment around where your stitches are," he says, brandishing a tube. "Let me take those glasses off. I guess it's just one glass."

"I guess."

"That's a shame. You'll have to get new ones or something."

"Bifocals, too, they're a fortune."

"Tell me about it. I've got this new kind, where you can't see the line. They cost even more, but I just can't feature someone looking at me and thinking I'm so old I wear bifocals. As if I were fooling anyone."

"Well, you certainly fooled me," I say.

But he is all business again. He squeezes a little white ointment onto his finger and starts to rub it in. "This may sting a little," he says, after it already has. His head is tilted back so he can see what he's doing through the reading part of his confessed bifocals. It makes him seem disdainful. Just as he is squeezing out another dollop, the intercom breaks in: "Michael, Michael, you have a call."

"I'll be right back," he says. He sets the tube down on my nightstand, looks for someplace to wipe his finger, finds none. He hurries out, his finger held aloft with a pearl of cream at the end.

I wake to the sound of the TV, one of those shows about a new kitchen gadget, but the volume is down and I can hear soft snoring from the next bed. I don't know if Michael came back and didn't want to wake me or if he just forgot me. His tube of ointment is still on the nightstand. I squeeze a little out. It is tacky but better than nothing. I squeeze a lot more out.

Masturbation has changed like everything else. Time was, I would just shut my eyes and start flipping through memories as through an erotic Rolodex, from the boys of my adolescence to the latest trick. Tiny memories: a second or two culled from a whole evening, a snip of beauty artfully edited from a month of tedium. How was it that one picture or another would take command on a given night, push out the other memories and draw me in, so that I would run and rerun the same frame or two of film until I was finished? What misfiring circuit would bring to the fore that hustler with the pimples on his back, that furry Canuck with the bad breath, that German boy who bit? Something in my mood or in the air would give each of them his turn with me, his moment of stardom in the cinema of Onan.

I started buying porn when you could start buying porn. Not because my memories had ceased to satisfy, but just because it was there. Ripping open the sheath of plastic on a new purchase was like starting a new affair, or five at once: Rip and Chuck and Butch and Chris and Paul. I became a connoisseur, choosy as I never was in life. What an unbecoming mustache. Why did he ever get that tattoo? This one's too small, and this too big. Goldilocks with a hard-on, flipping through the pages until she finds the one that's just right. Now I have a whole big carton full of the stuff, two decades of despoiled youth in the back of my closet. What has become of them all? How many have turned respectable, worrying every minute that someone will find those ancient pictures of them in the dainty posing straps they used to wear? How many are dead? Did the cops find the box when they were going through my apartment?

Tonight I am thrown back on my own repertory. It's funny, but none of the two-dimensional images creeps in. You would think they could find their place with all the other, equally frozen, *natures mortes* in my gallery. But the real ones crowd them out, filling me with a longing to go back and turn again even the most ghastly trick.

Every picture dissolves into the one who hit me. I keep trying to cut away, force into my vision one or another of my golden oldies, and there he is again, looming above me at the very last instant before he struck. Why not just give myself up to him, what could it matter? It wouldn't really mean, would it, that I wanted it, that I was as degraded as that? Just an inconsequential jerk-off, over before I'd know it: why do I feel that to allow it would be to cross some fateful line? To let him through would be to turn into one of those creatures who wears a dog collar and waits for the stroke of the belt from an accountant with a leather hood. Still, he insists, he will not get out of my sight. I must be that creature. I flip through my Rolodex with mounting frustration. Nothing. The boy from the other night has chased away every rival; he is my only memory.

Forty years now I have spent walking into bars, from the Garland to, the other night, the bathetically misnamed Corral. In that time, I have been transformed from a starlet awaiting discovery to an accident scene from which all eyes are averted. All but those of my contemporaries, who waved briefly as I came in the other night, before resuming their attempts to score through telepathy or knee rubbing. I took my place at the square bar in the middle of the room, the territory of old men and their hangers-on. Younger men in search of their peers lined the long bar at the far wall.

Cochran was across the square from me. He's as old as I am, but he doesn't show it: all the forces of nature couldn't carve so much as a laugh line in his smooth, fat face. He was wearing make-up, you could see it even in the careful, soft light of the Corral. Nothing outrageous, like eye shadow or Aschenbach's rouge, just a little foundation. So his face was like the ones in the Sunday funnies, an outline filled in with an even, lifeless flesh tone. His neck was a bluish white; he hadn't brought the make-up down for fear of staining his shirt collar.

A couple of boys were hovering around him, dressed too well for the Corral. They work for him, probably, at his design firm. The Associates in Cochran &, working their way up, performing other duties as assigned. I wonder if he took both of them home. There is certainly enough of Cochran to go around. They could clamber over him, like whalers over their trophy. The evening climaxing in a little CPR.

The boy who was looking at me was, ipso facto, a hustler. So I felt free to stare at him, instead of playing the monotonous peekaboo I learned at the Garland. He stared back, expressionless, like a mug shot. (I lied, I could probably pick him out.) I looked away, at one or two of his competitors — appraising the goods like a K mart shopper — before meeting his stare again.

I'd been out to dinner, by myself. I knew the waiter winked as he offered me another drink only because he wanted a better tip. I knew this, knew that I ranked just above his grandmother in the roster of sexual possibilities. Still, I was foolishly excited as I watched him walk away, his buns saluting me through the gap in his apron. I read the menu and I decided — no, realized, my heart thumping out its old one-note song of trepidation and desire — that I was going to go out after dinner and try to forge a contract. So I stopped at two drinks.

My friends, some of them, use the services. You call up and give your Visa number and pretty soon the boy is at your door, certified, safe, versatile. That's what I should have done, of course. But it isn't at all the same, not like meeting someone in a bar. Even if you know that a price will sooner or later be quoted, it feels like making a connection.

There doesn't come a day when you just say, oh hell, I'm never going to attract anybody, I'd better start paying for it. You slip into it gradually, as slowly and imperceptibly as your hair turns white. At first, once or twice, you're talking to somebody, still exploring, a little flattered that he might be interested. You notice that his beer's empty and, quite casually, order him another. When he goes off to pee a friend happens by — Howard, probably, always looking after you — and well-meaningly bursts your little bubble of self-satisfaction by announcing the boy's profession. You nod and force a smile: of course, I guessed that, I was just talking to him. As he comes out of the john you can see that maybe he was a little too good to be true. But you're not entirely over the hill yet, lucky surprises do still happen. When he sits down again and offers you a friendly and unmercantile smile you wonder if Howard might be mistaken. You start talking again, and you begin to imagine that the boy might be enjoying a night off. Then he drains his beer, sets it down, goes on talking. He expects you to order another without his asking. You excuse yourself then, irritated that you've wasted an hour and it's almost closing time, worried that your friends have seen you and are entertained. You must be scowling; nobody cruises you and you go home alone.

Another time — it's 1970 or so, you're in your mid-forties and have shifted to a bar with dimmer lights — you are on the way out the door with your catch (scrawny and stoned-looking, but with a pretty, gap-toothed smile, and he actually bought you a beer) when he says, man, I'm a little short, you think maybe you could help me out. You say you're kind of broke yourself. Hey, that's cool, he says. Listen, you got any dope? You say no. He kisses you and says catch you later.

Soon you are fifty, standing at a bus stop, and you have struck up a conversation with a boy in a pale polyester suit with the impossibly wide lapels of that year. Your bus comes, the 43, and it must be his too, because he let a 37 go by just a few minutes ago. You wait for him to board, he waits for you, the bus rumbles away, leaving a great black cloud in its wake. You say, all these packages, I thought maybe I better catch a cab after all. Then, can I drop you anywhere? In the cab you announce your destination, look to the boy. He says that's close enough. You ride along, unable to believe your luck, a pickup like this in broad daylight, it could be thirty years ago. You get to your place, the two of you get out, you are standing there trying to remember the right thing to say. He looks down at the sidewalk and murmurs, you know, I usually get paid. He's wearing a suit, it's two in the afternoon, how could you possibly have guessed? You hear yourself asking how much.

As the bard of my younger days said: after the first death,

79

there is no other. At last you are sixty-two. You've left the restaurant and you know you need cash. You stand at the bank machine awaiting its judgment and worrying a little bit about the guy behind you, who doesn't look like he has much of a balance to draw on and may be coveting yours. You hear the gratifying thuck-thuck of the money dropping down. It is the sound of possibility, the way a certain look in a bar or a park spelled possibility years ago.

The boy at the Corral was looking at me steadily now. His hair was cut close on the sides, fuller at the top, in the fashion of the magazines. His hands and feet were proportionate to the rest of him. So he wasn't jailbait. Twenty-one or -two, maybe more. The rest of him — oh, the rest of him: a fine surging chest, shoulders raised a little, tensed a little. Who would not be tense at the prospect of a contract with hideous old Reeve? And the belly not too flat. I cannot abide a boy with no soft spot anywhere. He had had a beer or two, this one. His teeth, which he now displayed in a hesitant but deliberate smile, were straight, and all present. He was a prole, but not a lumpenprole. Not dangerous. Perhaps he would even turn out to be one of those boys for whom the money is an alibi and who give more than full value. Our contract was concluded, across the square bar, long before I sent him a beer.

Back at my apartment, the contract concluded, the boy waited in the bedroom while I went to the john to spruce up. I looked in the mirror, saw no possibility of improvement, and just sprayed a little breath freshener to give the whiskey a bit of competition. When I emerged in my bathrobe, the boy was standing at the far side of the bed, as far away as possible.

He was still wearing his pants. A nice touch, made it seem almost as though he just happened to be there. If he had been standing stripped he would have been too obviously a commodity. As I approached him, he raised his arms a tiny bit and tensed his shoulders once again. He had the face of someone who was about to get a typhoid booster and did not intend to wince. Too bad; I wouldn't have hurt him. I sat on the bed. He sat, too, hands on his thighs.

He cleared his throat, and said, "We can't . . . you know, the way things are, there's things I don't do."

"My dear, I couldn't undertake to do those things without a hydraulic engineer and a respiratory therapist."

He gave a little laugh, "Huh," catching from my tone that he was supposed to. "I mean, I only do safe stuff."

"Me too," I said, with minimal clairvoyance. I took off my glasses and put them on the nightstand.

As a last withholding he had sucked in his lips so that his mouth was a straight, unwelcoming scar. The look he gave me was clinical. It was an experiment: how far would the old rat proceed without any reinforcement? But the old rat had been through this test before, entered the maze, not at the forbidding mouth, but at the open glowing hollow above the collarbone. And with a tongue light and tenacious as a rat's paws threaded a way up the vessels of the boy's neck, pressed the familiar lever just below the ear, and got the reward: the boy inhaled sharply, closed his eyes. His mouth just drifted open, and he pulled my face down to it. In a minute I was on my back on the bed, he on top. He broke the kiss, sat up. I disentangled myself from my bathrobe and lay back. Then he was kneeling above me, still with his pants on. I looked up at his little beer belly and his smooth chest and his face, which was frowning and thoughtful now. I was about to reach up and touch his face.

I have lost my erection. Whatever started me off has passed, and the ointment has lost the little slickness it had and is sinking into the skin of my diminishing cock. I ought to try to sleep. But I want to finish, just to feel that I still can. That I haven't been robbed of this, too, along with whatever worthless odds and ends the boy scraped up from my apartment before he crept out. I get some fresh ointment — I have nearly depleted Michael's tube, I'll probably be billed for it — and try to think of anyone but the boy looming above me.

I open my eyes and look over at my roommate. He is still on his back, snoring more robustly now. I picture him as he was, coverlet down, gown up, offering himself ambiguously. This time I take him up on it. My impediments and apparatus are swept away. I fly to his bed. I bury my face in the golden down on his chest, he is stroking my hair, he leans forward to kiss me on the top of my head. He raises his hand. The bandage is gone. He is going to hit me.

My cock is chafed and my headache is coming back. Still, I shut my eyes and return to my Rolodex. At last there appears, like a visitation, Arnaud. He looks a little like the boy from the other night, but it is definitely Arnaud, from fifty years ago.

Finally my climax: abrupt and meager, like a burp, a mere relief without even the usual teasing glimpse of the sacred. Even as it arrives my eyes are already drifting toward the television. I know I must get up and find something to wipe myself with, but I cannot. I doze.

I watched Winslow, my home town, die in the thirties. It wasn't just the Depression. Some of the mills had been shut up even earlier, as the absentee proprietors sent the machinery south, where the cheap labor was. The thirties just finished the job: the whole city ran down and stopped, like a mechanical toy someone had forgotten to wind up. If my father had been alive he would have been out of work and we would have starved. As he had providently died, my mother had a little pension, on which we starved more genteelly.

The Wonamaddock went first, right after the war. The Great War: I hadn't even been born when they shut down. We never called it the Wonamaddock, we called it the Khaki Company. Maybe they called it the Wonamaddock on Wall Street, or maybe they had uglier names for it. The market for khaki got a little soft after the Armistice.

Their mills were a good way from the center of town, off the canal altogether; they were steam-driven. For the older, water-powered mills the canal was a discipline. Having to hug close to it they built vertically, five or six stories and a cupola. The Khaki Company, freed of the water, built horizontally — low sheds sprawling across what had been a town park, sacrificed by the aldermen for the war effort. After, they were simply abandoned. One shed stayed open, I guess, turning out janitors' trousers and boy scout uniforms. The rest were silent, their machinery intact. Built in a hurry, those looms, to weave one kind of twill and nothing else. So there wasn't anybody rushing to buy them, dismantle them, ship them off to Carolina. The machines stood in their deserted barracks like lines of noncoms in the peacetime army, waiting for the call.

As the thirties wore on, and abandoned mills began to litter Winslow like bodies no one cared to claim, the old khaki mills took on by contrast a rather pleasant air. The people who had worked at Khaki had blown into town with the war and drifted away with the Return to Normalcy; it was all nothing to us. The vacant shells hard by the canal stood for Winslow people, our people, out of work. But the Khaki was just a ruin left by strangers who had never touched our lives. Children played among the sheds; daring ones climbed the spiral staircase round the smokestack. Lovers met in the shadows of the looms — it was easy to get in, and where else was there to go in winter? I myself learned many of life's mysteries lying in the dust of those dark sheds. Cotton dust, that turns your lungs the color of khaki.

No one in Winslow was ever quite sure who owned the Wonamaddock. But it was the whole of Tom's fortune. In 1920, the year Tom's father put the common stock in trust for him, the shares were worth a dime for every dollar he had thrown in just three years before. Through the twenties, the place produced exactly the amount of income Tom was meant to have, no more. In the thirties it produced nothing, not a penny, and Tom actually had to live on his salary. But for the irrevocable trust, the company would have dissolved. Instead it remained in suspended animation until the next war. Then it rose to the call, and suddenly Tom was richer than he was ever supposed to be.

We were arguing once about Thomas Jefferson, one of Tom's heroes, predictably. I was young enough to be indignant at his hypocrisy in never freeing his slaves. I got rather hot about it, and had the temerity to draw an analogy to Tom, friend of the workers, and the wartime revival of his fortunes at the eternally nonunion Wonamaddock.

Tom's answer was jesuitical. "I can't sell the shares, I'm not allowed to. And, even if I could, to do so would only be to pass the crime from one hand to the other. I could go and run the place myself and try to be a kindly father. But at best I should drive the place to ruin and throw them all out of work. And at worst I should succeed, and be a kindly father. Don't you see: the capital is there, it is held, by my hands or someone else's. All the labor that's been stored up, all the blood in which my very certificates are printed, I cannot give it back. It can only be taken back, when the revolution comes. Until then, as well in my hands as any other."

I said, "The shares, fine, but the dividends: you could do something with them. I mean, give them to the poor or something."

"I give away every cent I can spare," he said. Probably he did, the war profiteer writing his dutiful checks to the Joint Anti-Fascist Refugee Committee and the National Council for American-Soviet Friendship. But what he kept, what he could not spare, was plenty. He lived modestly at great expense. In New York he would go to the Colony and order a bowl of soup. At the opera he would take a box and then stand at the back of the orchestra, because the sight-lines were better. His suits were bespoke — from Wetzel, or from Dunn in Boston — but he would affect a ratty cardigan in place of the waistcoat. He was at war with his own extravagance. I don't think he ever meant to impress anyone. He simply had the habit of money. If he had been governed only by his own needs and desires, he could have lived on his salary alone. It just never occurred to him that he could do things any differently from his father.

We dropped the subject. I never brought it up again, though it was an interesting coincidence, his owning half my home town. When he left it to me, in that will his brother broke, I could see that he was sort of making amends. I was much older when it first occurred to me that the coincidence was not one he had inadvertently uncovered. Maybe it was my ticket to him in the first place, the reason he had ever let me in to his world of Wheaties eaters. At least it's the only reason I can think of.

When we talked about the Wonamaddock, it must have been '46 or '47. There was, I suppose, a lull in production in that interval of peace. Since then, peace has never cast a shadow over the place; the company has never gone a quarter without declaring a dividend. I haven't been back to Winslow since my mother died in '69, twenty years now.

85

But I keep up, check in the papers, watch the fortune of my lost estate. The only mill still running in all of Winslow.

My Winslow is now the quarry of persons who call themselves industrial archaeologists. They have actual digs — I read about it just the other week, how they are systematically excavating a parking lot where the old Winslow Looms once stood. Next thing you know, the whole place will be a national park.

Arnaud worked in Spinning Three before they shut it down. Even now some graduate student is unearthing a Moxie bottle once touched to my lover's lips. It got closer than I ever did, that bottle. The student whisks the dust from the bottle and marks it: Section D-7, Stratum II, c. 193(9?). Another student, not an archaeologist but a social historian, wanders the streets of Winslow with a tape recorder, innocently supposing that the geezers on park benches will be able to tell him how things really were. If those old wrecks are anything like me, they remember how things weren't. Our might-have-beens are not footnotes to the main text of how-it-was; they are the text. The real things that happened, if we can remember them at all, seem no more than sarcastic marginalia.

At the northern end of the canal, just where it parted from the river, was a kind of granite watchtower. It was built right into the canal wall, just at the end of the Canal Street bridge, a little piece of a castle, someone's romantic conceit. You could lean out over the edge and watch the water hurtling toward the first man-made fall, and on south, to the next fall — West Mills — or the next after that, Winslow Looms. And on down, eleven falls in all before the canal rejoined the river: a sparkling and treacherous staircase for a giant. Or you could look to the north, back up the river, to the desert unworkable farms that had given their daughters to Winslow and their sons to the West a hundred years before.

If you were ten years old, though, you could see ever so much farther. From that outcropping I could scan the besieging army; I could order my archers to let loose their volley; over the rampart I might pour, if that army came too close, the requisite oil or molten lead. My solitary reading had given me a name for the place — a bartizan — and had taught me what it was for. After school I would perch in it and spin out long chivalric fantasies. I had with me a sometime foot soldier, sometime prince, Arnaud. A Canuck.

What could he have made of it all, those spring afternoons when I babbled away about knights and damsels and feats of arms? I may have been the only Anglais he ever knew. Perhaps he thought we were all like this, that this was what the American boys did. Anyway, he played along, did not refuse even to be my champion and wear my kerchief in the jousting; he knelt in fealty, I the princess swooned in the bartizan.

We were there after the last day of school. A cool, cloudy afternoon. Rain had darkened the stone of our little outpost, making it more credibly medieval. A summer of chivalry stretched ahead, then junior high. I announced a grand tournament for the following day. No, Arnaud couldn't; tomorrow he started at Winslow Looms. Matter-of-fact, so I was obliged to be, too.

He was eleven or twelve, I guess, and clumsy in small movements as he was graceful in large; probably they put him to sweeping or toting rather than at the machines. In any case, he promptly disappeared from my world as entirely as if he had moved to another hemisphere. When I started seventh grade after a grim summer without my chevalier, he wasn't there. By the time I left for school in the morning he was already at the mill, and he was still there when my mother and I were sitting down to our tasteless supper. I might have seen him Sundays, I suppose, might have ventured into Lower Falls and found him after Mass, if he still went to Mass. But it didn't take much prescience to know what kind of meeting that would be. I didn't seek it, and I didn't seek it that winter, when the Winslow Looms closed for good. His afternoons were free as mine were then, but I knew he wouldn't want to play.

Years later, not long before I left for college, I was heading home one night from the library, just coming over the Canal Street bridge, when I saw a dark figure in the bartizan. I didn't know him at first. In the dark, at sixty feet, one Canuck was like another. Hair trimmed close at the sides, full and spiky at the top, like neglected privet. A sweater. Trousers close at the hips, billowing at the knees.

As I got closer I stopped looking at him. I only needed to get past the bartizan. Then streetlamps, safety. I listened to my own footsteps on the stone. Steady, taking me right past him, no need to run.

I was almost to the light when I heard, "Fuck you. Don't say hello."

His voice had changed. I knew it only from the accent: not quite perfect American, a little extra play of the vowels across the roof of the mouth. The years had thrown muscle about his chest and shoulders like gobs of clay on a sculptor's armature. The legs were still a boy's, and would never catch up. His were a top-heavy people.

"I didn't see you," I said.

His eyes might have been drawn by a department store fashion artist: lightless wedges. Below them a perfect smile. Where did a poor boy get teeth like that? I can remember the smile, but only a little of the talk that followed when the smile faded.

"You're going away." He must have seen it in the paper, when I won the scholarship. It was news when anyone escaped Winslow.

"Pretty soon, yeah." Then, proudly, "To college."

He snorted. "To play football, you."

"To get an education," I said, primly. It was lost on him; the phrase meant nothing. He understood that the rich, among whom he classed me in contrast with himself, went someplace called college. But it was just something they did, like playing polo in the newsreels. It wasn't for anything.

"And after that," he said. "You go to work?"

"I guess. If the war's over. I don't know what happens."

"Yeah, we have a college guy in the mill. Dumb, that one."

"You're working again."

"Yeah, a year almost. They opened up part of the Khaki. Uniforms."

"Uh-huh."

"Not all. The north line is still closed. People still go there, you know?"

We stopped talking. Arnaud turned and looked down-river, off toward the old Winslow Looms. I began to think of going home. Still looking away, he said, "I hear you get browned."

Heard it from the other mill boys of Winslow. All through high school I was a harbor of last resort for boys — and sometimes men — too poor or too lazy to hunt themselves a real piece.

They would just happen upon me, or they would make assignations: Meet me in the alley behind Winslow Looms or I'll bust your teeth in. The threats were superfluous. I went unresistingly. I didn't know why. I didn't enjoy the act itself. It stopped hurting soon enough, but all I wanted was for them to be done. Still, I went with them. It made sense

89

somehow, it felt like what I ought to be doing. They could feel that, the boys. They knew what I was before I had an inkling of it.

So I would get browned, in the word they used back then. When they had finished, they would hurry away without a word while I was still picking myself up from the straw or gravel or, on cold nights, the brown dust of the old Khaki, the north shed that was still closed. Before I could button my trousers, they would be out of sight.

Some of them did surprise me. In the middle of the act, one might whisper rasping endearments omitted from my high school French book. Another might, at the end, offer forth a half-crushed pack of cigarettes. We would smoke, nothing to say to one another, and I would look at his dark eyes. And, once in a long while, one would take my hand. Awkwardly, not an idea in hell what to do with it, but feeling that he kind of ought to take my hand, as long as there was no one to see.

Arnaud said, "I hear you get browned." Half a century, and the shame of those words can still bring the blood to my face; I have to sit upright to relieve the pressure.

I stammered, "Sometimes."

At the north shed, I followed him down the aisle between the sleeping machines until he came to a stop before a pile of rags: our marriage bed. He stepped back and then just stood, waiting, not looking at me. I took off my jacket, draped it over a stool. I turned toward him again, but he was still motionless. There was nothing to do but take down my trousers, crawl onto the rag heap, and wait. He stepped forward, and I listened as he unbuttoned his fly. I knew he would not want me to look back at him. "You need to spit," I said. He understood, hawked twice. Then he was behind me, his cold hands on my butt.

I didn't expect him to make love to me; I wouldn't have

known what those words meant. But I must have thought that our being childhood playmates would count for something, that I would feel some shadow of our courtly playacting, so long ago.

He rammed into me so hard I had to bury my face in the rags to keep from crying out. I think I understood at once that he was punishing me. Because I was privileged and would escape Winslow? Or just because we had been friends once and he had to be rough with me to show that what we were doing wasn't friendship, I wasn't his princess, he wasn't my knight. It didn't matter why he was doing it: he was doing it to *me*. For everyone before I had been a mere public convenience. They didn't care what I felt, they just did their business and left. Arnaud's violence was, in contrast, a sort of recognition. He was slamming into me personally.

He stopped for a second, caught a breath. When he resumed he had slowed down: as if he were lost in thought he shifted to a quiet, walking rhythm. He fucked me *andante*, and soon I was moving with him. Until that night I had always lain still. My raptors might as well have been fucking a milk bottle. With Arnaud, for the first time, I gave myself up entirely. And, well, graduated from princess to queen.

As I sat picking cinders and stray bits of cotton from my belly, Arnaud examined himself with evident distaste, as if I had left something that wouldn't wash off. He pulled up his pants and walked away, like all the others, before I could even get up. Outside, I followed as he headed back toward the bridge. He seemed to slow down, and I hurried to catch up with him, though I should have been walking the other way. He stopped in the dark between two streetlamps. When I had reached him, he said, "You're not going to tell anyone."

Of course I never did; it was the others who did the

telling. But I said, "Why should I tell? It wasn't anything special."

I stayed where I was as he went on, into the light of the next streetlamp, into the darkness beyond it. And again, smaller in the next pool of light, smaller still in the one after that. I had turned to go home when I heard him running, hard soles clicking on the stone walkway of the bridge. When he caught up to me he was a little out of breath, though he hadn't run so far. Only a few years in the mill, and it was already doing its work. He said my given name and put his arm around my shoulders. That wasn't, back then, such an uncommon thing for boys our age to do.

His face was close to mine, but I could not, in the darkness, make out his expression. I raised my face toward his, near enough that I brushed — or told myself I had, could feel the charge of — his stubble against my smooth skin. I thought he meant to kiss me, but he stepped back.

"When are you going?" he said.

"Couple of weeks." I added, feeling absurdly coquettish, "Maybe I'll see you again before that."

"I don't know. We're real busy at the mill." My first rejection, harbinger of my life in the bars.

I turned away, but he grabbed my arm, and then he really did kiss me. Not at all far from the mouth. He ran away, soles clicking on the stone bridge.

Michael is back, looking for his ointment. He sees it, and also sees that it's practically used up. He looks at me; I try to look back blankly but cannot suppress an embarrassed grin. He shakes his head and says, "You probably need a towel or something." He thinks he'll be over it at sixty-two.

In the john he runs water for a minute; he emerges with a hand towel, warm and damp. He starts to pull back the covers, but I say, "I can do that," and take the towel from him. While I dab at myself under the covers, he gets what's left of his ointment and starts again to rub it over my stitches and over the little cuts that were too small to stitch. He works with a businesslike concentration that is a kind of tenderness.

"That's going to heal real well," he said. "You'll hardly see it, just a little line."

"Just one more."

"No, go on. I've got as many lines as you do. You know, I looked at your chart and I just couldn't believe the age it said. You look terrific."

We both smile; I feel that I am being welcomed back into the social world where such gracious fatuities are uttered. He looks at the back of my hand, the little puncture wound from the tongue of my belt buckle, when the boy bound me. He rubs some ointment on it, then just holds my hand a second. "You've been very brave," he says.

Brave is a word for children. It makes me want to cry, the way you do when you don't have to be brave any more. He lets go of my hand and gently smooths my hair back. I look at him through my tears, and he goes on stroking the top of my head for a minute. Then he puts the cap on his ointment and goes.

$\mathscr{F}$IVE

Friday morning. I have actually slept through the night, for the first time since my episode. The boy is sitting up in the visitor's chair, wearing street clothes, jeans, a T-shirt with the legend WTFS: Power Rock. On the bed is his duffel bag.

He is watching his cartoons apathetically, as one might dutifully page through the foreign news in the *Times*. His left leg is bouncing slowly up and down like a piston: on the upward stroke, a hole in his jeans widens and I glimpse his bare knee. He must be waiting for the doctor to come and send him home. Like a prisoner whose sentence is up, waiting for the gate to be opened. Already, just by getting dressed, he has distanced himself immeasurably from me and the other inmates. Probably he cares more about getting out, just now, than he cares about the future of his thumb.

The boy's doctor eventually appears. The boy stands up: he is about to be discharged, passing out of my life as quickly as he entered it. Another of those small, unconsummated passions — the guy who smiled from across the aisle once on a long bus ride, the man in a hotel bar whose signals were too ambiguous to take a chance on — who wind up not in my Rolodex but in a special file of their own. From which they leap out, unsummoned, at inconvenient moments, giving me a pang briefer but also deeper than the memory of any real lover I've had and lost. Maybe because only what you haven't had might have been perfect.

The doctor is thirty, if that, a resident I guess, with a cool, ex-surfer air and a tiny smirk. He says to the boy, "Hey, how's it going." The boy shrugs, does not look up at his face, fixes instead on the embroidered Dr. Harris on the resident's white coat. Dr. Harris sits on the edge of the bed, says, "Let's take a look," and begins undoing the bandage. The boy turns his eyes to the television and soon I do too, neither of us eager to look at the thumb.

"That's looking a whole lot better," the doctor says. As he starts rewrapping the thumb, he covers with a smooth, lay-talk narrative about test results and how things could still go either way and, in short, how he'd rather the boy stayed another day. The boy looks him in the face for the first time but says nothing.

"Hey, I understand how you feel," the doctor says patronizingly. To him the boy is just a dumb kid, carpenter's helper or apprentice plumber or whatever it says on his forms. Maybe he can see that the boy is good-looking in a lower-class way. But he doesn't acknowledge an aristocracy of beauty, isn't awestruck by the boy as I'd be even if I had a dozen M.D.s. "We'll just see how it goes for another day." Needing no answer, he gets up, throws the used dressing in the toxic can, the one with the red liner, and starts out of the room.

He pauses at the foot of my bed, looks at me but does not speak. I am just a curiosity, somebody else's patient with some entertaining wounds. He regards me as he might a picture in a gallery. Back at the nurses' station he will glance through my chart as through the catalogue of an exhibition.

I feel the boy's eyes on me; I am a regular attraction today. He has returned to his visitor's chair and is sitting there looking at me. I keep myself from turning for a moment. Let him look. He must be trying to figure me out. Or no — he isn't in the business of figuring things out. He is just taking me in, as he might stare at some creature in the zoo.

To him I am an impossible exotic, strange as a platypus or a bird of paradise. He has never met one of us. No one is out, in his world. If you have to come out, you leave the neighborhood. He sees us on television, of course, the wacky neighbor in the situation comedy or the serial killer. He has known sissies, and he has heard things said about that substitute English teacher he had for a while. Perhaps in junior high friends of his made a quick ten bucks letting someone blow them, perhaps he himself did. I never went in for that, the skinny children with acne leaning against the wall at McLellan Square, waiting for the cars to pull up.

He has never known a gay man in full flower. Now here he is, caged with one for three days, as if he had been abandoned in the zoo and left to dwell with the platypus. A big old one with tubes running out of it and a funny, plump mate that dropped by yesterday. I turn, finally. He is slouched in his chair, fingers drumming softly on the armrests, looking straight at me. I look back. He is counting my wounds, I can see his glance moving from my bandaged eye to my bruises to my split lip to my punctured hand. I hear him thinking as clearly as if he were saying it: what happened? He knows I wasn't mugged, he's heard enough by now that even he must be able to piece the story together. He looks straight into my sighted eye. What happened to you?

I want to tell him, everything, as long as he is caged with me why not tell him everything? He looks at me so steadily and calmly, I find myself imagining he would accept it all, just drink it in without question or judgment. No, one thing he would judge: the part where I didn't fight back. Maybe he could accept my being a fairy, an especially stupid and imprudent fairy who ran into what I had always dreaded and found it just as bad as I had thought. But he wouldn't be able to accept or forgive that I hadn't raised a hand to fight it off.

I could lie easily enough: I tried to fight him, but you can see, I'm an old man, he was too much for me. That would round the story off, and he could nod and turn the volume back up on the TV, his little flicker of curiosity satisfied. But I just look back at him, wordless as a platypus, until he loses interest and turns away. I didn't even try. I was as cowardly as, say, a suicide.

Sharon the day nurse comes in. As she is wrapping the blood pressure cuff around my arm she says to the boy, "You need to get back in your gown." He starts to protest; she can tell without looking at him. "I'm sorry, but it's a rule. If you're staying you have to be in the gown."

When she is gone, he starts to change. But he has only just lifted his T-shirt up to expose his ridged belly when he thinks better of it, grabs the gown and his duffel bag, and retreats to the john. As if he had any modesty to defend after last night.

He is still in the john when Janice comes in. "Hey, where'd he go?" she says, turning to me. "You're looking better, a little. I was supposed to take him home. He didn't leave already?"

Before I can say anything, the boy answers with a flush, the voracious, world-swallowing flush of a hospital toilet. He emerges, in his gown of course, and she says, "Jeez, ain't they let you out yet?" He shakes his head, eyes down, as if it were his fault. "I don't see why they keep you lying here just so they can watch your damn thumb. You could bring

97

it in to them once a day and they could look at it. That's all they look at it anyway, once a day."

He shrugs and gets back into bed. She sits on the edge farthest from me. He sits up with her and puts an arm around her. They both have their backs to me. She is saying many things I cannot quite hear; he is not answering. Can it always be like that, her merry babble crashing against his silence?

He is holding her more tightly now. His unbandaged hand is out of view, probably at her breast. Their faces are very close together. Whatever she is murmuring now is making him laugh; the muscles of his back dance.

What can it be like for her? Wrapped in his great arm as in a fur, her cheek grazed by his stubble, she holds his hand to her breast and whispers gossip, family stories, lewd suggestions, whatever it is that makes his back shake. So lively and voluble, and she spends it all on him, just so he'll hold her. I wonder where her other hand is.

I thought yesterday that what I was feeling was jealousy. But it's not so simple; we are not even the same species, I can no more be jealous of her than I could begrudge a doe her buck. Of course I cannot imagine what he sees in her, any more than I can picture what Bambi's father found so alluring about the white rump of Bambi's mother. But I am equally baffled by what she might see in him. Partly I am still a captive of the old myth, that women didn't really go for looks, that they were taught in infancy to evaluate career prospects and aptitude for bringing home the bacon. Now we've all learned better. Still, I had thought that women tended to fix on the odd detail, cute ears or a lopsided smile. Here Janice has homed in on an archetypal hunk who will never be able to take care of her and who may never favor her with so much as a complete sentence. She must do it because she sees what I do, that he is an angel. Therein my jealousy, if that is the word, that she not only can have him, but can know what she has.

He whispers something to her, finally, and she suddenly looks around at me, too fast for me to pretend I haven't been watching them. She shakes her head, he mumbles a little more. He is telling her that I am a disgusting old queer who stared at his penis last night.

"I gotta go," Janice says. "Oh, and I won't be back tonight, I'm supposed to watch my sister's kids. I didn't know you was still going to be in here." She jumps to her feet. "Come on and walk me to the elevator. If you're going to live here you ought to at least walk around the halls or something, so your feet don't fall off."

He gets up and starts with her to the door. "Put your robe on," she says. "You can't walk down the hall with your butt hanging out." He grins, pleased that she is the proprietress of his butt, and obeys.

At the doorway they kiss. At first a perfunctory smooch like a handshake, but he doesn't let go. He buries his face in her neck, reaches under the hem of her miniskirt with his unbandaged hand and grasps her panty-hosed behind, pulls her closer. Now her face is tight to his chest, her lips brushing the skin above the V of his gown. Her legs straddle his, he is practically lifting her off the floor. His hips move slowly up and down.

I believe it is an exhibition for my benefit, to put a period to last night and ensure I will not mistake him. How I flatter myself, to think the boy's rutting should be a pantomime for me! No, he is merely taking what he can, the third point of his life's triangle of work and cartoons and balling. As he goes on, she draws her face back and looks at me, but she does not stop him. She, perhaps, has some meaning? To warn me off, this charming and insidious threat to her boyfriend, this bruised and betubed seducer? Her arms cannot reach around his great terry-clothed back.

After a minute, she disengages herself. She holds his hand primly and starts to lead him out into the hall. He has an evident hard-on and stops to rearrange his robe. She gives him a last teasing grope, then they are gone.

I take advantage of their absence to switch the channel. I feel a little like a hijacker, since I didn't pay for the TV. But I want to see the news. I still have an absurd fear that I am a headline.

Traffic is backed up halfway to Richmond. A man in a helicopter describes it, with amused disinterest; helicopters don't get stuck in traffic. The weatherman feigns a shiver as he describes the front that is on its way. People outside the hospital will be cold tonight. President Bush has vetoed something or other. The new Soviet legislature has just passed a law giving workers the right to strike. They have footage of the members, giving their ten-hour speeches, and then of a Russian anchorman, vapid and solemn as any of ours, reading the announcement.

No one cracks a smile at the notion that the workers may now strike against the workers. In one last writhing the Party has absorbed this comical paradox and thinks it can go on being the Party. Could the members of Tom's study group have followed that shift as readily as they did the popular front and the Nazi-Soviet pact and all the pirouettes after that? What if the Pope were to announce one day that they were just kidding, there was no Heaven, but meanwhile they hoped everybody would keep dropping by the Christian Social Club? Well, some people would, just to see the familiar faces. But, even if they hadn't put Tom through what they did, no one in the Party was a friend of his. He had comrades but no camerados.

It is hard to be a leftist fairy. You may, with the best of will, desire for the workers such a paradise as they are capable of dwelling in. But it isn't your paradise, not in any of its features. It's for them, those workers. You see them in the murals of Tom's day: those sexless giants did not, after a day at the mill, go bowling, or have a few beers, or sit at home listening to *Amos n' Andy*. They were just workers, building mighty America. Everything that made their life bearable was a mere symptom, to be wiped away by the revolution — the church, the corner bar, the racetrack.

After the end of history, the workers would go to concert halls and listen to American tone poems with titles like *The Corn-Husking*. They would go home to nutritious meals — things made in a pressure cooker, to preserve the natural colors and save the vitamins. After dinner they would retire to living rooms furnished in blond wood, like Tom's last ghastly apartment. There they might read a newspaper devoid of rape or gossip or publicity stunts. Or they might, if it was summer and still light, go out to the common space and play with the children — play some nonviolent, cooperative game like volleyball. At last they would go to bed and have intercourse with their odorless wives. Healthy and simple intercourse: as their lives were without frustrations, there would be nothing to be worked out, worked off, in bed. Nor in their dreams; what dreams would they need?

Tom would try to talk about it sometimes. I can hear him say it, in his alto simper: "The revolution." If there was not a hint of doubt in his voice, there wasn't any passion, either. Perhaps he really had fully persuaded himself. But if he honestly did believe that we were about to see the twilight of history, how could he be so matter-of-fact about it? The revolution, no capitals, no italics. I had seen him, countless times, more excited about a single line of verse.

There are, I guess, revolutionaries who pause now and

then to speak concretely of the world they mean to make. Mao, perhaps, did so at off moments in his cave dwelling period. But of course nothing was further from Tom's mind. Tom would only joke about it. Red flags over Broadway. The United States Steel Collective, and the People's Transport Assembly Facility at River Rouge. FDR wheeled jauntily off to the firing squad. Silly. Inevitable, bound to happen, but at the same time preposterous.

And of course the notion that the university would become the State Institute of Technical and Useful Arts was no part of Tom's postmillennial agenda. It must have been hard enough for Tom to trudge off every week to undergo constructive criticism by his peers, as if he had any. Could he have imagined his life after the victory, with some pipe fitter turned political officer sitting in on his Melville seminar and suspecting revisionism every time things got too elevated?

Once or twice Tom did admit that a political officer, or something of the kind, was in attendance at the study group. He wouldn't say any more about it, just that they'd had a "guest" from New York; he was skirting treason even telling me he was in a cell. To this day I wish I knew which of his tweedy buddies had a direct wire to Moscow. Tom would just tease me: "We all have pseudonyms," he said. "We have to call each other by names like Mr. Jones. Silliest thing — there isn't a man there I don't know."

"What's your name?"

"Hyacinth Robinson. Nobody gets it."

"You know all these people."

"Of course."

"So . . ."

"So? Oh." He shrugged. "Yes, you know them too." He grinned hugely, schoolboy with a secret.

"When are you going to take me?" I said.

The grin vanished. "This is — you understand, it's for people who take things rather seriously." His tone was the one a dedicated bridge player might use to let a potential fourth know that it wasn't a social game.

"Well, then you'd better leave me behind," I said. "I can't take it seriously. I just don't think it makes any difference to people like you and me."

"How is that? Doesn't make any —"

"Stalin doesn't like fairies either, does he?"

"Oh." He took out his cigarette case. I never noticed, at the time, the irony of a fellow traveler with a platinum cigarette case. No one ever said, after all, that Tom was obliged to start the revolution in his own person. Anyway, he was silent, and I was so satisfied with my own retort that I didn't speak either.

Finally he said: "Well, you know, there won't — when it's all over there won't be any . . ." He wouldn't bring himself to say fairies. "There won't be any people like you and me."

I said — not as a comeback, I really wanted to know if he could possibly mean what he seemed to be saying — "You mean they'll get rid of us."

"No, no. I mean, the sorts of tensions or dislocations, whatever it is that makes us the way we are — after society is reformed and children can grow up in a more wholesome world . . ." His voice trailed off.

"You mean the revolution will eliminate the Oedipus complex."

"Yes. You make it sound silly. But if it doesn't do that, what good is it?"

We didn't, as many times as we talked politics after that, we didn't ever return to this peculiar theory, about how the withering away of the state would be accompanied by the withering away of the fairy. It was, I think, improvised then and there. He wasn't given to brooding over the contradictions in his world.

Anyway, the revolution wasn't about his problems. He thought he was a happy man. Even his endless series of failed romances could not shake this bizarre conviction. It was hard for him even to make himself think of the awful lives the rest of humanity was compelled to endure.

"Comrades," someone would say at a meeting. "Let me tell you how the Spanish-freedom-fighters-jute-pickers-Scottsboro-boys-auto-workers are suffering." And everyone else would lean forward, lap it up. Capitalist atrocities were the pornography of the old left. Tom would make himself stay, make himself listen and believe. Of course the only workers he ever encountered were Sam the custodian and Martha the maid, shuffling along despondently, as befits the casualties of the class struggle. If he had once forsaken his Wheaties eaters and ventured into my part of the woods he would have learned that the workers knew faster routes to ecstasy than he had ever discovered.

But no, he could imagine for the proletariat only that dry, Ville Radieuse sort of contentment, a world in which they would neatly reproduce, raise their young to be clean and productive, die on mattresses with no bugs in them. His own life, with its occasional — once a semester or so — rapture: that was, of course, impossible for the mass of men. So I suppose it was fitting, the way he wound up, in that awful apartment on Marsden Street. With every prospect of living out his remaining years in the adequate, the acceptable circumstances he had mapped out for the rest of the world.

Whether he was in fact what they used to call a card-carrying member I never was sure, not exactly. I remember a conversation a few years earlier, not long after the war. Truman had just started his loyalty program for federal workers, the one that was still clanking along when I got to Washington ten years later. It was all very far away as yet, had nothing to do with us in a private university, but I was a little worried about Tom's fellow traveling. Tom was saying, "This is just a little flare-up. You're not old enough to remember, are you, the Palmer raids, after the last war?"

"I wasn't even born."

"Then you wouldn't remember. At any rate, it will burn itself out soon enough."

"So you're going to stay in the Party?"

"The Party?" he said. "Oh, I'm not really in the Party." That was — I thought then — a lie, told so gracelessly that I think he actually wanted me to believe it. I knew everything else about him, down to the things he said in his sleep. If he wanted to imagine that he could keep this one thing from me, perhaps it was not the thing that mattered but the keeping; he just didn't want to be known utterly. Or perhaps he was afraid that his politics were too fine. He was so proud of being in the van of history that — like any good St. Martin's boy — he kept quiet about it for fear of being thought a show-off. "Oh, I'm not really in the Party," he said, just as he often said, "I'm not really rich," or even, "I don't know German nearly well enough."

I think he must have been. After everything that had happened, the non-aggression pact, Masaryk pushed from the window, the blockade of Berlin. He rode through all of it, until they threw him out. I did once ask him how he managed to go to the study group on Saturday night and a high church service on Sunday morning. It was like asking someone who is eating dinner how he manages to keep the food out of his windpipe. For Tom living with irreconcilables was just about as natural as that.

"Never thought about it," he said. And never thought about how he could go from that same church service to a long, flirtatious, and inconclusive Sunday brunch with his latest boy. And never for a moment thought about how he could write a very *subjective* — that was the word the Party would have used — treatise called *The Invincible City* and still call himself a Marxist. Never thought about it until that awful conclave at which he was invited to render himself up for a little constructive criticism.

Again, he didn't see it. The great enterprise, the book he'd been working on since the day I met him, was done, and he rushed it into print without getting whatever kind of imprimatur the Party was supposed to supply. I don't know if, by then, he didn't care, or if he honestly believed that he had written a good Communist book.

By the time he brought it to the study group it was already in galleys. He let me see a set at the same time they did. I understood it to be an enormous honor, and I was sorry I couldn't show my gratitude by actually reading it. I peeked at parts here and there. You could, if you struggled, find a bit of Marx in the odd paragraph. After the catastrophe, people did focus on all those harmless fatuities, like calling Huck Finn's Pap a member of the lumpenproletariat. But they were a tiny part of the book. His comrades in the study group were not distracted.

The secrecy of the Party was permeable, but randomly so. You heard a lot about some things, nothing about others. Everyone heard about the meeting where Tom was denounced, but no one heard a word of what was said. One thing was generally current: Tom was finished in the Party (or, if he wasn't really in the Party, finished hanging on).

Even Tom, when I got up the nerve to ask just what had happened, would say only, "I — you won't understand this, but I am lost without the . . . study group."

"After all of that?"

"All of it's true, what they said. I cannot print that

book and stay in. There are correctable deviations, and then there are deviations so enormous that criticism, argument, are irrelevant; you either see the light, give it all up — for there is not one salvageable word in that book — or you leave."

"But I've read the book. It's wonderful. You can't —"

"You haven't read it."

"Well, not the way your comrades have, picking apart every sentence."

"You haven't read it at all. This is Tom, dear boy, you're talking to Tom."

"I read the first chapter or so. I want to wait till summer, when I really have the time to —"

"Till summer? You're going to carry it about with you as you go trolling in Lowell Park? All those galleys?"

This was a little close to home, but he said it in the flat tone he reserved for his best jokes, so I went along. "Well, it will be in print by then. Not so much to lug around."

"I'm sure it will help you make many new friends. The title alone is not without its suggestive qualities."

"Anyway, what are you going to do," I said, "withdraw it?"

"They've set it, my dear. Every *op. cit.* and *ibid.* It will be out next spring, will I, nill I."

"Well, what's the procedure, then? Dramatic recantation? Sackcloth at the cell meeting?"

"It is in print. I sold it and allowed it to be printed without letting anyone see it. I am irredeemably apostate."

"Then you're out. You're out of the Party."

He didn't bother, for once, to remind me that he wasn't in the Party. "You make that sound so simple, like being out of Grace. The only human institution that ever deserved my allegiance, the only place where anything ever made any sense, and I am out of it. Outside."

It seemed to me that he recovered quickly enough. The book duly came out the next spring, '49, and he was suddenly a famous man, or as famous as English teachers get. A success in his little field, as his brother said. There were the prizes, and the chance to write for the *Partisan Review*, and the visiting semester at Stanford. (I rather lost my moorings that semester, with him out of town. I saw much more of the Garland and Lowell Park than of the library, and Tom had a time of it getting my assistantship continued after he got back.) Outside the Party he was having the best times he'd ever had, capped at last perhaps by the arrival of Jimmy in '51. It was as if his life had begun the day they threw him out.

So it seems more than just unfair that his new life should have been brought to a close by the Party, those years in which he had only half lived coming back to bite him. It is almost a cruel joke, like the one about the workers striking against the workers. Maybe the whole twentieth century is a joke, all its heroism a mere detour on the way to McDonald's.

The century sort of crept up on us. Other states might have had their own little un-American committees, catching in their nets the fish too small for the grander inquisitions in Washington. Our state seemed for a while to have escaped the hysteria. Not that the legislature was especially enlightened; it was run by farmers like any other. But they were Yankee farmers, no more frivolous than their slaty fields, and not at all hungry for headlines. When they were pushed, finally, by the American Legion and the Rotary and the Catholic assemblymen from the big city wards, they undertook the narrowest possible investigation. The Public Instruction Committee was to report on foreign influences in state-funded institutions of higher learning.

Well, that meant the state university, of course, and not us. So we watched with some amount of haughty amusement as the committee skewered agronomists with advanced ideas and prematurely anti-Fascist French teachers. It was all but over, the evil wind having passed us by, when the state comptroller pointed out that our little academy, ostensibly a private enclave, was in fact sucking up public funds like an erudite sponge. I suspect the city assemblymen had always known that. That was the point, maybe, to get at us. While to the farmers we were still the place great-uncle Hezekiah had gone to a century before, to the Irish pols we were just a black hole in the city's tax base, a devourer of real estate. What we did not devour, or even admit, were the Irish assemblymen's sons. A tactical error.

So the committee moved on to us, lackadaisically. They'd been through a score of witnesses, none of them more than faintly pink, by the time they got to Tom in the spring of '52. I'm not sure how they happened on him. He hadn't ever signed anything — he wasn't discreet, just picky; no one could word a petition well enough for Tom. He hadn't marched, or campaigned for Henry Wallace, or served as faculty adviser for the American Youth for Democracy chapter. Maybe they'd uncovered his donations, all those fellow-traveling groups that got his war dividends from the Khaki Company. Or maybe someone had actually read his book. Anyway, he was an S, late on the list. The committee was tired; they wanted only to get through the rest of the names. Tom just needed to affirm, for the record, that he had never had a deviant idea or attempted to impart one to a student. Then they could all go home.

The chairman had been, as it happened, a year behind Tom at Yale. When he was an undergraduate, before the first war. They had scarcely known each other then, but —

having wound up in the same city — they had been nodding acquaintances for twenty years. This slight connection made the chairman self-conscious, and his tone when he called Tom to the stand was at once jovial and apologetic.

Tom made his way up to the little witness table and sat, hands folded, with the air of a perfectly prepared doctoral candidate who hopes the orals will be stimulating.

"Would you state your name and address, please?" the chairman said, openly smiling.

"Thomas Frick Slater, 233 Brewer Street."

"What is that address?"

"That is Winthrop House."

"Yes. And your occupation?"

"I am a teacher."

"Thank you." There was a long silence, as if Tom had been called forward only to declare himself Tom. Finally the chairman said, rapidly, almost mumbling, "Professor Slater, are you now or have you ever been a member of the Communist Party of the United States." There wasn't even a question mark at the end. He looked up at the ceiling, where foreshortened Pilgrim Fathers strode forth from an armada of rosy clouds.

Tom spoke the formula that became so familiar in those years. There was, afterward, some debate as to whether he had said it at the right time. Some said you had to take the Fifth right when they asked you your name; some said the address was where you drew the line; some said profession. But of course there wasn't any right time to do what Tom had done.

The chairman looked straight at Tom now, his face baffled and furious. Not because Tom had been a Communist, if he even had, but because he had perversely disdained to lie about it. No one had expected, or especially wanted, to find anything: maybe not even the city pols who started it, and surely not the farmers and lawyers whose job it was to finish it. All Tom had needed to do was tell a brisk lie and go home. Now there would be no end of trouble.

Well, from that point the story is elementary, tells itself. Ex-Communist, or maybe not so ex-, refuses to rat. Like a schoolboy: he takes the Fifth because it's what a St. Martin's boy would do. Even if he wasn't ever in the Party, or if he was and they threw him out, either way you didn't talk. You just stood silently before the headmaster and took your licking. Or in this case before the president of the university. What was his name? He was so famous once. Van Leunen, the wonder boy — van Leunen starts pressuring him to co-operate. Because he needs the episode finished, it is bewildering the alumni, gifts are dropping off. Tom can't be fired, but he's thrown out of Winthrop House, barred from teaching. Loses, in short, everything that matters. Then bang.

Making of his life a bald illustration of the times, an archetypal drama like all those plays from the thirties. The ones in which the characters' very names tell you which side they're on. That Tom, eccentric and contradictory, should have given his farewell performance in such a play: it's as if Lady Bracknell had gone through the wrong stage door and stumbled onto the set of *Waiting for Lefty*.

All a joke, as cruelly silly as history itself. Tom died searching for his fabulous city: he died because he was queer. As I nearly have. Except that my assailant didn't, at the last, plunge in the knife. Tom's did, that's the only difference. Maybe one other: my predilection for the working classes (in the flesh and not on post office murals) has always exposed me to the possibility of getting a little . . . roughed up. Even the other night I was indignant but not surprised. I hadn't asked for it, but I had asked for it. Whereas the worst Tom ever courted in his procession of Wheaties eaters was tedium, passion fading to a yawn. He was surprised out of this world. Even if he, too, had asked for it.

$\mathcal{S}$IX

Tom held his last sherry of the term in May of '52, just before exams. This would have been a week or two after the hearings. I had tried for days to catch up with him. I don't know what he was doing — there was some talk of meetings in support, but I'm rather sure he didn't attend them. I wonder if he wasn't just going about his business with a parodic intensity, as if showing himself indispensable.

His rooms were jammed; anyone I'd ever seen there had come. Martha, his housekeeper, was overwhelmed. She tried to hide in the kitchen, but there were people even in there. All of them talking quite openly about Tom, who was out of earshot, sitting bolt upright in his usual seat in the living room. They exchanged the rumors that had been going around for weeks, that Tom was covering for somebody, no, that someone in the Party was setting him up, or no, that it all had to do somehow with Tom's . . . tendencies. I wanted to hear more of that, but whoever was saying it clammed up when someone nudged him and he saw I was there. Martha listened with bewilderment: she didn't seem to know why anybody would be saying all these things about Professor Slater.

In the living room, Tom sat quietly smoking, answering greetings with monosyllables — physically at the center, as usual, but not dominating the room as he always had. The throng in the living room couldn't talk about him, not like their brothers in the kitchen, and without Tom to listen to they were left chatting dispiritedly about exams and what they were going to do for summer vacation. They were all handsome, of course: Tom's private sherries always looked like a casting call for an Arrow shirt ad. But without Tom to energize them they seemed like so many mannequins.

Someone tried to get Tom going on the Rosenbergs, who weren't dead yet but had already become a bit stale. Tom agreed wearily with everything that was said, how they'd been framed or, even if they'd done it, whatever little secrets they'd passed on had been trivial, not worth going to the chair for. It was the sort of cause Tom used to seize on, good for an hour or more of wit and historical comparisons and Socratic back-and-forth with some willing second banana, the performances people came to Tom's sherries for.

This time, as his interlocutor prodded him, Tom finally said, "There are Negroes being hanged every day for nothing, for crossing their eyes. Why should I spend all my passion on the Rosenbergs?" That doesn't sound so unreasonable now, but it was shocking to us: perhaps because it had never occurred to us that his supply of passion was exhaustible. It was the voice of old age, for the very first time. And he went on: "I can't remember a year when I wasn't supposed to be outraged about someone or other they were doing in — a couple of semiliterate Italians, nine colored boys on a freight train, now a pair of dupes turned in by their own relatives. These causes, one at a time, when they're doing in everybody every day. Might as well petition God to lift Adam's curse."

A boy who was sheltered by the crowd from Tom's sight dared to say, "What if you're the next cause?"

Tom strained to see who it was, but couldn't. "I shan't be," he said. "I am not the sort of martyr for whom the machinery of orchestrated indignation is set running. Besides, whatever you're hearing, I am not in so very much trouble."

He raised his glass, the way he used to when he was on a roll, so someone would get him a refill (usually me). We thought he'd go on talking then, but he just waited for his fresh drink, took a sip when it arrived, and sat back looking at us. We were like a crowd in a theater after the first act curtain: not sure, until the houselights come on, whether there's another scene or whether it's really intermission. After a moment, everyone stirred, ready to make for the exit. The people in the kitchen and the quieter set in Tom's guest room took a little longer to learn the party was over. But soon they, too, had drifted out.

I followed, was most of the way to my room when I decided I couldn't just walk away from him like that. Well, actually I was broke, and I felt like another drink. And maybe I could cadge a couple of bucks for the Garland.

The sun was almost set, but Tom hadn't turned any lights on. He stood some while in the doorway before admitting me, and I had to peer beyond him to make out that Jimmy was still there. When I was ushered into the dark room the boy stood but gave no greeting. Tom went to pour me a scotch without being asked. The boy and I stood squinting at each other across the gloom.

Tom handed me the glass and sat down on the sofa. Jimmy joined him at once, sat tight up to him like a teenage girl in her boyfriend's jalopy. I took the club chair facing them, Tom's usual seat. I had been in the room a couple of minutes, and no one had said anything.

The few other times I had come upon them together, Jimmy had scuttled away as fast as he decently could, as if he felt himself the outsider. Now, not quite touching Tom but with an arm surrounding him on the back of the sofa, Jimmy was plainly saying that I was the intruder. Thus labeled, I completed the intrusion by turning on a light. A bit of Jimmy's shirttail peeped out through a fly only half done up.

Finally Tom said, "I'm sorry we couldn't chat when you dropped by the other day."

"I — it wasn't important. I just kind of thought up a — just the start of an idea for my thesis."

"That's very important. I am glad to have another chance to hear about it."

So I started telling him my plans for the thesis I never got to. He listened carefully, as always, putting in an appropriate word or two. It had been so many weeks since I had had his full attention that I babbled away excitedly, and it took a while before I noticed that his interjections had become briefer and less frequent. At last he was simply staring at me. Not cruelly, not as though I were making an ass of myself. As though he were still interested in what I was saying but I had perversely started talking in Welsh.

I wound down. Our two blank but awfully interested faces mirrored one another across the Bukhara. I couldn't look at Jimmy, who had slid to the end of the couch, away from Tom, while we talked shop. And it was as though Tom couldn't either; that's why he was still looking into my eyes. Jimmy was like a force at the other end of the sofa, a pure power, and we couldn't either of us turn to face it.

Tom looked down, swallowed, and said, "Yes, perhaps that idea might be stronger if you brought in — oh, Carlyle, say, as a counterexample. That is, if you can ever bring yourself to read Carlyle. Or —" He just stopped. Whatever energy he had mustered to bring forth that little bit of dreck, he couldn't keep going on it.

Then Jimmy spoke. "Last sherry hour." He was almost in the dark. Funny, I can remember the boy clearly now, picturing that visit, while last night I could hardly picture him at all.

"Uh, yeah," I said. "Till next year."

"Professor Slater won't be here next year." Imagine calling him Professor Slater, as if I didn't know. I could just picture it: "Oh, harder, Professor Slater, faster . . ."

Then I realized what he had said. "They're — they're making you —"

"They're letting him stay, but they're making him give up Winthrop House."

"Is that so?" I said to Tom. He didn't answer, and I looked toward Jimmy.

"They want him to cooperate. They can't take his job but they can take this. And maybe his classes."

"Gosh," I said, or something equally apposite.

"What do you think the professor should do?"

I thought he should do anything he could to go on living in those beautiful rooms. But I said, "Whatever he thinks is right." This sounded inane, so I added, "I mean, it's not anyone else's business, is it?" This was worse, sounded as though I were digging at Jimmy, but I let it go and so did he.

"What the professor thinks is right is just to do nothing at all. Just to —"

"Let the winds come," Tom put in, with an odd casualness. Breeziness, rather.

"You see," Jimmy said. "He's kind of lost interest. I think he ought to go ahead and give them what they want."

I just nodded my head foolishly, how was I to know what Tom should do? He went on, "This whole thing could be over in a couple of weeks. Hell, the Party threw him out, you know that. What does he owe them? He ought to turn in every stinking one of them. Reynolds, Fisher —"

"Stop that," Tom said, with an involuntary little smile, as if he were being teased.

Jimmy knew the names. He knew more about Tom than I did. Why should that have surprised me? I suppose I had thought we each had our niche. He might be the lover, but I was the comrade, recipient of secrets. He went on spouting secrets. "Every one of them: Fisher and Edelman and that guy, the one who called himself Henry Smith. Drag their commie asses out into the daylight."

That made sense to me. If Tom hadn't been a little too generous with his whiskey it would have occurred to me that Jimmy must already have exhausted his limited persuasive powers. But again: he seemed like a power then, sitting silhouetted in the twilight and speaking in a strange airy tone — the same tone Tom had just used, as if it were nip and tuck who'd break into laughter first at the silliness of it all. Their Olympian mirth at such serious things: it made me think the boy could somehow handle everything. "Maybe you're right," I said.

"You say that because he's handsome," Tom said.

"No, I —"

"Mr. Stivers thinks the same thing. That beauties are the unacknowledged legislators of the world. That because they've been given a bit of grace, because it has been vouchsafed them to move across the surface of the globe so lightly, there is nothing too hard for them. But this is. This is too hard for you, Jimmy."

"It is hard," Jimmy said. "I'm ready for that."

"You're ready? What has it to do with you?" Tom said. His awful alertness came back for a moment, then he let it lapse. "It's not your trouble."

"It is my trouble. I'm the only person in the world who gives a damn about you."

I was about to protest, but Tom was on his feet. "If that's so," he said. They were both standing now, facing each other. "If that's so, if after fifty-eight years on this planet I have secured the loyalty of no one but a confused schoolboy, then —" He stopped himself, perhaps thinking that — if it was so — it wasn't a very good idea to jettison the schoolboy along with everything else.

Tom sat again. I looked back at Jimmy. I thought I would see tears or anger or something spectacular. I had a shameful feeling of exhilaration. A lover's quarrel, two men, even quarreling they were showing what I wasn't yet certain was possible, that two men could feel something. But I saw nothing. Jimmy just finished the last sip or two of his drink, put the glass down, and said, "Mr. Reeve, we'll miss dinner." Then to Tom: "You'll think about it?"

"Of course I'll think about it. What else do you suppose I think about?" Jimmy frowned, and Tom added, "Button your fly."

The boy did, with no apparent loss of dignity, and left for the refectory. Tom closed the door after him but went on looking at it.

"What are you going to do?" I said.

"What do you want me to do? You get a vote."

"Not like his, evidently." I was still a little stung that Jimmy knew things I didn't.

Tom turned away from the door, as if to refute me. "Everyone gets a vote."

"I'd rather have voted before you went downtown."

"Yes, everyone says that. That's the best advice anyone can give me: let it be April again."

I must have waited a full minute, properly solemn and ruminative, before I said, "Listen, can you let me have a few bucks?"

A couple of weeks later, after exams, I went with Tom to East Station to see Jimmy off for home. I was surprised Tom asked me: you would have thought he'd have wanted to be alone with the boy. But perhaps he didn't want to be alone afterward.

We waited outside Jimmy's room while he finished packing. Tom showed me, in the inside pocket of his suit, two Trans World tickets to Paris. He had got them that very morning, and a passport application for Jimmy. "I would have preferred to sail," Tom said. "That new ship, the *United States*, is going on its maiden voyage first week in July. I thought that would be wonderfully fitting, to sail off together on a spanking new ship. The fastest ship they ever built, they say it might cross in three days."

"So why aren't you?"

"I don't know. Jimmy says he has to go home for a few weeks, back to Pittsburgh. He couldn't just leave without doing that. We've put off the trip to the end of July. By then the point will be gone, the *United States* will no longer be a maiden. So instead we're going to fly."

"Uh-huh."

"One way, maybe."

"What?"

"I don't know. I have the feeling they aren't finished with me."

Before I could ask what he meant Jimmy emerged, with just two bags and a tennis racket. Everything else he'd already sent on by Railway Express. Tom went off to hail a cab, and we were left standing there, lover and mere comrade. I didn't know what to say. I thought of talking about Paris, but I was frankly a little jealous: Tom had never taken me to Paris. So I just looked at him, rather boldly. He was an apparition in a summer suit, crisp blue cord. Above his white shirt his face had already taken on a little summer color, and his hair was bleached to a finer gold. I could grudgingly see why Tom was taking him to Paris.

By the track at East Station, Jimmy stood holding some impossible book Tom had pressed on him — he would get some magazines in Providence — and the tennis racket he hadn't wanted to check. Tom was speechless, for once; I'm sure he regretted bringing me. But even if I hadn't been there, even if they hadn't been surrounded by people, he couldn't possibly have said what he wanted to. No matter what had passed between them, there were words he could not utter to another man.

So he just stood looking down at the platform, hands in his trouser pockets. He was wearing the white linen suit he sometimes brought out of hiding on the hottest days. A perfectly idiotic thing to wear to a train station. It was already flecked with soot — now and then added to by an ash dropping off the cigarette clenched in his mouth.

Jimmy, for his part, was babbling away about the wedding he had to go to and the summer job his father had lined up for him. Oh, and in August, he and this friend from home were thinking maybe of going out west, in his friend's jalopy, just hitting the road.

That sounded wonderful. I pictured myself in the rumble seat, on the road with Jimmy and some equally comely friend, staying in roadside cottages or camping some nights, and —

Tom said, the cigarette still between his teeth, "I was still rather planning on getting away to France." With no particular emphasis on the getting away part.

"Oh, yeah, this is nothing definite. We still need to talk about that."

I edged discreetly away from them, but not beyond hearing distance, even though Tom lowered his voice: "I thought we had."

"Well, sure, but I didn't know — with everything happening, I wasn't sure that was still on." No hint of evasion crossing his excessively clean face. "I'll get in touch with you and we'll work it out. Do you have your number yet, at the new place?"

"No," Tom said. He waited for Jimmy to volunteer a Pittsburgh number, but had to ask finally.

"Oh, sure," Jimmy said. Tom took out his pocket memorandum book. The morocco one with his initials which I carried around for a while after he was gone but never wrote in. Lost years ago, in some move or other. Tom had his pen to the paper, ready to write, and for a second Jimmy said nothing. Then: "Well, listen, I don't know if that's a good idea. My parents and all, what if they picked up the phone or something, how would I explain? Or just, I don't know —"

"Very well. Perhaps in a week or so, when I'm settled in, the operator will have my number." Tom's voice had a chill in it that Jimmy might not have recognized. I mightn't have known it myself, if I hadn't heard him say one night, so many years before, "I'm afraid I'm too tired for any company." It was terrible to hear it again. Tom himself seemed to be listening to his own voice, the cold that should have been dispelled once and for all at the lodge returning, creeping back as subtly as a glacier.

"Okay," Jimmy said, apparently oblivious. "In a week or so." He was inching toward the train. Not actually turning away from Tom but, almost imperceptibly, backing up. "I wish I could have stayed to help you move."

"Thank you. I have Sam the custodian packing me at this moment. I should have stayed with him, perhaps, I'm rather afraid he'll get the books out of order."

Jimmy forced a smile. "Yeah, that would be awful."

"It matters to me. I think I shall go. I may not be too late to intercede."

"Sure, might as well. My train's leaving any minute."

"All right," Tom said. By now Jimmy was at some distance. Tom had to traverse it so that they could shake hands. Jimmy climbed the steps into the car, looked around and saw me. They must both have forgotten I was there. He looked startled, then waved politely and vanished into the car.

Tom didn't, as he used to when seeing me off somewhere, walk down the platform following Jimmy's progress through the car, see him properly settled, wave good-bye through the window. He headed straight out to the main concourse, leaving me to catch up. For a while he just stood there, the crowd of passengers and redcaps swirling around him. He looked up at the ceiling, the great glass skylights painted over during the wartime blackouts and never uncovered. Then he reached in his pocket and pulled out the tickets to Paris. I thought he was going to do something dramatic, tear them into bits or press them on a passerby. But he just gazed at them for a minute and shoved them firmly back in his pocket.

"Very nearly made a fool of myself," he said, and he strode out of the station so briskly I could scarcely keep up. But in the cab he seemed to be shaking: the lit end of his cigarette made ghostly lightning bolts.

I have to pee. They've given me a little jug to go in, but I can't bear to use it. So I stagger to the bathroom, even though it makes my head hurt to stand up and I have to wheel my IV along with me. I hike my gown up and do my business, like a nun, without looking at my body. As I wash my hands I finally let myself glance in the mirror, for the first time since leaving my apartment. No wonder Howard flinched when he saw me. I could be a poster boy for celibacy. There is even dried blood in my hair. They have let me lie here for two days with little flakes of black blood in my white hair. I scrape at it ineffectually with my fingernail. I hope Howard thinks to bring me a hairbrush.

As the boy is still absent I can go past his bed and look out the window. We have a view of a parking garage and, next to it, the empty lot where they are starting yet another hospital building. Beyond is a dismal vista of decaying tenements and forsaken churches, waiting their turn to be torn down for the next and next buildings of the ever-expanding complex. Our last growth industry: at this rate, the whole city will be a hospital one day.

I hold up my spectacle and survey the construction site, hoping for a glimpse of a worker or two. Yes, there's one, not bad from this distance. A shame it's October, else he'd have his shirt off. But I can at least admire how nimbly he strides the foundation wall, how gracefully now he bends to some manly task or other. I can watch for only a minute. Something about him makes me feel marginal and futile. Or just lonesome; I even wish my silent roommate would come back. I reach for my IV and stumble back to bed.

The next time I went to see Tom — the last time — he had finished moving into the one-bedroom apartment on Marsden Street. I can still see the awful stuff in his new living room, the blond wood furniture from Denmark or Sweden. It wasn't cheap, they weren't mass-producing it yet. But it was meant to be redolent of the world to come, meant to look as if it could be mass-produced if people ever came to their senses. I can picture him looking around at it, the decor of the revolution, and realizing that he could never become the man whose anthropometrically typical ass those chairs were meant to harbor.

Why is it that, as I try to think about Tom's collapse, I keep returning to the awful flat in which he spent his final summer? I am just like Howard, imagining that a man's decline could be summed up by the condition of his apartment. He never even unpacked; the room in which he died was lined almost to the ceiling with cartons of books and papers. Never unpacked, as though he knew his sojourn there or anywhere on the planet would be only one more summer. Maybe I should have guessed what was coming, just from that, his refusal to nest. Even a trick will take some pains to make himself temporarily at home: move an ashtray, change the station on the radio, something. Tom never even did that. He left the tags on the awful new furniture. He bought a rug and never unrolled it. He hung not one single picture.

This would have been late June. Commencement was over; he had not made his usual appearance in the striking blue gown of a Yale Ph.D. I don't know if he was told to stay away, or if it was another step in turning himself into a ghost. He'd been out of Winthrop House for a couple of weeks. He had been there so long, long before I'd known him: first in a cozy tutor's flat, later in that grand house-within-a-house that was the master's lodging. I couldn't imagine him living anywhere else. Neither evidently could he.

We hadn't been speaking. After Jimmy left, I had exams to grade, and I was in and out of the English Department offices a good bit. Tom and I couldn't help running into each other, but we were barely civil — he for whatever private reason, I from anger. That is what I felt, not just hurt.

Here the whole world had turned away from him, and I was ready to show what a splendid chap I was by continuing to be his friend. But he was so much a ghost that I couldn't touch him, and I blamed him for that. I could understand his wanting to be invisible, but not to me; for me at least he could now and then have taken on his bodily form. Not all his, after all: I was part proprietor. Part owner of Tom Slater, and with certain rights — those of a standing tenant, or a frequent traverser of a common law right-of-way.

Finally I swallowed my anger and went to exercise my rights by visiting him in his new diggings. I wanted to see what kind of cell he had chosen to atone in.

He was in a low and nameless apartment building, glazed brick from the thirties, cream-colored run to gray. There were still no locks with buzzers then; I could walk straight into the building and up to his door, 1-B. I knocked, and he opened instantly, as if he had seen me coming. He didn't say anything, just stepped back and let me walk past him into the living room.

I had fatuously assumed that everything would be as it had always been, all the Hepplewhite, the Bukhara rug, the portraits of dead Slaters. But the walls and the floors were bare, and the only furnishings were those few sticks of post-war hypermodern in blond wood.

"Where are your things?" I said.

"Things?"

"Your furniture and stuff."

"That wasn't mine."

"All your furniture?"

"All of that belonged to the university. It stayed in Winthrop House."

"Even the pictures?"

"God, yes. Do you think I collect portraits of former deans?"

"Is that who they were?"

"Who did you think? Anyway, none of it was mine."

"All of this stuff came with the place, then?"

"I bought it. I suppose I need more."

"You bought this?"

"This is what they sell."

"You could have gotten — well, reproductions, anyway, if you didn't feel like hunting around. Something cozier."

"Oh, but this is much more honest. Functional."

"Mm."

"Drink?" he said, leading the way to the kitchen.

It was a calamity, the kitchen. "You haven't got any help," I said.

"No. Martha preferred to stay on at Winthrop, with the new master." He was digging through a forest of glasses by the sink, holding each to the light, looking for a clean one. "Like a cat."

"Who is the new master?"

He stood still for a moment, gave an odd smile. "Fuzzy Walgreen."

"Really?"

"He — he was in line. Nothing to the job, anyway. Won't take him away from Pindar." He held out a glass for my inspection. "Can you drink from this?"

"Put a lot of alcohol in, disinfect it. Can't you hire some-one of your own?"

"A housekeeper? I suppose. But I'm off for France in a few weeks."

"Are you? Still?"

"Why not? I forgot to fill the ice trays."

"Maybe it will snow."

He didn't catch the reference. "Yes, still bound for Pa-ris," he said. He headed out toward the living room, leaving me to make my own drink, sans ice.

When I got to the living room, he was by the window, smoking and watching passersby. "They can see right in," I said.

"Nothing to see. No private life being led here."

"You going alone to France?"

"Why, did you want to come?" he said. It wasn't quite an invitation, and of course I hadn't meant to elicit it. I was wondering if he was still going to take Jimmy.

"No. No, I really should do some work this summer."

"You might as well come. Come back fresh this fall and start your dissertation."

"Oh, I will. I still haven't got it exactly pinned down." Still haven't, forty years on.

"No, I didn't think you had. Why don't you come? I've booked two seats."

"I know that. What happened to Jimmy?"

Tom looked around for an ashtray and, finding none, dropped his cigarette on the bare floor and stamped it out. "I believe you witnessed what happened to Jimmy."

"I thought there was still a chance. Didn't he ever call you?"

"What do you think?"

I thought about France. Tom and me, Americans in Paris, gamboling through the Dufy streets of that Gene Kelly movie from the year before, the taxis klaxoning Gershwin. I waited for him to ask one more time. If I had said yes, I wonder if he would have stayed on the planet a little longer, just because it would have been rude to break an engagement.

But he was quiet. I sipped my drink. Tepid whiskey makes me gag a little, so my sips were tiny ones. Tom was getting through his more rapidly; shortly he headed back to his war-torn kitchen for a refill.

From there he called out, "It's getting late. I should offer you dinner but, as you've seen, I am not entirely at home in this kitchen yet."

"That's okay," I shouted back, my voice echoing off the bare floors and the wall of cardboard cartons.

"We could go out, I suppose. We haven't been to dinner in ages. Perhaps that little Italian place, we haven't been there in so long."

I started to say I needed to study. But he would have pooh-poohed that. So I made the one excuse he couldn't laugh me out of. "I was going to head to the Garland."

He emerged from the kitchen. "Ah, your mysterious Garland. Where is that, exactly?"

"Down in the shopping district. The little alley next to Burton's."

"Right there? I've never passed it."

We sat for a while, I sipping, Tom more nearly gulping his drink. I felt a little bad about not going to dinner. Just a little; only in retrospect, and for no good reason, do I feel very bad.

After a while I said, "They're letting you go abroad? The committee, I mean. Don't you have to hang around?"

"What for? No sessions this summer. You don't suppose they're going to grill me in this heat? Oh, a pun."

"But they trust you to come back? In the fall?"

"I don't think they really care. I think they're sorry the whole thing came up. Sorry that they have to go on with it."

"But they will."

"I suppose. I've rather made them." He drew a cigarette from the platinum case.

"But if they don't care, well, what's the worst that could happen?"

"I'm not worried about them. It's the people here."

"Here? Oh, you mean President van Leunen and all? All the great liberals?"

"That's right."

"Well, what can they do, they've done their worst. Here you are, how much farther can they throw you?"

"To Paris, at any rate."

"I don't see why you have to run away. It's not like you've committed a crime or anything."

He looked at me sadly: how could he ever have taken on, as protégé or comrade or whatever, someone as stupid as I? "You and I commit a crime just by being on the planet."

"What?"

"It isn't my politics. It is my apolitical deviation."

I remembered what the boy at his last sherry hour had said, that Tom's problem had something to do with his tendencies. You never hear that word any more, "tendencies." Such a diffident word. I have just a wee tendency to commit crimes against nature. Tom sort of tended to subvert the moral fabric of the nation.

"They've got wind of that?"

"Who in all the world hasn't got wind of that?"

True enough. After he had chased a generation or two of Wheaties eaters, who didn't know, or guess, Tom's tendencies? They were tolerated. He was just one of those professors who had boys in for sherry, every school had a few of those. As long as he didn't lose his grip and actually put the move on one.

But of course he did, over and over, however unsuccessfully. In between me and Jimmy there must have been a dozen others I never even noticed, interchangeable, arcing through Tom's affections like comets and out of his grasp before I even laid eyes on them. Any one of them could have come forward and supplied the smoking gun. So to speak.

"Do they have something . . . well, concrete?"

"They have a statement."

"Jesus." I was drinking my whiskey faster, not minding any more that it wasn't cold. Tom took my glass and went to refill it.

A statement. As I sat waiting I tried to picture it. He wouldn't, whichever little bastard it was, have had much of a tale to tell. A hand resting just a moment too long on his shoulder. A tentative proposition so shrouded in rhetoric and hedged with qualifications that it required no answer. Hardly the stuff of scandal, unless fleshed out, embellished to the point that Tom's thwarted dreams turned into acts.

Still, maybe someone had done that, some duplicitous Wheaties eater connected Tom's hesitant dots and handed van Leunen the finished picture he required. To get a grade changed, or a job reference. Or just to punish Tom for having hinted, however delicately, for having even suspected that a normal American boy might be interested in — in whatever vile thing it was that Tom wanted to do. They would have had to prompt the boy for specifics, he would have feigned reluctance, then it would all have poured out. Stuff he had heard about, or read on the restroom wall in the library, over near the classics stacks. A conventional tale of perversions more orthodox and more conclusive than Tom's, dictated, typed, witnessed, and notarized.

Putting it away from him: no, it was all Mr. Slater, I was never like that. And then hopping the train to, say, Pittsburgh. If there had been a train to Mars it could not have carried him far enough.

As Tom came back I had a sudden, awful thought. I burst out without thinking, "Do they know about me?"

He looked confused. "Why? This has nothing to do with you." He started to hand me my glass. Then he understood the question and sighed. "No, this has nothing at all to do with you."

I realized how self-centered I must have sounded, in the midst of Tom's calamity. I tried to think of some way to apologize, but I couldn't. Instead I heard myself saying, "Listen, it's getting real late. I better get going." I set down my untouched drink and scurried out without even shaking his hand.

That would have been his last memory of me, then: bolting away from his problem, just relieved that it had nothing to do with me. It's a wonder he didn't change his will at the end. But I suppose he simply didn't have time. In a couple of weeks he was gone.

$\mathcal{S}$EVEN

HOWARD COMES IN. "Mail call," he says. "This must be yesterday's, today's wasn't here yet. I brought you some clothes and things, I hope all this stuff fits. And I checked at your front desk to see if there were any phone messages."

"And there weren't any."

"Well, no, how did you know? Don't you ever get any messages, poor thing?"

"Because my phone wire is cut. Everyone must be getting a busy signal."

"He cut the phone wire? How awful, you must have been terrified. Where's the cutie? Check out?"

"Down the hall somewhere. Didn't you see him?"

"Uh-uh."

"Well, he was with his girlfriend. It's been quite a while. Maybe they're in a broom closet."

He sits heavily in the visitor's chair; the vinyl offers a faint protesting ploop. "Anyway, there was this at the front desk." He hands me an unstamped letter. "And then all this mail. You do get an awful lot of magazines."

"It's about all I read any more."

"Me either. Such a burden keeping up. Ooh, what's this in the plain brown envelope?"

While he plays with the rest of my mail, I open the letter. It is from Culp Management, the people I write my rent check to. It says:

In response to complaints from other tenants and after an inspection of the leased premises, we have determined that you are in violation of your lease agreement, as follows:

(1) You have used or permitted the use of said premises in a disorderly manner and have created or permitted a disturbance to other tenants.
(2) You have failed to maintain the said premises in a clean and sanitary condition.

We must therefore inform you that the lease agreement is terminated, effective the 31st day of this month. Failure to surrender the said premises on that date free and clear of all furniture and debris will be grounds for additional action.

I hand the letter to Howard.

"The sons of bitches. What in the world are they talking about?" He hands the letter back.

"God only knows," I say, but I know too. I look at the thing again but I cannot see it. A wave of shame and anger brings so much blood to my face that I can feel my spigot throbbing again and I have to sit up right away.

The boy comes back in. At the sight of Howard, he pulls his robe a little closer. He starts to lie down on his bed, but then he sees that the channel has been changed. He flashes me a look of indignation as he repossesses the clicker and hunts for Bugs Bunny.

I call the building manager, Hurley. I can hear the lady

at the front desk call back to his office, and there ensues a muffled colloquy. He doesn't want to talk to me, of course, but finally he comes on the line.

"I got this letter," I say.

"I know. I'm sorry. I didn't write it."

"I don't understand."

"There were . . . some people complained." Then, gravely: "One of them called Mr. Culp. About all the noise in the middle of the night."

"All the noise? That was me —"

"I know what it was, Mr. Reeve. And then Mr. Culp came downtown and he looked at your apartment himself and he said you couldn't stay here, he couldn't have this going on in his building."

"I didn't want it going on either. It wasn't my idea of a party."

There is a silence, as if he were considering this. But he isn't. "I'm sorry, Mr. Reeve. You've been a very good tenant." He means this. I can picture the solemn look on his pudgy face. He is standing by his desk, wearing the dusty blazer that doesn't cover his ass. Now he is smoothing his red mustache; it's a wonder he hasn't rubbed it off. He says again, "You really were a good tenant. We never had any trouble."

His tone is so firmly valedictory that I am back in the room with Tom's brother, feebly negotiating.

"Look, I can't possibly move by the thirty-first. I'm in the hospital, I can't even walk around."

"Well, I understand that, but I'm not able to do anything about it."

"What do I have to do, call this Culp person?"

"No, no, don't call Mr. Culp. I don't think it would be a good idea to call Mr. Culp. It doesn't matter anyway, everything gets turned over to the lawyers when it goes this far."

"This far."

"When we have to do this. So I guess you could talk to the lawyers. This guy named BB."

"BB? Oh, Beebe. Like the diver."

"Who?"

"Never mind." Even I am scarcely old enough to remember Beebe the diver. I mime writing, and Howard comes up with a pen. "Okay, Beebe. And the number?"

He supplies it. I thank him and hang up before he can tell me again that it isn't his fault.

"So what is it?" Howard says. "What's happening?"

I look over at the boy; he seems to be well enough occupied with the TV. I say to Howard in a low voice, "I screamed. I bled on the walls. I was annoying."

"But you were the victim, for Christ's sweet sake." The sequence of angry, whispered sibilants, like steam escaping from a pressure cooker, makes the boy look over for a moment.

I dial. "Patterson and Patterson." The voice is male; males answer the phone nowadays.

"Mr. Beebe, please. My name is Reeve."

"May I tell him what this is in reference to?"

"It's a matter relating to Culp Management."

"Thank you. Please hold." While I hold, the telephone plays Schubert. I feel the way I do when I'm called into Mr. Pollen's office, guilty but ignorant of my transgression.

"This is Fred Beebe." One of those tenors who strives to be a baritone and winds up singing everything on one improbably low note.

"Hi, my name is Reeve. I live over in the Huntington Arms, and I've got this letter from Culp Management telling me that they're — well, evicting me."

"What was your name again?"

"Reeve. R-e-e-v-e."

"Reeve. Oh, yeah, I just got that folder. Wait a second. Uh-huh, yeah. You need to be out of there by the thirty-first."

"I can't get out by the thirty-first, I'm in the hospital, I can't even walk around."

"You're in the hospital, I'm sorry. What's the matter?"

"I got beat up. That's what this is all about, somebody beat me up in my apartment. I mean, that's what the noise was, and all. And here they're turning around and treating me like I was the one who did something."

"Gee, none of this is in the file," he says, in his actual voice. He is open to suasion. "How did this person get in?"

"How? He came in with me. I mean, I let him in." The boy in the next bed is openly listening.

"You were acquainted with the person who assaulted you."

"I — not really."

He takes a moment to reconstruct the story from my gratuitous "not really." Then he says, baritone: "You admitted this person to the apartment."

"I didn't know what he was going to do."

"No, I'm sure you didn't. But you understand, if you let somebody in voluntarily and then you let your guest break some law or violate a rule of the building, whatever, you're responsible for that."

I let this extraordinary concept sink in, that the boy was my guest and that I let him do it. I am the responsible party. I permitted my unruly guest to beat me up, thereby defacing the premises and causing a disturbance. I assent. "Well, I understand that I'm technically responsible. But I —" I hate the phrase even before I get it out: "I've kind of suffered enough." He is quiet, and I elaborate. "I had to have surgery, I almost lost an eye."

"Gee, I really am sorry." This sounds genuine, perhaps I can persuade him. "I understand that you didn't want it to happen. But you've got to see, like, from the perspective of the management, that you let that kind of person into the building. I mean, they could have gone on and hurt other people, something like that. So their concern, see, is about you letting him in in the first place." His voice is still down in the depths, but he is forgetting to talk lawyer. He must be in his twenties, not long out of school, in his first job. He has dreamt of winning civil rights cases or overseeing vast mergers, and now he is throwing old men out of their apartments.

"I won't do anything like that again. I've been there twenty years, nothing like this has ever happened."

"I can't argue with you about that. I mean, that's their position, and they have a legal right to do this. I'm not authorized to negotiate on this."

"Maybe if I talked to this Mr. Culp."

"I wouldn't. He has kind of an attitude."

"About —" I start to ask.

"Okay, listen," he says. "You don't think you can get out by the thirty-first."

"No, I can't even go looking for anything, I'm going to be laid up, and then I'd have to pack, and —"

"Well, under the circumstances I think they could give you another month."

"Till November thirty-first."

"Thirtieth."

Howard is gesticulating. "Could you hold on a second?" I say.

"References," Howard says.

"What?"

"You're not going to be able to find anything without references. And if they start telling people —" I had no idea Howard was so practical; perhaps he has been this route.

I uncover the mouthpiece. "You know, I'm going to need references, for the next place."

"So?" Beebe says. "Oh, I get you. You pay your rent on time?"

"Of course I do."

"That's all they ever talk about. I mean, they don't make written allegations about people. Just they paid the rent or they didn't."

"Okay. So you — you're going to send some kind of letter, about it being November?"

"No, no," he says, a tenor again. "I'll talk to Hurley, work it out. A letter, I'd have to copy Mr. Culp and all."

How they all shrink before this Mr. Culp, with his attitude. I thank him and hang up.

Howard says, "I can't believe they're doing this."

"They're letting me stay another month. If the terrible Mr. Culp doesn't find out."

"Maybe you should get a lawyer. I think this is defamation or something."

"It's all true. I did everything they said. What I need to do is get a newspaper."

"You're going to tell the newspapers?"

"I need to find an apartment."

"House-hunting, God. When my last place went condo I was out for weeks, looking at the most bizarre apartments."

"I don't have weeks. Maybe you could poke around a little."

"Well, there's something in my place. It's, I don't know, nine hundred."

"Nine hundred, Jesus. Do you have any idea what I've been paying? They were practically paying me to live there."

"I'd fight it if I were you," he says. Simultaneously we picture it, me in front of some rent court judge, Beebe waving the police report. Howard surrenders on my behalf. "You ought to think about my building. You can afford it. It would be fun."

"Dear yes. In and out of each other's places, borrowing a cup of Crisco."

"Well, I'll go get a paper. No, it's Friday, there won't be anything. I've probably saved Sunday's. We're recycling now, and I always miss the day to put it out. I'll see if I've got it, bring it this afternoon."

"Oh, no, you don't have to come back today. This can't be any fun."

"Just wait till you retire. This is the high point of my morning."

"Okay. And why don't you check exactly what they're asking at your place?"

"Are you going to be all right?"

"I'm fine. Angry more than anything else. I think I hate this Culp creature more than I do the, the guy who —"

"Me too," Howard says. He looks at the boy, who is deep into television, then he touches a finger to his lips and goes.

I've been there so long, I thought I owned the place. Not entirely: I never went so far as poor silly Howard, who once poured money into a rented apartment until it looked like something from *Architectural Digest* — tore out walls, built multilevel platforms with industrial carpeting, put up wallpaper each roll of which was as priceless as a Dead Sea scroll. I remember the night he found out it was going condo and he couldn't make the down payment. He ran shrieking around that overdone flat like Vivien Leigh when she gets the tax bill on Tara. I was as comforting as I could be, but I couldn't help — chums though we are — savoring the crude justice of it. I'd always been jealous of that apartment.

I at least retained some consciousness that I was a mere tenant. I have never repainted the regulation white walls. The venetians left by the last occupant are still there. I even hang my potholders on some ancient predecessor's hook. Still, after twenty years, it is like my body. I could find any book or bibelot in the place blindfolded, as easily as I could touch my nose. More easily, some nights.

I used to think about moving. Once a year, when renewal time came, I would head out, looking for a bigger kitchen — one I could get one of those little bistro tables in, if a pachyderm like me could sit at a little bistro table. Or a better view, something besides a parking lot. Or a balcony! A balcony like Howard's, in the place he's rented since he lost Tara. Where he can sit on a summer evening looking down at the street, at the endless parade of — what did he used to say? — queers and jugglers. Boys on their way to the Laundromat or, later in the evening, the bars, and the deranged on their way to no place special, a constant circus.

But every place was too much, or laid out wrong, or on a street that was just a wee bit too scary. Lots of English basements, so named I assume for their Dickensian character, where I had the creepy feeling that behind the woodwork lurked water bugs the size of Howard. I would always come home. Even when the condo fever hit, the plague that cost Howard his plantation — I could have made the down payment, and everyone told me I was crazy not to buy, what was I going to do in my old age? I would joke with my friends about how I wasn't going to go spend my life's savings to become landlord of a cube of air, and I stayed put. The Huntington Arms never turned over; there were too many old people in it, and some ordinance made it impossible to budge them. So I never took it seriously. This was folly, I suppose — if I owned some place no one would be throwing me out right now. But it all seemed like an elaborate scheme by the landlords to extort a century of rent in one swoop. And I thought I already had a home.

Home most of all those mornings — back in the days when I was making friends for free — when I'd close the door on some overnight guest and feel that I owned myself again. I'd always wake up first: I slept fitfully and untrustingly with strangers. After I examined my bedmate and felt the usual wry amazement at my lack of discrimination, I'd get dressed, creep out into the living room, sit in my facsimile of Tom's grand club chair, and wait. And wait, for the interloper to get up and fly. I'd make coffee as noisily as possible, even turn on the radio if the creature was an especially sound sleeper.

At last he would emerge, giving me a look not unlike that of Elsa Lanchester in *The Bride of Frankenstein* when she first lays eyes on her betrothed. He would sit and drink his coffee — crossly, I never had cream and they always, without fail, wanted it. I would feel on display, holding my stomach in and unable to fart. We would exchange, incuriously, the same information we had shared and ignored the night before: I'm sorry, what was your name again, where was it you said you worked? Oh, you didn't say. At last one of us would invent an urgent engagement and off he would go. I'd shut the door behind him with the breathless relief of an astronaut managing to seal off an air lock.

Home. There in solitude, surrounded by my things, not having to hold my stomach in one more minute, able to breathe. At home in my skin and the second skin of white wallboard I'd nearly forgotten I only rented. Even the other night I felt it. When I got up off the bedroom floor and, on my way to the bathroom and my rendezvous with my face, closed and bolted the front door my tormentor had left open. Home, safe: until I actually saw what he had done I even thought of just going to bed.

Now I've lost it. I am an exile, if that isn't too grand a word. I already was, I guess, many times over: from Winslow, and then from school, career, love. Finally, just the other night, from sex, even C.O.D. Banished to a chaste old age as decisively as if the boy had handed me an eviction notice. So the actual eviction notice is just one more banishment on a long list, one more station on the Trans-Siberian. Why should one station more or less make any difference?

Perhaps it is the very literalness of it: a sheet of paper I can hold in my hand and that tells me unequivocally I must go. With all the doors that have closed behind me in my life, I never heard one shut so firmly before. When I drank my way out of the university, after Tom was gone: it was ages before I acknowledged that I wasn't ever going to return and finish up, pass the prelims this time, write the dissertation. At my job, every election has revived the fantasy that the newcomers will rediscover my virtues and bring me back from the margins of the organization chart. Even at the Corral — not two months ago, a kid glanced over my way and allowed me a brief unmercenary smile. I felt for a second the tug of possibility, the chance of a coupling that would not involve, in the role of matchmaker, an engraving of Ben Franklin.

Never anything so final before. After I have moved they will paint over the bloodied walls and it will be as if I had never lived there.

Lunch has arrived. I've been lying here for I don't know how long, having it out with the invisible Mr. Culp. The usual range of fantasies I used to conjure up when a boyfriend left me for something better, or when someone else got the promotion I wanted: I have Tom's fortune after all, the release his brother made me sign is invalid. So I can buy the damn building, I appear in Culp's office with the papers, he whimpers — There is a terrible accident, Culp and I are the same blood type, I'm the only one who can save him, I magnanimously — It is Judgment Day, I am a sort of deputy deity, Culp stands before me, trying to defend himself. His face is my father's, and he repeats, in Beebe's strained voice, that it is my fault, I let the boy in.

Of course, here is what is so different about this particular banishment. Not just that it's in writing, a veritable deportation notice at last, my walking papers from the decent world of Huntington Arms. But this sour feeling that I sort of deserve it, that they have a case.

I've been violating the lease since the day I arrived, using or permitting the use of said premises in a disorderly manner. Hanging pictures without standard picture hooks. Failing to separate newspapers from other refuse. Playing my Piaf records too loud. Disorder, disorder. There are a hundred reasons to evict me, I should probably be grateful for the forbearance Mr. Culp has shown all these years. He asked only discretion, that I keep it behind closed doors, that I not rub his face in it.

I let a bit of the underworld into the Huntington Arms, where it could have gotten loose, ravaging old ladies. I am myself the underworld, hidden away behind my door until my demonic screams, breaking into the other tenants' sleep, betrayed me. An outlaw as much as my assailant. All a joke, except Mr. Culp has found his way into the part of me that has never left that life.

We were in terror for so long, not just in the dark time when Tom died but for years afterward. When I got to Washington in the late fifties it was still going on, the raids on the bars, the pickup who turned out to be a cop, the fear that you would never be promoted if you didn't bring a date to the department picnic. (Sally, the phys ed teacher in the next apartment, used to rescue me on those occasions. She was credible, if perhaps a touch too formidable at softball.) Most of that is gone now — at least here, at least for the time being. The new kids who get off the bus today have plenty to worry about, skinheads and preachers and microbes. But I think they will never feel, as we did, that they are fair game.

We thought it was just in the natural order of things that the world would force us underground and punish us unremittingly if we dared to show our faces. We all thought it: it underlay every joke and every song. At the old Piazza, where we gathered on the balcony while the straight families slurped up their spaghetti on the main floor, the piano player would launch into "When Irish Eyes Are Smiling," loud as hell, if he saw a cop outside the front door. We would, fast but in good order, make our way to the back stairs. Our drinks still on the bar, our cigarettes burning in the ash trays, our tabs to be settled the next time in. This seemed ordinary. I'm not sure any man my age has quite got over the feeling that this was ordinary, the way it was always going to be. By the time we were let out, like prisoners freed from a camp, we just stood around, dazed, to this day never quite believing that we had actually been liberated. Carrying our Culps inside us.

For lunch I have some kind of salt-free soup and a dry sandwich, by far the most foodlike of my blind selections. The boy doesn't sit up on the edge of his bed as usual to eat. Instead he lies as I do, the head of the mattress elevated, the tray table over his belly. As if this extra unanticipated day of confinement has broken him, he droops like an invalid and pokes mournfully at his lunch. So I'm deprived of my usual mealtime recreation, counting the muscles on his back. Instead, I can see now that he grips his fork with his unbandaged hand as one might clutch a dagger. And he is not scrupulous about closing his mouth as he chews. These lapses seem more childish than vulgar: he lacks manners as he lacks guile. Still, I look away.

I'm going to be moving. They'll slap some white paint over my blood and I'll be someplace new. The more I repeat it, the less painful it sounds. Indeed, I seem for the time being to have worn out my grievance against Culp, the Culp in me, and I feel an odd excitement. I'm going to be moving! I'm going to be starting life again all over.

Maybe Mr. Pollen is right, this is the time to do it. Retire, move on to another place. Key West, maybe, a little bungalow. Just one bedroom. Well, two, one for my liver: if I ever retire I know I'll start drinking at ten in the morning. And why not? What am I supposed to do now, finish the damn dissertation? Or whatever make-work projects Mr. Pollen is dumping into my in-box at this moment? Why don't I just grow a beard and live in a bungalow at the end of the earth and become a village character, the old geezer at the end of the bar, where it's shady?

I have been, not a transient, but too firmly fixed. One address, one job, even cruising ever more fruitlessly the same bars and the same faces, year after year. I am root-bound, I would have stayed in this same damn pot forever if the boy hadn't smashed it. Forever, never enough nourishment to bring forth a new flower. Here I've been thinking of shutting down my systems, one by one, until I just turned into an old heap on a gurney. When I should be getting ready to move, on to a new life, with the new face the boy has made for me, rakishly scarred.

We were never meant to stay in one place. It's different for straight people, maybe, with their kids growing up around them and then scattering, blown away like maple seeds. But we don't send life forth, we have to pick up and move ourselves or wait until we are felled by some storm and turn into rotting deadwood. We are supposed to move: exile isn't a punishment, it's our condition. It starts our lives, when we are cast out from the straight world we expect to grow into, and it starts them over again and again. Moving Day should be our national holiday, Saint Mayflower our patroness.

If I pray to her maybe I'll persuade myself. I can't say that I've felt like a potted plant in my old digs, or that I have any great hunger for new vistas. But I don't feel, the way I did just an hour ago, as though I'd been hurled out of Eden, with the baleful Mr. Culp hovering above me, brandishing the flaming sword. I am able to go, and it really is just a little bit exciting. Maybe even new furniture, get rid of that formerly white love seat and the silly brick-and-board bookshelves that seemed so bohemian twenty years ago.

So why mightn't Tom have felt, picking his avant-garde furniture for the new place on Marsden Street, as though he were starting a new life? He was an exile as much as the rest of us. Long before he left Winthrop House, after all, he was thrown out of the Party, and eons before that thrown out of the cozy world he had grown up in. Expelled from the country of his youth and living thereafter in a world of his own devising. Every banishment a shove on the way to freedom.

He felt that way himself, or said he did. Not long after we'd met, during our pajama party period, I showed him a bizarre letter my mother. She began by wondering if I were dressing warmly and ended by pointing out that the war had brought to Winslow all sorts of wonderful jobs that didn't require a college degree. So why didn't I stop wasting my time and come home, to my semi-invalid mother and her hospital cookery?

Tom was entertained, but I was outraged. "I have to go home for Christmas. And I just know she's going to be at me the whole time."

"Don't go," he said.

"What?"

"I always spend the holidays in New York. Why don't you come along?"

"New York!" The name has lost its shine. I don't think anyone growing up now can imagine what that faraway place once meant, or how just mouthing the word "Manhattan" could give you a nervous, jazzy thrill. I felt, even more than when I first glimpsed Tom's beautiful rooms, that he was carrying me to a new world. But I said, "I can't, she'd never speak to me again."

"Judging from her little epistle, I should think that a piece of luck."

"You make it sound so easy. I mean, she's the only family I have."

"And one too many at that. I sometimes think the very best thing that ever happened to me was being ejected by my family."

"You were?"

"Absolutely, aren't we all? In writing, no less. Would you like to see?"

"You still have it?" I said.

"Of course I have it."

"Why 'of course'? You always say you don't save stuff." An untruth, as I would discover when I rummaged through the cartons he left behind.

"But, my dear, do you think any freed slave ever threw away the Instrument of Manumission? It's a wonder I haven't framed the bloody thing, except that it's so depressing to look at a wall and see framed documents, as if the tenant had decided to start a little museum of his life. Why is it, do you suppose, that they hang only the degrees and not their birth certificates?"

"The letter."

"Two letters, you have to read both letters."

Slater Brothers
38 Broad Street
New York, New York

August 4, 1920

Thomas:

Your mother says that this will find you in Newport. She has some ideas about what sort of mission you are on. If she's right, I wish you the best. I'm awfully happy to see you settling down.

I want you to know that I have thought carefully about your next step. I have concluded that it would be better if you did not start off here at the firm. While I know that you're nothing like your uncle, that unhappy experience has left me with the feeling that this is not the kind of business that can be run as a family affair. You can point out the obvious exceptions, but they're all Jews, exceptions that prove the rule. I suppose it may be something in my own character, but I cannot envision myself as the senior partner in Slater and Son. Though I will admit that the idea used to cross my mind when you were very little.

"He does run on, doesn't he?" I said. "Practically free association."

"He dictated this letter."

"It's handwritten."

"By a male secretary. Imagine: not thirty years ago, and he still hadn't given in and bought a typewriter."

"Imagine dictating a letter like this."

"He was a busy man. He might, though, he just might have found the time to sign it himself, don't you think?"

I went on reading.

I think, though, that we both have to face up to the fact that you are very nearly thirty, and that it won't do for you to start in business the way I did, or the way younger men do. Of course your age isn't such a serious disadvantage, because everybody understands that the War interrupted so many boys' lives, and you're not the only one who took a year or two to settle down after. Well, you earned it, and I don't have to tell you again how proud your mother and I are. I'm almost sorry that your brother wasn't old enough to go.

I've been asking around, and it is pretty well agreed that Mr. Lamont is going to find something for you, one or two of the less speculative issues, and take you on as a sort of junior associate handling just those until you've found your feet. Of course, you'll be on commission only, and with conditions as depressed as they are just now you cannot expect to be pulling your own weight just at first. But I honestly can't think of a better way for a man of your age to get started in business. I think, if you and Pauline can wait a little longer, that it would be best for you to do so before trying to set up house. For the time being, you'll go on staying with your mother and me. When you've learned the ropes and are ready to go out on your own, we'll get you started.

I suppose you'll want to dally with your sweetheart a few more weeks. I have told Mr. Lamont to look for you in the second week of September.

Affectionately,
Andrew P. Slater

"You were engaged?"

"I was."

"You were — what? Twenty-six, and you didn't know?"

"I knew. But I — that didn't seem to have anything to do with it. One married, that was all."

"Kind of a heartless 'all.' You can't have cared for her."

"I think. Maybe not by then, not after the war. She was just the only one I could think of, and I — maybe I had made some promises, or what she took as promises. But we'd been together before the war, and then the foolish girl had waited all those years. And, since it had to be done, it was obvious that it had to be done with her."

"But even before the war —"

"Before the war. It was a different world, you know. I was pretty sure I loved her. Chased her all the way from New York to Newport. Quite a stir; we were an item, she and I. It was all circumstantial, you know. She led me on the chase, I suppose she led me every step after that.

"I'd been calling on her most of the spring. Once or twice we went for a drive, and occasionally someone found it entertaining to seat us next to each other at dinner. It was all harmless enough, people just enjoyed seeing us together, the dashing, serious youth and the laughing beauty. I had just graduated, I was loafing about in the city. She would be going away for the season soon enough. Whatever one might call what we were doing, there was no certainty we would resume in the fall.

"One morning I came down to breakfast, very late. I'd been to the theater the night before, with a college chum, and then to the old Mouquin on Sixth Avenue for a bite to eat. That's where all the writers went, it was exciting. We thought we recognized Dreiser. When I came down, there waiting for me was her card, so she had to have stopped off on her way to the morning train. I have that card somewhere." I was already beginning to wonder about his never saving anything.

"It was in roman type, and without plate marks, rather mannish. Miss Pauline Winston, and in the lower left corner, handwritten, the letters P.P.C. *Pour prendre congé*, to take leave. Which meant that she was bound for Newport a week early.

"You must understand, a card like that was ordinarily the coldest and least encouraging of leave-takings. That she had stopped specially made it a little less daunting than it might otherwise have been. Still, she was hardly begging me to follow, and I wouldn't have done, except that the summer had been as tedious as any I could remember.

"Other people recall it differently — the few of us left to recall it at all — but that is only because they know that the summer of '16 was the last before we entered the fight. Of course nothing was ever the same again, so memory colors that summer with the hues of every summer that went before it. But at the time it looked to us as though season after season would crawl by forever. Given the choice between sitting through just one more of Momma's at-homes and prancing off to Newport to court Polly Winston, I chose the latter. My uncle Edward had a little place up there —"

"This is the uncle who didn't work out in business?"

"Yes, rather in our line, I suspect. He was one of those men who liked to hang about with society women, rather like that awful Harry Lehr. Except of course Uncle had his own money. At any rate he wasn't there yet. The season was late starting that year, some people were already worried that we might be dragged into the war and that ostentation might be inappropriate. As I remember, they were well over that by midsummer.

"Since of course I couldn't open up Uncle's cottage all by myself, when I got to Newport — a day after Polly, I took the Fall River Line overnight — I had to take a room at the Faisneau and then drop cards all over town. It was only a couple of days before someone got the hint. Mrs. Perry, whose cottage was, even by Newport standards, a monster, was happy to put me up. Especially when she learned, through the gilded grapevine, that she was abetting a romantic mission. Because no one had failed to observe that I had stepped off the steamer at the Old Colony Wharf just one day after Polly Winston had arrived.

"I was so awfully naive, you know. I'd never even heard the words for what I was. And, while I knew in a mechanical way what it was men and women did, I didn't have any feeling that — that I should want to do that with Polly."

"What did you think marriage was for?"

"Oh, I understood that we would do that, when the time came. But I didn't understand that other men felt more than I did, looking at a woman. And I certainly didn't understand that what they felt was what I felt, looking at a boy.

"I thought it was enough that I liked the look of her bright face over a white shirtwaist. I thought it was enough that she laughed for me — that soft stabbed laughter when I would say something perverse or meaningless. It was an invitation to say or be anything I felt like at the moment. It would always make her laugh.

"We'd stroll along the Cliff Walk, her brother a little ways ahead, protecting her virtue. He was just eighteen, just on his way to New Haven, and I felt awfully grand, a graduate and courting his sister. Today, you know, if it were today I should have carried her off to some country lane in my convertible automobile, and there in the dark I should have found out. But then, skipping along the Cliff Walk with her in the middle of the afternoon and watching the boats, I thought: this is how it feels for a man and a woman walking together, this is what it is. And those other feelings — what stirred in me when I took my eyes off her face and gazed ahead at our stripling chaperon — I had no name for them. I could wake in a cold swamp of a bed knowing perfectly well that I had been dreaming of Jack —"

"Of course he'd be named Jack."

"People were, in those days. I could know that my — I could know that it arrived just as I was dreaming of Jack naked and poised for a dive, and I could simply decline to interpret the conjunction of the two events. You're different, you. You can't ever decline to interpret. But most of us humans are simpler than you are."

"So: you were engaged."

"After the war. I proposed, like an automaton. Strolled with her, those last August weeks in 1920. A very much beefier Jack still leading the procession. Back from the war he was, like me. And discreetly looking straight ahead — we could kiss now, if we wanted to, we were engaged. I did kiss her, those twilight walks, and I did feel some stirrings: twenty-six, and I'd never kissed anyone — I did feel something.

"The reception, finally, that September, back in New York, when the Winstons were to announce what everyone knew. I had started work already, peddling my 'less speculative issues.' Or rather, trying to imagine how one peddled them. Did one stand on a street corner and cry, 'Hey, get your American Telephone! Right here, Standard Oil, red hot!' Well, I suppose a few years later, when things got frantic, one practically did.

"It wasn't until the very evening of the announcement, it wasn't until I stood at the foot of that staircase in the Winstons' ballroom, looking up at her mastodon of a poppa and hearing him say my name, that I knew it was impossible. Even then I didn't know why. I just heard myself described, in the third person, as the intended of Pauline Winston, and the sentence sounded — dissonant, strangely ungrammatical, there was something wrong with it. It was my name, that's what was wrong, my name didn't belong in that sentence.

"I had been living my whole life in the third person. Mr.

and Mrs. VanNitty request the pleasure of Mr. Thomas Slater's company, Mr. Slater accepts with pleasure, Mr. Slater regrets — all that pleasure and regret might have been real enough for this Mr. Slater, whoever he was. But I, in the first person, I wasn't feeling anything, or wasn't letting myself. So I stood amid the crowd in the Winstons' ballroom, hearing that Mr. Slater had affianced himself and receiving the claps on my back. And I realized, as though awakened by those claps from a very dry dream indeed, my God, they're talking about me. I am this Mr. Slater. And if I do this — why, I'll have to spend all my time with her. And I'll never, oh never, have a chance to —

"To go diving with Jack. I swear, I stood in that ballroom, while Mr. Winston went on droning out some apposite sentiment or other, and I saw Jack, up on the landing with his father, naked and poised for a dive. And I finally, in that instant, understood."

"Well," I said. "It could have been worse. You could have been at the altar. Thinking about the minister."

"Bishop, it would have been. And that wouldn't have been very much worse. Things were as bad as they could be, we were quite far enough along. I didn't say anything that night, nor for several more nights. I couldn't think what to say. I just went on calling on her, sat numbly discussing plans for the wedding journey, picked my ushers, looked at her and listened to her laughter. Couldn't think of how to tell her.

"One day — it must have been a good two weeks later, I think the invitations were already back from the engraver, with the name of this strange Mr. Slater in raised letters — one day I went to see her and was told that she was not at home. The butler said, 'I'll tell her that you were by, Mr. Slater.' He started to close the door, and I said, 'Wait.' I took out a card and wrote P.P.C. in the lower left-hand corner."

"How elegant."

"How terribly, terribly craven. How despicable."

He picked up the second letter. "I went back to New Haven. It was some days before anyone in New York fully understood what I had done. Even Polly must have thought at first that I was only on a little trip, that the card meant nothing more than that. The term at Yale had already begun, but I persuaded Wilbur Cross to take me on at the graduate school. I managed finally to write Polly a correct little note, and then I wired to Momma to send on my things. Then this letter. I think my father must have written this himself. I'm not sure, I never saw his penmanship except on checks."

> *Slater Brothers*
> *38 Broad Street*
> *New York, New York*

> September 28, 1920

Thomas:

Your mother says that you're in New Haven. I can't say that I understand why I have to rely on your mother for news of your comings and goings. And I surely don't understand why you are running back to school at an age when a man ought to be well along in his career. But then I am not at all sure you have a career. In the business world a man's word is the most important asset he has. Maybe that isn't so of the newer sort who are starting to appear on the Street. But it's so of the men I deal with, the men you would have been dealing with. Now you have shown what your word is worth.

I suppose I have some inkling of what the problem was. But I cannot imagine how a son of mine would destroy all his prospects simply to escape an unfortunate engagement. Some of the most successful men in New York rarely see their wives. If you entered upon this thing too hastily, that is too bad, but there was no excuse for not going through with it.

I have been thinking very hard about what I might possibly do for you now. My old idea, of getting you a seat on the Exchange, is out of the question. I suppose you might still think about the law, but I can't see you coming out of school two or three years from now and setting out to compete with a lot of smart Jew boys ten years younger. You will have to find your own way now.

I have put the Wonamaddock in trust for you. I can't say that it is doing very well just at present, what with the demobilization, but it should yield about enough for the scholarly life you appear to have settled on. If not, I suppose your mother will find a way of supplementing it, although I would be prouder of you if you did not ask her. Putting something in trust means that I don't trust you to take care of it. I guess I really only mean that I don't think you're worldly enough to take care of it.

Your father.

P.S. Your mother will expect to see you at the holidays.

"What was that about having an inkling?"
"Oh, he spoke of it once."
"He actually talked about it?"
"Thought I ought to cut it out."
Of all the things that ever happened to Tom, this is one I cannot picture. After a family dinner, perhaps? Mother and sister withdrawn and Tom left uneasily with his father at the table. Retainers hovering with the port but tacitly invisible, like Japanese puppeteers.

All right, then. The father cutting the end of his cigar, Tom drawing a cigarette from the platinum case. Why wasn't that among his effects, the case? I never picture him without it. A retainer hands Tom's father the matches but doesn't light the cigar. That takes too long, is too intimate, men light cigars for themselves.

The old man lights the cigar, draws on it slowly but shows no satisfaction. Clears his throat and:

Speaks of it. Ought to cut that out. No outrage, evidently: when he did finally write Tom off, it wasn't for this. He only thought Tom should discard an unappealing habit. What words could he have used, in those days before the World War, what could a man like Tom's father have known about such things? Who in his round of office, racquets, obligatory soirees, could have told him about it? I don't mean told him about Tom; no one could have done that. I mean, when did a man like that find out that other worlds even existed?

At school, old St. Martin's in the seventies, a generation before Tom: all those boys shivering their way to Christian manhood under the icy eye of the Reverend Northwind? Could they have told him? At Yale, at the Exchange, in the steam room of the Racquet Club — one glistening walrus turning to another and murmuring, "Say, Slater. Have you heard? Some men —"

He would have known the words, of course, pansy, fairy. Sister: that's what a man of his generation might have used. But those words had nothing to do with Tom. Whatever it was he saw, Tom's father, whatever he had to speak of, cannot have been so distinct. Something, perhaps, that made him think of rakehells and Brummells, sinful dandies who drank and gambled in French and made love in some even less accessible tongue. Or even vaguer: some faint sign of *sentimentality*. That was the word old headmaster Northwind would have used, when obliged to caution against the second most common schoolboy vice (to the most common I was reduced last night, come full circle).

Sentimentality, yes. A friend comes up to Newport with Tom for the summer holidays, some fellow Eli. Tom's father happens to notice that they stand too close, murmur to each other, go off for a dip at the pond when the Misses Dewlap, over for luncheon, are plainly set for a stroll. When Tom and his pal return, their hair slicked back, they laugh at some joke Tom's father cannot understand. No hint of incipient buggery. All just a little distasteful, a little off.

And it is this he speaks of, quite casually, over his cigar and port. As easily as he might point out that Tom's neckties are too garish. "I think you ought to cut it out," he says. Confident that a word will be enough.

A father needs no heavy hand at the helm to pilot his son through the calm waters of that world. A word will do. The ties at Kaskel & Kaskel are good. You oughtn't to hang about so with that — what's his name? — that fellow.

So he puffs away, Tom's father, motions for the invisible hand to refill his glass. Not imagining that the faint side-current for which he has just made ample correction is only the visible eddy of the real current, rushing hot and strong under the calm of the Narragansett, bearing Tom's vessel on to shores his father has never imagined.

$\mathcal{E}$IGHT

THE BOY SHOVES the tray table aside and is on his feet, all
in a motion, as if he had felt himself — lying there just like
me, our postures virtually parallel — sinking and had to get
up before it went any further. He stalks to the window and
stands there a minute, giving me quite the most prolonged
view I have had of his stalwart and inadequately gowned
ass. In a gesture of unconscious provocation, he restlessly
bounces up and down on the balls of his feet, until I am
nearly surfeited with the sight of his cheeks, tensing, letting
go, tensing again. It is too much, I am almost grateful when
he stops and just stands for a second, quietly looking out.
His ass in repose like a psalm, simple and profound. Now
he is in motion again, putting on his robe, slipping on his
hospital-issue booties, heading for the hall. The poor caged
child must be horny as hell, ready to jump the first live thing
he comes across. Present company excepted.

There is a knock. The door is wide open; no one before
has thought it necessary to knock before breaking in on the
boy and me, in our little nest of celibacy. God, I hope it isn't
anyone from the office. "Yes," I say, in my feeblest voice.

A woman comes in. "Mr. Reeve?" she says.

"That's right."

She is forty or so, holding a clipboard and wearing one of the severe suits all the women in my office affected a few years ago, before they got their mysterious fashion bulletin and started wearing dresses again. She is chubby, but firmly so, one of those women who does brisk walking in the morning, striding along and gripping teensy dumbbells. On bad days they do it right in the office now, making the round of the endless corridors, with that determined look that makes old slouches like me step aside for them.

"Mr. Reeve, I'm Sarah Freund and I work for the School of Public Health." She extends a hand and I offer mine, but limply, so she'll understand I'm very weak and mustn't be bothered long. "We have a federal grant to study the follow-up needs of people who have suffered accidental injuries or violence. Your admitting diagnosis code was 801, so you're potentially a candidate for this study." All this is recited; she's said it a thousand times.

"No, thank you," I say.

"All I want to do is administer a survey." Odd word: administer it, as one might an enema. "It would just take a few minutes, and it's completely anonymous. I mean, I know your name, but I won't use it. See, just this identifier." She shows me the top sheet on her clipboard. I am F-319, old F-319, victim of an 801. What is that code: blowout fracture? Trick-induced trauma? "This study will help us improve our care systems, and your participation is very important."

"Okay," I say. What else am I going to do, try to read Tom's book for the millionth time? Peek into that plain brown envelope Howard was so excited about?

She goes to the remote control and turns the TV off without asking, then sits in the visitor's chair, in the crater left by Howard. "What is your age?"

"I'm sixty-two."

"Really?" she says. No one seemed to think I was especially youthful-looking before I got my face smashed in. Or maybe she means I look older than that. "And you're a white male."

"Uh-huh."

"And what is your address?"

"I thought this was all anonymous."

"I mean just your zip code, that's all I need."

"20036."

"Are you married, widowed, divorced, separated, or never married?" I am at least three of the above. Divorced a half dozen times, separated a thousand. Widowed once. But I supply the expected "never married." Me and Emily Dickinson.

"Do you live alone?"

"Yes."

"What is your occupation?"

"Federal employee."

"That's all the basic identification, you see. It really is all anonymous."

"That's fine."

"Now what I'm going to be asking you about are some activities of daily living. We call them ADLs. These are activities that most people perform in daily life and that contribute to self-sufficiency or to social integration. We want to know which of these activities you could perform before your injury and which you expect to be able to perform after your release from the hospital." She has memorized this, too; she recites it like a poem, an ode to social integration. "Now here's the first one. Before your injury, were you able to walk without assistance?"

"Yes."

"Do you expect to be able to walk without assistance after your release from the hospital?"

"Yes."

"Before your injury, could you climb stairs?"

"Yes."

"Do you expect to be able to climb stairs after your release from the hospital?"

"Yes."

"Before your injury, were you able to prepare your own meals?"

"Not very well."

"You had some limitation in this activity prior to your injury?"

"That's what all my friends say."

"Oh, I see," she says. She essays a smile.

"This is like the old joke: Doctor, after the operation, will I be able to play the violin?"

"Yes?" She tries to look interested, though she would rather administer her survey without digressions.

"No one has ever told you this joke?"

"I don't believe so."

"Never mind," I say. If I told it, I would probably have to explain it. "Yes, I was able to prepare my own meals."

"Do you expect to be able to prepare your own meals after your release from the hospital?"

"I guess. I suppose it'll be a while before I feel like whipping up a soufflé."

And so on and on. Dressing. Toileting, as she calls it, which makes me think of Belinda at her dressing table in *The Rape of the Lock*, though apparently she means going potty. Shopping for groceries. Paying bills. I begin to fall into the rhythm of the thing. It isn't before and after. That may be the point for her, but for me it is a catalogue of my before. I am stunned at the number of capacities I have displayed every day of my life. All these ADLs that I have performed unthinkingly and that must be — why else would she be asking? — accomplishments for some people, or hopeless dreams.

The boy comes back in, looking calmer and smiling a little, as if perhaps he has been flirting at the nurses' station. He looks at my visitor and raises his bandaged hand in greeting.

"Mr. Sikorski, how are you doing today?" What is he, then, Polish? I wouldn't have thought so: I have the standard picture of a Pole, broad face, high cheekbones. Well, maybe his are, a little. "Mr. Sikorski completed our survey several days ago." Mr. Sikorski nods, then looks up longingly at the blank TV. He wants to turn it on, but is afraid of disturbing us. So he resumes his post at the window, stands in his robe like a monument waiting to be unveiled, and pretends not to listen.

Ms. Freund continues. "Would you describe your most recent employment as involving mainly active physical labor, standing in place, sitting and standing, or mainly sitting?"

She could be a spy for Mr. Pollen. "Mainly sitting."

"Do you expect to be able to resume your employment after your release from the hospital?"

"Yes." I am conscious that Mr. Sikorski is listening. His answer would have been active physical labor, and he must be less confident than I about his ability to resume it, possibly sans thumb. I picture him, active and physical. Labor, one of those workers in a post office mural who were, for Tom, a distant abstraction.

"The next question," she recites, "is of a personal nature and may be omitted. It's not really a standard ADL, but we're adding it on a test basis because it relates to what can be for many individuals an important part of a fully satisfactory post-discharge adjustment. Before your injury," she begins. She hesitates, starts again, "Before your injury, were you able to engage in sexual activity? Again, this question is optional."

This is clearly the part of the survey she least enjoys administering. She must be especially embarrassed to be asking a sixty-two-year-old, nearly as embarrassed as I am to be answering in front of the boy.

"Yes I could." Mr. Sikorski is picturing, if he can exactly, what sort of sexual activity I was able to engage in. Sixty-odd years on the planet, twenty of them now since the day we were supposed to be liberated, and I am still embarrassed. Not unhappy about it, nor truly guilty, merely abashed, as if she were asking me whether, before the episode, I was able to pick my nose. This is as far as we got, I think, my cohort: from mortal shame to faint mortification.

I brace myself for the question the rhythm of the survey demands. Ms. Freund swallows and says, "Do you expect to be able to resume your employment after —"

"We've done that one." Unless she thinks, flatteringly, that what I do for a living is engage in sexual activity. In which case "mainly sitting" would not be especially descriptive.

"Oh, yes, I'm sorry. I lost my place. Do you expect to be able to engage in sexual activity after your release from the hospital?"

I have said yes to every other question, confident of my ability to resume every other activity of daily living, every last ADL. My injuries — trivial ones after all, not so much worse than a lot of men take without a whimper in a Saturday-night brawl — my injuries will not prevent me from climbing stairs or toileting. Why should they cut me off forever from the key, the indispensable ADL?

"Yes, I do," I say.

She checks her last box. On her questionnaire is an uninterrupted column of yeses. I am all but omnipotent, jack-of-all-ADLs. Ahead of me lie whirlwind days of walking and toileting, mainly sitting, engaging in sexual activity. I can hardly wait.

She gets up. "Thank you very much, Mr. Reeve. Your cooperation has been very important in helping health professionals improve our discharge planning. Did you want the TV back on?" The boy takes the cue at once, practically leaps to the clicker. "It was good seeing you again, Mr. Sikorski." He nods, but he is already busy, hunting for anything other than a soap opera.

I am content that he be Polish; it gives him a little depth. A childhood of stuffed cabbage and pierogi, maybe a term as a golden-haired altar boy at St. Casimir's, shy but mischievous. Now that Ms. Freund is gone, he slips off his booties and doffs his robe. Everything is back to normal now, and we resume our respective ADLs of watching TV and puzzling over Tom.

I can walk and talk and sort of cook, and maybe some day I'll make love again, my late resolutions notwithstanding. I can even, under the threat of Culp's flaming sword, move on to the next place. So why couldn't Tom? Why couldn't he have improvised a home once again, opened his cartons and made a life again? What could they have done to him that was so very much worse than my being thrown out of Huntington Arms — my books and bibelots and all the suits I plan to get into again as soon as I lose a few pounds — practically in the street? He could, with his money, his contacts, his name, however sullied, have lived a very pleasant life as a ruined man. Could have lived in New York, maybe, written an occasional piece for the *Partisan Review*, gone to the opera. Could have had one or two more long, no-touch affairs with collegians. Perhaps even, with whatever skills he acquired from Jimmy, some more conclusive dalliance. And could have had finally his rehabilitation.

The coroner said he was in good health. That is, aside from the fact that he had become brainless, he had the body of a forty-year-old. Every organ, squeezed by the coroner like produce, was intact and resilient, every vessel pliant and unobstructed. Ready for every ADL. He would have lived to be a hundred. That is, he would be alive today, crotchety and sclerotic, still calling himself a modern. Peppering his later essays with timely allusions, but the allusions shopworn, a few years out of date, as if the world took longer to penetrate. He could have had a future, a fourth or fifth start in a life of pink slips. There wasn't any reason to do what he did. Unless he just couldn't see another shore to land on.

When the boy the other night struck the first blow, my initial protest — hey, no — was in the simple language we use in bed. It was like when someone used to bite my nipples or undertake something else beyond the edges of my limited repertory: I muttered my faint *hey, no*, and I just assumed he would stop. I thought we were still in the realm where what we would do with each other's bodies was a subject for discussion. I didn't realize that we had been hurled back into the common world. Or rather, as he must never really have joined me in the separate world of bed, that he had pulled me back into it.

We were well launched into the scene — I was already on my knees on the floor, he was already cutting the phone line — before I understood that he was robbing me. Wrenched so rapidly from one world to the next, naked and half-blind, kneeling before him: I had never been so lost. I couldn't recognize anything in the room, nothing to hang on to. I had landed in a new country and saw no chance of sailing away from it. A country where the boy was king and I was deeply out of favor. I am not back yet — here in this strange room, the pink slip from Culp on my nightstand —

I am not back yet, not entirely, no matter how extensive my repertory of ADLs.

So maybe it was this: love coming so late, that morning at the lodge, and then letting him down so unmercifully. Would that have done it? Coming on it so late in life, and losing it so suddenly, hurled back into the common world with the tickets to Paris still in his pocket. Dragged from one country to the next, with no landmarks to hold on to, while Saint Mayflower averted her eyes.

Howard is here, with the Sunday classified. "And I checked back at your building and got today's mail." He hands me *The New Republic*, my college alumni magazine, and three letters telling me I've already been accepted for this or that credit card. They seem to come in waves, these letters, drowning me in approval. I wonder if they'll subside when the credit agencies find out about my sins. But Beebe promised, they won't tell stories about me.

"You shouldn't have gone out of your way."

"It wasn't far," Howard says. "I wanted to get another look at those horrible people."

"I guess it isn't their fault. I mean, the manager's just a petty functionary."

"I don't mean the manager. I mean the ladies in the lobby. The ones who hear someone screaming for his life in the middle of the night and call up to complain."

It's funny: I don't remember making any noise. I must have, for all I know I was screaming the whole time. But what I recall is all silence, broken intermittently by our quiet discourse, the boy's and mine, on modern banking practices and their implications for my life expectancy. During which the harpies sat up in their beds and listened through our paper-thin walls. Doing nothing to intervene, any more than I intervened in Tom's last weeks.

Howard goes on, "There they all were, so ghastly. They must be there every day, watching everyone go in and out."

"Every day. They had a lot of excitement a few weeks ago. They noticed that Muriel hadn't contributed to the conversation for a while, so somebody tapped her on the shoulder, and what do you think?"

"She hadn't!"

"Right there in the lobby. It's just as well I'm getting out. Pretty soon I'd be down there with them. Counting heads every morning."

"Then we'll have to rescue you. Let's see what there is. You want to stay near the Circle?"

"If I can. Oh, I don't know, there doesn't seem much point."

"We're not going out any more?"

"I don't know about we, but I suspect I'm destined for a quieter life."

"That doesn't mean you can't look. Anyway, you'll get over it."

"I don't know." I do know, I will get over it, master of every ADL. But for some reason I feel impelled to keep my revival to myself. As when a child in tears is made to laugh by a little tickling and laughs grudgingly, even angrily: no, you can't make me happy so cheaply. The little tickling in my groin cannot bring me back to life so cheaply. "I've been thinking about Tom."

"Tom?"

"Tom Slater. My old teacher."

"Oh, him. That's a cheery way to spend your time here."

"Well, you brought the book."

"I should have left you with *Daniel Deronda*. So restful. Two pages last night and I was sleeping like a baby. Here we go," he says, eager to get off the topic of Tom. "'Dupont.

Sunny one-bedroom with CAC, wall-to-wall, dishwasher, high ceils. Eight fifty a month.'"

"Eight fifty!"

"Oh, don't take on so. You can manage eight fifty. What are you, an eleven?"

"A twelve," I say, with offended dignity.

"A GS-twelve can certainly afford eight fifty, my God. This is 1989, you're not going to find anything decent for less than that."

"Go on."

"Oh, this sounds nice. 'Cozy one-bedroom near Metro. Remodeled kitchen/bath, custom closets, hardwood floors, CAC, pool, twenty-four-hour secretarial desk. A pool!'"

"Someone would harpoon me."

"You don't have to get in it, silly. You just take a thermos of daiquiris up and offer the young people refreshments after their brisk swims."

"How much?"

"Eight seventy-five. 'Cozy': it must be tiny. But still."

"I barely have the energy to get up and pee. How am I going to go look at apartments?"

"I can go check a few of them out. I know your furniture and things, what'll fit where. I'll find the perfect nest and we'll whisk you in there the minute you're able to get around."

I should be grateful, of course, I am grateful that anyone would take so much trouble over me. But I've never liked people managing my life, not since Tom tried; I was supposed to be grateful then, too. "I don't want any of my furniture," I say.

"I can't blame you. A man our age living like a college boy. You should get all new things." And he'll help with that, too. Until my place is just like his, with dark walls and pinspots and obelisks and tortoise-framed photos of Mums.

"I want to get a train," I say.

"What?"

"I want to get an electric train. I want to get a new apartment and just have a bed and a big electric train set. With towns and tunnels and things. I've always wanted that." Well, I have always wanted a train, it isn't exactly a joke. If I'm going to start over, why shouldn't I have exactly what I want? That money can buy.

"Oh, what fun!" he says. "And we can do up the bedroom like a Pullman car. We'll get you a little uniform, with one of those caps — Oh, and I saw up in Frederick, you know, in that huge barn where they have all the antique places, someone had a whole set of B&O china. Blue, like willowware, but with trains and bridges and tunnels on it. Maybe we can get you that."

This little burst of fancy from Howard makes me turn so I can check on my roommate with my good eye. Sure enough, he's staring at us, mouth open. Well, let him, I don't care how much Howard flames. We have been flaming in unison, keeping the darkness at bay, for eons.

We went to bed together, just once, in the twilight of the Eisenhower administration. We were both willowy little things in matching V-neck sweaters: the two of us could have slipped into one pair of Howard's 1989 trousers, or mine. We met at the Piazza, up on the balcony. Howard was singing along with the pianist. He knew every word of Rodgers and Hart — not just the refrains, but the verses. He sang them straight at me. *In our little den of iniquity* . . . I was embarrassed, it was so corny, someone I'd never met singing these lyrics at me as if they were about us. He wasn't my type at all, not even back then before he turned into a dirigible. My type didn't sing Rodgers and Hart. But I loved instantly the way he smiled, a big wide smile because he knew he was embarrassing me, and knew he'd caught me, for a night anyway. I kept looking away, hoping to spot someone a little less ethereal. Then I'd turn back and he'd go on crooning at me, his happy smile ever wider.

Of course nothing came of it. We were two tunnels with no train. After we gave up, we just lay there for a while. I was cross, angry with myself for having skittered home with something so evidently unworkable. He got up, put on a little kimono, and came back to the bed where I lay naked and fuming. Then he spoke my thoughts. "You know, you should have gone home with that jarhead."

"You too."

"I could never have fought my way through all those bobbysoxers around him. But he was looking at you, I could tell."

"Do you think so?"

"Oh yes. Anyway, we should have known."

"Uh-huh."

"But I thought you were kind of butch."

"Me?" I could have seemed butch only to Howard, for whom Kinsey might have added a 7 or 8 to his scale.

"Yes indeed. Not a marine, exactly."

"Not exactly."

"But I thought it was worth a try."

"Well, we tried." I got up and started putting my clothes on. I wanted to get away from his kimono and his all-white bedroom — that's what he had, before he went in for the industrial carpeting. No, there was some stage in between, in the sixties; paisley, probably.

"It's only eleven," he said.

"I'm not spending the night."

"No, of course not, how ghastly. You're heading straight back to the Piazza to see if your marine's still there." I turned around. He was smiling his enormous smile, a smile all out of proportion in those days, before his body grew to fit it. "If he is, he'll be in his cups. We'll have to line you up something better."

"You're not coming *with* me?" I said.

"I most certainly am. Just as soon as I freshen up. Don't you want me to?"

"I don't know," I said. I didn't want him to at all. The two of us in our identical sweaters flitting around like a matched pair of Staffordshire dogs.

"I won't get in your way," he said. "As soon as something catches your eye you just nudge me, and I'll fly off to the piano and sing mood music. 'Getting to Know You.' Or 'Begin the Beguine.'"

"Terrific."

"Or 'September Song': 'When the autumn weaaa-ther turns the leaves to flame, one hasn't got tiiiime for the waiting game.'"

"Get dressed," I said. "Clock's ticking. And I'm not a day past April."

My doctor comes in. Hoff-something, with the manic fringe of thin, rusty hair that has receded to the very top of his skull, so he looks like a thoughtful clown. My roommate's doctor, the surfer, is following him; mine must be the chief or whatever, though the sum of their ages wouldn't equal mine. Hoffman, it says on his jacket. I don't think I've seen him since they put me under. But maybe I did, yesterday morning, when I was still a little groggy. He wouldn't have let a day go by and not have seen me at all, would he? My doctor, with the soft, tired voice.

I'd been in the emergency room for hours and hours, just lying there, and they hadn't done anything. Tests, insurance forms, and a lot of people in and out, but nothing to make me feel any better. I had stopped shaking, I hadn't gone into shock after all. All I could think of was going home.

His face just appeared above mine, upside down, so at first I saw a man with a rusty Amish beard and horn-rimmed glasses, but no mouth. This apparition started speaking through a hole in its forehead. As his features rearranged themselves I began to make out something about his needing permission to operate. I said no, I was going home now, and we could talk about it in a few days.

He called me by my given name and put a hand on my shoulder. Still upside down, he mumbled, almost inaudibly, "You can certainly go home, this isn't a jail. But you know, that's going to start to heal, and then it'll be a whole lot harder to fix. If you go and come back it'll be a whole lot harder."

"What's there to fix? They said I'd be able to see again as soon as the swelling went down."

"Oh, you will. You're very lucky. I'm just afraid you're going to be . . . there could be some scarring."

"I don't care. I have to get home."

"I mean there could be a little disfigurement."

I was too tired to explain that it wouldn't matter, a little disfigurement more or less, as my face had ceased to be an object of aesthetic contemplation and I was planning to keep it indoors. What came out was a childish summary: "No one wants to look at me."

He held my shoulder tighter and said, "They sure as hell won't if you don't let me operate. You're going to look like the Phantom of the Opera."

I could sort of tell that was a joke. But it didn't matter if it was or not: I didn't care if I looked like Medusa, and I was determined now not to give in to him, this balding child who called me by my first name and tried to make jokes. "I'll call you," I said. "Do you have a card?"

"As a matter of fact I don't. People act kind of funny if a plastic surgeon steps up and hands them a business card."

He walked away from me and scratched his head. "You know, I had a kid in here last week, he was working under a car and something fell on him — I don't know what, some part that's under a car — and I don't know if he's ever going to have a face again."

This stratagem, which he must have thought surefire, irritated me even more. He went on, "Anyway, this kid, he's trying to be very tough, you know, he's at the age when that's the most important thing, to be cool about it. He's going to need, God knows, a dozen operations. I had to tell him, look, this is going to hurt and you still better not sign up for modeling school. And the kid said — just like you, it's amazing — no one's going to want to look at me, no one's ever going to want to look at me. I didn't know what to tell him, what could I have said to him?"

How cute, how therapeutic, making me supply the answer. I declined to play. "I don't know. What did you tell him?"

"Nothing, I couldn't think of anything. He was probably right." I waited for his obvious next line, and instead he said the opposite. "I wasn't telling you he had it worse, you shouldn't feel sorry for yourself. I never tell people that. Most of my patients have very good reasons to feel sorry for themselves."

"I don't feel sorry for myself."

"That's good. It's just funny you'd use the same words. Like nobody needs to see you, whatever you look like, nobody needs you on the whole planet."

Who does, I thought. Think. Howard, that's about it. "I'm just tired. I need to get home."

"Oh, I know. They've had you here umpteen hours and you just want to get home and heal yourself."

"That's right."

"But you can't, any more than you could do your own

root canal. Oh, you'll heal. Your face will put itself together the best it knows how, with whatever spare tissue it can scrape up from somewhere. The body's wonderful that way, it improvises, somehow or other it'll make sure you don't have any unplugged holes. But you'll wind up looking sort of . . . ad lib. So my job, see, isn't to heal you. It's to stop you from healing too fast. That's the worst thing you can do, is heal too fast."

He waited to see if I was won over by this paradox, then sighed and went on. "I'm not trying to take over your life. It's just that I can fix your little blowout fracture with my eyes closed. So why don't you let me? Just let somebody take care of you for a couple of days, and then you can go home and hide if you want to."

"I'm tired."

"I'll bet. Listen, I'll make you a deal. You can sleep through it."

I laughed, finally. I had never gone so many hours without laughing. It was like returning to earth, back to real time instead of the eerie slow motion into which the boy had hurled me. Hoffman handed me a clipboard and I signed over my face.

Howard is entranced with the surfer, but he snaps out of it and gets up. "I'll go," he says.

"No, don't," Dr. Hoffman says. "We're only going to be a minute."

"I really should, anyway." Then, to me: "Maybe I'll have time to check out that place with the pool on the way home."

"You're doing too much," I say.

"It's right on the way." He goes.

Dr. Hoffman watches him thoughtfully as he waddles out. He turns to the surfer. "This is that blowout fracture I did the other day. Bled like a sonofabitch. You take a lot of aspirin?" he says to me.

"Once in a while. Keeps the hangovers away."

"Uh-huh," he says. He is of the generation that doesn't drink. If I were of that generation, I would drink much more than I do. "Well, that must be it, the aspirin. You know, we had to give you three pints."

"Is that safe?" I say.

He gives me a one-sided smile. "Safer than bleeding to death on the table." And, I imagine him adding, safer than bringing home whoever did this to you. "So how are you feeling? You still got that pressure in your head?"

"Not so much."

"No, you're pretty well drained out. I think you can get that off," he says to the surfer. Meaning, I hope, the faucet in my forehead. "What did you do to your glasses, break them just so you could see in here?"

"Yes."

"That's a shame, just for a couple days."

"I would have missed a lot."

"Uh-huh. Well, listen, I'll be back in the morning and probably we'll release you. Dr. Harris is going to get that tube out so you won't feel like a rhinoceros. But I want you to go on keeping your head elevated, okay?"

"Okay," I say, earnestly, wanting his approval. He goes.

I'm going to get out tomorrow. Home to a bloodstained apartment they're getting ready to throw me out of. But home, anyhow, away from here, a step back to my familiar world. The surfer rips off the tape that was holding my spigot on, so fast I hardly feel it. He hands me a piece of gauze. "Now, as soon as I get this tube out you press this there and just keep holding it." He pulls out the tube, I press, and he wanders out of the room. I wonder how long I'm supposed to go on pressing.

The boy has found an old episode of "Star Trek." He watches listlessly; they talk too much on "Star Trek," it's almost as bad as the news. The man with pointy ears is explaining one more time that love is the juvenile emotion of a juvenile race, something his wise people are lucky to be without.

The boy frowns. He is surrounded by aliens. Vulcans. Queers, scads of them. Me, Howard, Michael the night nurse. How unnerving for him: he must feel as though his starship has landed him in a galaxy of fairies. Trapped here, no one to beam him up. More alone than if he had no roommate.

The captain makes a long speech about how those of us who aren't Vulcans know love is all that matters. The actor is embarrassed by the pap they're making him utter. Like Beebe the lawyer, he forces his voice into a lower register, the proper baritone of the spokesman for all earthlings.

All this love talk makes my roommate as uneasy as it does the captain. Why doesn't someone come along with a ray gun? Not that he doesn't believe in love, of course he does. Love is Janice talking baby talk to him and making him listen again about the wedding she wants to have, and the honeymoon in the Poconos with the heart-shaped bathtub. Or the way she holds his hand during the scary part of the movie, when the music gets louder and you know the monster's right around the corner.

He knows all about love. If we could speak, we could talk about it and we would mean the same thing. But of course we can't: he and the captain both feel the same way, that it's a woman's job to talk about love. Here is what's so alien about a fairy — not what we do in bed or who we do it with, but that we talk about love, we have made love the center of our days. We have abandoned the seemly reticence that makes men talk only of sports and cars and bosoms.

There is an explosion. The starship is careening toward an unknown planet, you can see it get bigger and bigger on the telescreen, alarms sound, the power has failed on the lower deck, everyone springs into motion, no more talk. The boy sits forward, rapt, now that there is some action.

Sharon the day nurse comes in. "What are you doing?" she says.

"The doctor told me to keep holding this here."

"When was this?"

"I don't know. Half an hour ago. Is he coming back?"

"Not tonight. He isn't even on the floor any more. Half an hour, you're one compliant patient. We should have prizes. Why don't you let go of that and see what happens?" She goes over to my roommate as I take off the bit of gauze, half expecting my brain to start oozing out.

"Hi, hon," she says to the boy. "Are you okay? Do you need anything?" He shakes his head and looks up at her. Looks her over, rather. She must be twice his age, and her body in the white uniform has an indistinctness about it, like an ice cream mold that is starting to melt. But he stares with plain enough meaning that she laughs and steps back. "Other than that." He gives her a big smile and scratches his head with his unbandaged hand.

She returns to me. My brain is intact. "Well, it's discharging just a little," she says. "Let me put something on that. You're going to be getting out tomorrow."

"That's right."

"Well, I hope you're going to be more careful." I glance over at the boy. I wonder again if my whole story is right there in my chart and she's about to spill it. "There, that should do for tonight. I'm getting off now, but I'm on tomorrow. I'll probably see you before you go."

"Okay."

I look once again at the boy. He has a hand under the

covers and a pensive expression. Imagine: he is having impure thoughts about an enormous dish of ice cream. Cage him here long enough and I'd start to look good.

After a minute he hops out of bed, restless, as if the news of my imminent release has made him feel even more a prisoner. His face has a look of candid bafflement: mouth open, brows furrowed constantly. The lines will be permanent before he is thirty, and people will think he is always angry, when really he is just making his way through a world that is an endless puzzle to him. Even his cartoons are filled with enigmas that he drinks in with incurious delight.

When he stands for a second on his way to the john and looks out the window, the blasted landscape that surrounds the hospital is a vista of wonderment. He comprehends everything up to the reach of his bandaged thumb. Past that all is mystery, alive with the spirits of pagan gods. But he owns himself, stands there indomitably in the present tense. I wish I could join him there, in the present, cast off the layers of history in which I am immured as in my geological strata of fat. I wouldn't even have to touch him, necessarily. We could just stand and look quietly out the window together. He could teach me not to talk.

Nine

I AM STILL NOT SURE about Jimmy's face. I seem to picture him clearly enough now, the almost voluptuous mouth
and above it, as if in rebuttal, the razor-straight nose and
gunmetal eyes. Maybe I'm not remembering, just piecing
together an acceptable facsimile from various snapshots in
my Rolodex. Still, I'm almost sure I can see him as he was
the day he snared Tom, at that reception in Winthrop
House. It was Jimmy that day, I'm nearly certain now.

The receiving line had dissolved, and Tom was happily
orating to a clutch of ephebes. So I might have escaped to
the Garland, except that I was curious about the boy who
had endured Tom's laying-on of hands. Jimmy was by the
window, looking out as my roommate just did, holding his
sherry gravely and pretending to listen as a pair of gnomes
argued about Ezra Pound. He turned to look at them; his
eyes went from one to the other — not in the rhythm of
their sophomoric debate, but slowly scanning their faces,
trying to make them out as a sensitive dog might, their
words just meaningless noise.

He smiled for a second, as if having solved the riddle,
tossed back the last of his sherry, and headed for the bar. I

gulped mine, to have an excuse for intercepting him there, and it went down the wrong pipe. I was in the middle of the room, coughing, quite the floor show, and by the time I had recovered he had got his refill and wandered over to the piano. There he stood, looking at the music on the lyre with the same alert incomprehension with which he had listened to the babble about the *Pisan Cantos* and whether treason mattered.

If I could have thought of something to say, about the music, anything, I could have gone to him. But he was already moving to the edge of the group of Wheaties eaters surrounding Tom. Tom went on discoursing, gave him only the tiniest glance, but enough to draw him in. From then on, I never really had a chance to speak with him. So in my memories he has no insides, only the sort of redundancy I always attribute to beautiful men. Inside and outside just the same, like a saint.

Like my roommate, who emerges now from the john, blessed and impenetrable. He looks over at me: today he is looking at me a little, as if I were a human being. He gets back into bed, but only for a minute. Still restless, he returns to his window and stands again, staring out at the diminished world. So alone, in this galaxy of fairies. Not a friend around, no one he can nudge, no one to share a joke about Sharon the nurse's big ice cream cones.

I cannot endow him with an interior life — as if a soul were mine to confer. The very surface of him is so complex and resonant, eyes, mouth, shoulders, each like a well-formed thought, thighs like a dissertation, the witty dialectic of his buttocks and the simple *ego sum* of his cock: spinning all this forth instant after instant, how could he have time left over for an idea or a motive beyond just being?

So, again, with Jimmy. It isn't that he told on Tom, I can think of any number of reasons he might have. But that *he* could think of them, all by himself. That he had a will, any will left over after what it took to sustain that body in being. I cannot imagine him spontaneously going to van Leunen, making whatever bargain he made, coolly writing out his affidavit. I cannot picture, inside that body, a calculating machine, plotting out its future.

I have always preferred to think that he was trapped somehow. I suppose that is only because he was pretty: I am happier believing that Saint Jimmy was just an instrument. Because it would be too much to tolerate, wouldn't it, if beautiful objects had motives and powers of their own?

The phone rings. My second call in two days. This will be Cochran, maybe, or one of my other colleagues from the square bar at the Corral. They heard about me last night probably: I am sure Howard told the story with his usual vividness. Then everyone was busy all day. Now, getting off work, they will start to call, one after another. How awful for you, dear, tell me again how it happened. Hoping to elicit some detail Howard hasn't shared or invented.

"Hello," I say, as vigorously as I can. Cochran, or whichever vulture it is, mustn't have the satisfaction of hearing me sound miserable.

"Hi. You're sounding better." It is only Howard.

"I am. They're going to let me out tomorrow."

"Wonderful! You can come see your new home."

"Oh, we've settled on something?"

"That one with the pool. You know, I thought it was going to be the size of a shoebox. But it's just as big as your old place, and wonderful views, nice little kitchen. It's a steal."

"What was it, eight seventy-five? Who's stealing from whom?"

"Oh, don't start that again. You'll love it. And the building is just packed full of us, in the lobby, in the elevators, all up and down the halls. It could be the YMCA."

"Sounds noisy."

"Oh, if you'd rather go on shacking up with a bunch of old widows trying to outlive one another, I'm sure I can find just the spot. Bethesda, somewhere like that."

"I'm afraid it's more my speed than the Y."

"You're so right. I'll go hunt a little more. Now, you're going to be spending a lot of time in the lobby with the other dowagers. Which do you like, the kind of somber ones with wing chairs and gothic paneling? Or something a little more Eden Roc, long sofas and a modernesque chandelier?"

"Oh, definitely the Eden Roc. Would it have a fountain?"

"With a little boy peeing, I know just the place." I hear laughter behind him, he is calling me from the bar. "Oh, Cochran says there's a vacancy where his mother lives. You'll be such friends!" It's happy hour, they're all at the bar, and Howard has told every damn one of them that I've been thrown out of my apartment.

"You told them," I say.

"Well, maybe you shouldn't move after all," he says loudly. "Just dodder into your golden years at the good old Huntington Arms. But I did tell everyone you were thinking about it, just looking around."

"Nobody thinks it's odd that the first thing I want to do when I limp out of the hospital is go apartment-hunting?"

"Honey, these queens would climb out of their own graves and go looking for a choicer plot." More laughter behind him. "I wish you'd think about this place I saw. Live around some younger people."

"I'd just feel all that much older."

"No, you wouldn't, you'd be surprised. I don't mean you're necessarily going to get into anybody's pants. But you'd be a wonderful den mother."

"Or a resident adviser."

"There you go, school days. Tea and sympathy. Anyway, we'll check it out tomorrow, as soon as you get out. You can at least look. What time should I come for you?"

"I don't know when they're letting me go."

"Well, I'll call you as soon as I get up."

"Okay. But I'm not sure I'm going to be ready for any grand tours."

"I understand. Everyone says hello." They do, with quite a flattering racket. We hang up.

He's got me. I know he's exaggerating: the halls will be as long and deserted as in the Huntington Arms, and — if there are beauties in the lobby — they are merely passing through on their way to lives I will have no part of, not even as resident adviser. Still, as long as I have to move — Have to, this isn't my annual hypothetical house hunt. I have to move. It doesn't matter if Howard is persuasive or not.

Well, good, even if it took a shove. Already I am almost eager, coveting this new apartment and the dream life it seems to hold forth. Just the way, almost fifty years ago, I looked around at Tom's rooms, the master's suite at Winthrop House, and thought it would be worth doing anything — reading Spenser, even — to have a chance at that life, those rooms.

Those rooms that wound up in the hands of Fuzzy Walgreen, the replacement master. The only person I can think of who got anything at all out of Tom's demise (leaving aside his horrid brother). So whenever I speculate about who might have got the goods on Jimmy and set the wheels turning, I always wind up with Fuzzy. It's hard to picture someone as unworldly as squinting old Fuzzy Walgreen doing someone in for a nicer flat. But who else? All for those wonderful rooms.

It doesn't matter so much who it was. I know I require a suspect at all only because I won't grant Jimmy an inside of his own. But I am entertained by the picture of it: virginal Fuzzy blindly stumbling onto Tom and Jimmy's story. And then Martin van Leunen, in turn, stumbling onto Fuzzy.

I saw President van Leunen only once in all my years at school. He was out of town a lot, serving on commissions, speaking at dinners, doing radio shows and even television. The little time he was in residence, he seemed as impossibly distant as a pharaoh. This was not his reputation: on the contrary, one always heard how personable and unassuming he was, sitting in the stands at the Yale game, stopping by for lunch at the freshman dining hall. Perhaps these apparitions were vouchsafed only to the faithful, or perhaps I just didn't hang out in the right places. In any event, I was as likely to run into Martin van Leunen as into the Blessed Virgin.

The one time I did see him was at East Station, where he descended from the parlor car of the train I'd been on (I'd been in the bar car, chatting up a sailor) and made his way to a modest chauffeured Buick. He was moving very fast. I don't mean that he was running to his car. But it always seems to me — the few times I've encountered celebrities in person — that they are zipping along at a different pace from the rest of us. Partly this is just surprise, that the still picture can move: as in a cartoon, van Leunen had leapt off the cover of *Look* and come to life. Moreover, he was doing it in three, count them, three dimensions. Somehow keeping in place his public being and also acting human, and that seemed so enormously complicated that he just had to be moving faster than anyone else.

He was moving very fast that spring, the *dynamic* Martin van Leunen; the adjective so inevitable it might have been his real first name. He wanted to be governor. Or rather — since no sane man would have wanted to be governor of that

185

fractious state — he supposed that the nation's unconscious clamor for him would be more audible from the statehouse. Then, another four years or so . . .

When the uproar started, on distant campuses, he had crafted a response that was truly presidential, in the derogatory sense we have only more recently learned to attach to that word. We all saw him on television, the new Dumont console they'd just put in at Winthrop House. The incongruous object seeming a harmless novelty, its mock–Duncan Phyfe cabinet almost blending into the common room, until it turned around and devoured everything.

"Mr. Spivak," van Leunen said. "The issue isn't whether a Communist teacher is indoctrinating his students. We think our students have questioning minds and aren't likely to be turned into apparatchiks by one biased lecturer. But anyone with an allegiance to a fixed way of looking at the world, a school of thought that's supposed to explain everything: well, I think most open-minded people would agree that someone caught up in that particular way of thinking just can't carry on thoughtful scholarly inquiry."

This was a new way of talking back then. Some of the boys in the common room laughed in disbelief. The rest of us sat with our mouths open, not understanding that we were hearing for the first time the voice of modern statecraft.

Anyway, the message was plain enough. He was all for academic freedom and against hysteria, but he was poised to join the posse at the first alarum. So it was no surprise that, when the hurricane reached our campus at last, van Leunen took measures, from his pharaonic distance. By letter probably: you are relieved of your duties as master of Winthrop House, your classes are canceled, and so on.

May turned to June, school let out, Tom's silence persisted. Van Leunen's train to Washington — on which he was so far the only knowing rider — might have been derailed by Tom's perverse intransigence. For it would have done no good to fire him. There would still, after all, have been a coven of anonymous Bolsheviks skulking around the quad. Merely getting rid of Tom would not have satisfied the Board of Overseers, or the alumni, or the papers. The papers above all. He needed to sweep the place clean, flush all the vermin from their tenured hiding places, so the name of the school would be out of the news and back in the sports pages, where it belonged. The sports pages and the groom's résumé in the bridal announcements. He needed Tom to complete the standard ritual of contrition and finger pointing, and he happened at last upon a weapon. Maybe in the astonishing form of Fuzzy Walgreen.

I can picture them: van Leunen sitting in his palatial office; across from him, like an emissary from winter, an anemic, elfin figure in a worsted suit, clutching a green bookbag like a freshman. The first video politician faces the Pindar man.

"I'm awfully glad to meet you finally," van Leunen says, with the breezy man-of-the-people air he has lately been cultivating. "It's funny, isn't it, that we've never crossed paths? Sometimes I think the alumni are right, this place is just getting too damn big."

Fuzzy is obsequious but also peevish. "I have been trying to see you for some weeks."

"I'm sorry. There was a little mix-up. Obviously I'm always available to my senior faculty."

"I can understand, given the many more pressing matters with which you must deal, that the classics department might not always occupy the foremost place in your thoughts," Fuzzy says. That is how Fuzzy used to talk, as pedantically as Tom but with less juice. "I take it that you have read my memorandum."

Perhaps van Leunen has seen a page or two, out of thirty: one of Fuzzy's perennial missives about how the classics were the fount of all et cetera and how urgent it was to restore the Latin and Greek requirements. "I've read most of it," he says. "But, as you say, I've been pretty tied up." He counts off his burdens on his fingers, so that Fuzzy will understand how trivial his memorandum is. "The commission I'm chairing for UNESCO, and then the curriculum reform proposal, and of course this problem with Tom Slater, now commencement coming in a couple weeks, and —"

"Mr. Slater?" Fuzzy says.

"Hm?" He hasn't used all his fingers.

"There is a problem?"

"With the Assembly, his testimony. You haven't heard about this?" Possibly Walgreen's grasp of current events stops with the Gallic Wars.

"I believe I have heard something," Fuzzy says. "I am not an attentive student of politics."

"No? I think these days we could all pay a little more attention to politics. Mr. Slater's in very serious trouble."

"I am sorry to hear it. We have been colleagues for many years. And of course I am the senior fellow at Winthrop House."

"Are you?" van Leunen says, leaning forward. "Of course you are, you live right there, don't you?"

"I do."

"Well, you can take it from me, he's got himself in quite a jam. And on top of that, I've been thinking back and . . . it seems to me I used to hear some pretty disturbing rumors about Mr. Slater." He sits back again in his huge chair and says, casually enough, "Maybe you have, too."

"Rumors," Fuzzy repeats, tonelessly. He is impatient to return to his own agenda.

"I didn't used to pay much attention. You know, I try not to get bogged down in faculty gossip. But I really am starting to worry about these stories. You must know Slater pretty well: maybe you can tell me there's nothing to it."

"It?"

"His relations with students."

"Oh. I —" Fuzzy looks down. Van Leunen is wondering how explicit he'll need to be when Fuzzy mumbles, "I myself have had some concerns on this point."

"You know something about it?"

"I had better say no more." He clutches his bookbag like a shield.

Van Leunen is quiet for a minute. He can already see, probably, that he has struck gold. But such a bizarre little man: how to handle him? At last he says, "I understand. Anyway, being in classics, I guess you're a little more tolerant on these matters than a lot of people."

A trace of pink invades Fuzzy's pallor. "If you mean that students of the classics endorse that deplorable weakness of the Greeks, you are mistaken. Speaking for myself, I have always been dismayed by this one lamentable defect of a culture otherwise so exemplary. I do not tolerate it, I am obliged to overlook it."

Van Leunen says, not at all sharply, "And I guess it's the same way with Mr. Slater."

Fuzzy stammers, "He is my friend."

"So you overlook this little defect. Well, I can respect that; there are worse things than loyalty. I wouldn't be asking you about it if I weren't so very concerned about the welfare of our students. They're more important than anything, don't you think?"

"I suppose they are," Fuzzy says dutifully, though really only Pindar is more important than anything.

"Even friendship."

Fuzzy doesn't speak for a minute. Then he says, as if summing up, "I have breakfasted with Mr. Slater nearly every morning for twenty years."

Van Leunen waits, oddly patient for such a fast-moving man. Fuzzy peers down into his bookbag as if it contains an oracle. Finally he murmurs, "Perhaps it isn't right, what he's done."

"I seem to recall that the greatest crime in Athens was corrupting the young."

"That is incorrect," Fuzzy says coldly. "Any number of transgressions were regarded with equal gravity." Even Fuzzy can detect that he is being played on. But he also believes it, that Tom has transgressed.

The more I think about it, the more sure I am it was Fuzzy. Chaste Fuzzy, honestly scandalized by Tom and reluctantly doing his duty. And besides, there was that odd Pindaric line he declaimed the day Tom died, as my streetcar pulled away. *Nó one can have thóught he would do thát.* It had to be Fuzzy. Fuzzy pulling the trigger and then astonished at the mess he had made.

Fuzzy sits up straight, ready for his recitation. "Very well. As it happens, my rooms at Winthrop House overlook Mr. Slater's. They are on the facing leg of an ell, do you see?"

"Uh-huh."

"I am often up nights. My studies require it. And I can scarcely help, when I look up from my work, observing . . . what occurs there, in Mr. Slater's suite. I regret to say that Mr. Slater's fondness for fresh air sometimes makes him less than scrupulous about drawing the curtains. I have not spied on him, do you understand? I just happen to look up."

"Of course."

"Naturally Mr. Slater has always entertained students. His position demands it. And while I have — as you say —

occasionally heard rumors, I had until lately dismissed them, just as you have. Until this last year, such activities as I witnessed were at least susceptible of an innocent interpretation."

"Activities?"

"Mr. Slater would, from time to time, touch a student. I mean that he would put his arm around him, thus. It is not a gesture that I should comfortably have made, but one I suppose that could be attributed to good fellowship, or perhaps an offer of solace."

"Uh-huh."

"On one occasion a young man removed his jacket, and Mr. Slater . . . felt his arm. Even this, however — Mr. Slater has always had an interest in athletics. I believe athletes sometimes feel one another's arms."

"I believe they do," van Leunen says, through his teeth. "But this last year . . ."

"These last months, more precisely. One young man has been a frequent visitor to Mr. Slater's rooms. And —"

"Who was this kid?"

"I am not certain. A resident of Winthrop House, I am afraid I often neglect to learn their names."

"Okay, anyway, a frequent visitor."

"I have observed much that I wish I had not."

"Such as . . ."

"I wanted very badly not to see. I am — do you understand? — not a gregarious man. But for Mr. Slater I call almost no man friend. I have tried not to look, but I cannot help it."

Van Leunen nearly shouts. "What were they doing?"

"I . . . they were . . . I do not know exactly how to describe what they were doing."

"Uh-huh," van Leunen says wearily. "But — what's the saying? — the Greeks had a word for it?"

Fuzzy seizes the opportunity to digress. "Perhaps they did. I mean to say, there are words that appear in the lexicons and that one understands to refer to some form of . . . correlative posture. But they are never defined, and I am, I suppose, too deficient in imagination to know precisely what —"

Van Leunen cuts him off. "Then you'll have to fall back on English, won't you?"

Fuzzy continues, finally, in a near whisper. Unable to say simple words like "fuck" or "suck," whatever it was Tom and Jimmy did. Obliged instead to describe it flatly and mechanically, as an entomologist might detail the copulation of mantises. Or perhaps the way an infant would recount the primal scene. Daddy put his peepee here, and then . . . He gets the details right, every act in proper sequence, he just doesn't know what they were doing, what the various frictions and insertions added up to. And of course nothing in his experience tells him what they were feeling. Van Leunen feels the oddest chill; he might be hearing the newspaper account of an atrocity. He is grateful when Fuzzy is finished, and not just because he has his ammunition now.

"I know this has been hard for you," van Leunen says. "But I'm going to need something in writing."

A statement: Fuzzy pictures his breakfast mate reading it. "I have already done too much."

Van Leunen shrugs. "That's all right, I can see how you must feel. You've been of some help, at any rate. I guess I can go ahead with my own inquiries."

"I am sorry."

"While this matter is pending, of course, I have had to ask Mr. Slater to step down as master of Winthrop House." Fuzzy looks up at him. "So I'll be looking for a replacement."

After a minute Fuzzy says, diffidently, "I believe I remarked that I am the senior fellow."

"Yes, there's no doubt you're highly qualified, definitely a candidate. I'll certainly keep you in mind." Van Leunen stands and offers Fuzzy his hand. Fuzzy is too encumbered with bookbag and hat to take it. So van Leunen just steers him to the door. When they get there, van Leunen says casually, "Of course these are unusual times. As we were saying. Maybe the most important thing, just now, is finding someone who'll put the interests of the university ahead of anything else." He lets that sink in a moment. "This student, I suppose you could find out his name if you wanted to."

Fuzzy swallows. "I suppose I could."

Dinner is here. The girl sets it on my tray table and speeds out of the room with a neutral look in her eyes, as someone walking a dog will give passersby a blank expression that says, I have nothing to do with what Rover left on the sidewalk. I lift the plastic cover and find chicken à la king. Escorted, as they say in the restaurant reviews, by broccoli. I pick up the little slip on the tray, to see if this is actually what I checked off in yesterday morning's fog. It isn't. I had fortuitously checked meat loaf, and someone has altered it. No, he shall have chicken, the dietician says, with an enigmatic smile.

The boy also has chicken. He is eyeing it with his usual puzzled look; he didn't order it either. But he can't just cogitate that body of his into being; even if he has nothing else on his mind, he has to eat. He sits up and digs in. His back is to me once again, so I don't have to look at the way he holds his fork. I push my tray table away. Tomorrow, if I am up to it, Howard will take me to get a huge hot pastrami sandwich with melted cheese. Then we'll go to look at my dream house, with all the cuties in the lobby. I'll sign a rent application, list Culp Management as a reference, and pray for the best. Howard will drop me off at the Huntington Arms. I will run the gauntlet of the gossiping biddies, nod curtly to Hurley the manager, ride the elevator up, turn my key, and step into a room whose walls are splattered with my blood, dry and black now. Like Tom's walls. I don't think it will be very hard to move.

I am looking freely at the boy's back for the last time. No, maybe breakfast tomorrow. But nearly the last. Just a couple of days and I am almost accustomed to seeing it, marvelous though it is, as a Mellon or Annenberg must scarcely look up from his plate at the Cézannes in the dining room.

I wish I could memorize it somehow. Fifty years ago I had *The Lady in the Lake* by heart. Haven't I room enough now to hold somewhere, always, the eloquent sweep of his shoulders and the forbidding, mysterious declivity at the base of his spine? Not in my heart, necessarily. *Of the Lake*, *Lady* of *the Lake*. Everything goes. I will forget him just as surely. In a year or two, I will forget what happened the other night.

The boy abruptly pushes his tray away, turns, and catches me staring at him. There's no point pretending I haven't been, so I continue, now trying for a Polaroid of his face. Maybe it is, yes, rather Slavic. He looks back at me, his eyes unreadable, nothing behind them. He isn't really looking into me; the shades of cruelty that pass over his face are just the flickering blue light of the television. It is only in my imagination that straight men look right into me.

My first job here, back in the fifties, had a long title, program analysis technician trainee I (no one was ever a II, for some reason). PATT-I, everyone said Patty. It was just clerical work, mostly, and hunting for records. That was the worst of it, the day or two a week descending into the sub-basement of the south building, in search of some file that no one had thought would ever be needed again. There, in the dank memory cavern of our republic, boxes of records were stacked on shelves twelve feet high, rank after rank of them. If there hadn't been a river in the way I expect the shelves would have stretched on to Virginia.

I would climb a wobbly ladder — wobbly myself, often, from the night before — and try to make out the faded labels on the boxes. I was too good for this. I had a consolation-prize master's degree and a long title and, besides, that clerk at the entrance was supposed to find the files, you were just supposed to give him a little slip. But if you waited for him to find something the government could just come to a halt. So I climbed. And, too fine though I was, I would feel an idiot satisfaction when I actually put my hands on the right file. Coming down the ladder, clutching my quarry, I would feel that I had accomplished something. Not an everyday feeling in the civil service, not one I've had many times since.

Even then I spent most of my days in a cubicle with my fellow Patty, a guy about my own age named Dave. He sat on his little office chair as if he were on the bench at a football game, legs wide apart, hands on his knees. He wore, as I did, a short-sleeved dress shirt and the narrow tie of those days, skinny as a bolo. He would loosen the tie and unbutton his top button, as I never did; a whisper of dense black hair would peek out at the base of his neck. More on his powerful forearms. He was a Patty with a penis.

The way our desks faced, I was usually looking at his back — I'd spend much of the day looking, the way his shoulders strained at the cheap fabric of his shirt. Sometimes he'd turn around and try to talk to me. I wanted to talk, so he wouldn't turn back for a minute and I could drink in his dark eyes and blue chin. But of course all his opening lines were about cars or baseball or girls. I would just mumble or, when the subject was the new floozy in the steno pool, try to arrange my face into a leer. Pretty soon he'd give up and go back to staring at the papers on his desk, papers that never changed from day to day and that he is probably reshuffling at this moment. He must have thought I was a terrible square, never thinking about anything but work and getting ahead.

As it happened, I did get ahead, was rewarded with a couple of promotions for the little bit I accomplished during those long summer days spent dreaming on Dave's back. Pretty soon I was Dave's supervisor, but our department was short on space and I was left in the same cubicle with him, his back now sending forth waves of resentment and envy, or at least that's what I read in it. He still wasn't doing a damn thing, I had to do his work and mine.

At the start I tried once or twice to give him an order. He would swivel around and look attentive, no insubordination apparent in his face. His eyes gazed steadily into mine and — while he was probably thinking ahead to lunch or happy hour, depending on the time of day — I thought he was peering straight into me. Musing at the irony of our situation, that a prissy little queer was trying to give orders to a real man. Maybe he thought nothing so definite, but he surely knew, after a few of these episodes, that I had no power over him. After a while he started coming in late and taking a couple of hours for lunch. I said nothing.

My next promotion took me a floor away; in the great warren of our building I rarely saw him after that. Over the years, though, I would pass him sometimes in the hall, and would be gratified to see that he was looking more and more beat down. An eternal Patty, his muscles sagging, conquered by the years and a family and, I hoped, a supervisor who could meet his stare. But he had beaten me first. On my first foray into the grown-up world he had taught me that, if I got all the way to assistant secretary, there would be some men I could never give orders to. The world belonged to them, and any place I might make for myself in it was just a temporary usurpation.

Some days I feel that they are all, even the most polite and tolerant, my enemies. From Arnaud to the boy in the next bed, they are all looking deep into me with utter contempt. Holding themselves back: any minute they could turn and start hitting me. I know I don't want that. Last night, when I was playing with myself and couldn't get that awful boy out of my mind — that was an aberration, I have never wanted that. But I think there has never been a night, in bed with one of the butch numbers I have always fatally pursued, when I wasn't a little afraid — even if he gave himself up entirely and everything was magic — that he might turn on me and beat me up. Give me the licking, not that I deserved, but that I somehow was bound to get, in this world that belongs to them. No wonder Tom yearned to obliterate them, one after another. No wonder he dreamt so hard of that city where violence would be washed away and men could make robust love.

And no wonder, when he thought he'd found it, he fell so hard when Jimmy turned and gave him the licking he was bound to get. Sudden as the first slap from the boy the other night. But delivered from a thousand miles away.

Jimmy would already have been in Pittsburgh. Tom would have put in his new telephone. For a day or two he must have sat at home waiting for Jimmy's call. He didn't really believe it yet, that the boy was lost to him, no matter what had happened at the station. He was still hopeful that, with an eloquent speech whose outlines he hadn't managed to pin down, he could still persuade Jimmy to join him in their new life. One way, to Paris.

The phone rings. It is van Leunen's secretary. Can he stop by later in the day? So it's here, whatever final step van Leunen has in mind. It doesn't matter: Tom has the tickets to Paris in his desk drawer. Whether he flies solo or accompanied, he is ready. He is almost relieved, looking forward to facing off with van Leunen at last. It will take his mind off Jimmy, anyway.

It is nearly summer. Tom would be wearing the white linen suit. They're in van Leunen's office, it is stifling — no, '52, van Leunen would have air conditioning already, an unheard of indulgence in a private office, but van Leunen has it. So Tom shivers involuntarily as he comes in. Van Leunen probably has planned to stay seated, in a rudimentary bit of what we were just learning, that very year, to call one-upmanship. But the gleaming presence of Tom, in an outfit as anachronistic as a suit of armor, forces him up involuntarily. Having stood, he finds himself shaking hands.

Tom says, "I see — more exactly, I feel — you have air-cooling."

"Yes indeed."

"This is the only place on campus, isn't it?"

"No, some of the labs." He gets the point. "I — this is just an experiment, we'll be putting it in lots of places soon."

"I wonder if it's altogether . . . healthy," Tom says, in a tone that suggests air conditioning is a step on the way to the fall of Rome.

"Well, I'm the guinea pig, I guess we'll find out."

They sit. How well do they know each other? It wasn't such a small place, even back then. And Tom was not much given to grown-up socializing. They would have run into each other at the occasional party or meeting, but they can't be well acquainted. Perhaps van Leunen feels a little one-down, president or not, in the presence of Tom's name and money and white linen suit. Or am I wrong to assume that Tom seemed as huge to everyone else as he did to me?

In any case, van Leunen would begin formally: "You understand why I've asked you to come up?"

"I suppose I do."

"You've caused quite a stir."

"I can imagine."

"Some of the alumni are very upset."

"The alumni are upset if you paint a wall a new color or move a shrub."

"Well, yes, they are. But this is a little more momentous, isn't it?" Tom shrugs, and van Leunen goes on. "I want you to understand that I don't care very much what your private beliefs or affiliations may have been. That isn't the point here."

"I thought that was the point."

"The point is that we just happen to be at a time in history when it's important to get things out in the open. I'm not personally very alarmed that people with . . . wide-ranging intellects might have some passing interest in new ideas or causes. That's natural. It's just important to get it all out, so everyone can be assured it wasn't anything more than that."

"More?"

"I mean anything dangerous."

"I am happy to set your mind at rest. I have never been dangerous."

"You mean that you weren't really in the Party?"

Tom smiles. "I am so awfully tired of that question. It seems to me I haven't been at a gathering in fifteen years without someone sidling up to me and asking me that tedious question. And — do you know? — I have never answered. Not even years ago, when the answer was inconsequential, not even when my interlocutor was the closest of chums. I have never answered that question."

"You think it's nobody's business."

"Precisely."

"Well, you know I could almost support that as an abstract principle. But you have to understand my problem. You may think I run things around here, but there are people even I have to answer to."

"I never thought otherwise," Tom says flatly.

"They want this all cleared up. Now, I think I've been pretty patient. Even with all the pressure on me."

"Patient? You have already deprived me of my domicile and of my daily work. By letter, without having even the courage to face me. You have left me a title and a salary, and I assume I have been granted an audience in your air-cooled aerie so that you may take those as well. You will pardon me if I fail to remark upon your patience."

"I could have done a lot worse. I'm not the one who got us in this jam. I don't like it any more than you do. But it's the times."

"To which you are rising splendidly. Truly the man of the hour, precisely what the times demand. It shouldn't surprise me if you were destined for greater things."

As these are van Leunen's exact sentiments, it is unnerving for him to hear them spoken with Tom's ponderous irony. For it is the times after all: why do I get to make Tom a victim and not van Leunen? A man of adequately liberal instincts who sees his job as getting through these times intact, so that he can do right things later on, and meanwhile causing no more harm than he absolutely has to. A deputy inquisitor who is squeamish about the fire and who feels even a little aggrieved that the heretics are so obstinate, forcing the match into his unwilling hand.

If he could only get Slater to stop focusing on his own little problem and consider van Leunen's, they could get through the times together. And van Leunen wouldn't have to . . . use the other thing. If they could just talk like grown-ups. "I'm on kind of a tightrope, you see. I can't fire you, all those magazines you write for would be on top of me in a minute. And on the other hand I can't just sit here know-ing that a lot of anonymous subversives are running around on the campus. I have to get everything out in the open. And then, you understand, once everybody's made it clear that it was just academic curiosity, what have you, and that they've thought better of it now, once we've been through all that —"

"Then you can go back to being a liberal."

This is without sting: van Leunen takes it with a con-spiratorial laugh. "That's right." Tom smiles back at him, and van Leunen believes the thing is almost done. "That's right. Nobody has to be fired or anything else."

Tom looks down, clears his throat. Van Leunen has an odd urge to reach for a pen, as if Tom were about to re-cite the names then and there. Because Tom is evidently a grown-up, if a rather spoiled one. It's the only thing he can possibly do.

Tom looks up again, and says, "I am sorry, but I cannot help you off your tightrope. You will have to dismount on your own."

If Tom smiles just a little, it is only to express a sort of sympathy, that he and van Leunen should be caught up together in the snare the times have set for them. But van Leunen would misread: he thinks it is the smile of an aes-thete, perversely relishing the situation. Here is this degen-erate in a white suit — he has almost wanted not to believe it, the story Fuzzy told with such innocent explicitness, the more elaborate story he has since extracted from Jimmy. The few times they've met, Tom has always seemed like a regular fellow, but he can see it now in Tom's twisted cosmopolitan smile. Here is this cocksucker blocking his passage to the White House and grinning at him. He very nearly lets himself get angry.

"There are a lot of people like you in jail," he says. Just like Tom's brother, the day I gave away my fortune. He doesn't specify what kind of people he means.

"I've had that researched," Tom says. "My lawyers aren't at all certain the Assembly has contempt powers."

"Congress does. I know people. I could give you an opportunity to display your loyalty to your friends on a bigger stage."

"What becomes of the liberal then?"

"Oh, he's done for. There's no question about it, you can do me enormous damage." And van Leunen would have to take whatever consolation he could from knowing Tom was in Danbury. He is already a little consoled, picturing it: Tom in a suit of gray, not white, trudging mournfully across the exercise yard. Tom in Reading Gaol.

The image of it calms him. "In any case," he says, "I'm confident that it won't have to come to that."

This is the point at which van Leunen wordlessly slides Jimmy's affidavit across his desk. Tom is puzzled, begins to read. Memoirs of a Wheaties eater. An involuntary smile, of bafflement and disbelief, creeps across his face. Van Leunen sees it, again that smile on the face of a pervert so utterly corrupted that he thinks it's all funny, the awful things he managed to lure the boy into, all like some locker-room joke.

Or worse: they are sitting there and van Leunen turns

on a tape recorder. Tom sits motionless, listening to a boyish voice he once found charming, as it spills forth a detailed and fabulous account of Tom the seducer. No, not a tape recorder, I think they were still too rare then. A wire recorder, that's what he might have had. A war-surplus wire recorder, gray metal, on van Leunen's desk.

Tom sits, watching van Leunen try to make the machine work. He almost intervenes, it's obvious you're supposed to turn that dial there. What will be on this spool of wire? Which of his comrades in the study group has broken ranks? His curiosity is academic. He cannot keep himself from smiling. It wouldn't matter if van Leunen had an entire chorus of turncoats. Tom's future is in his desk drawer.

A wire recorder. It was different from tape: you almost felt that you could see your words being graven on that silvery wire, the living moment turned to metal and shimmering like breath on a cold day. Tape is frail and disposable. Wire is so much more permanent. Delicate like all relics, but also eternal. Somewhere in the archives of the university the voices of that ugly spring are frozen, waiting to be heard in some other spring. If it had all happened somewhere else there would be nothing left. But the university never threw away anything. It kept things. Fragments of Hellenic verse, lab notes by some dead chemist, memos from the dean duly filed for doomsday. It even kept people, doddering emeriti shuffling into the library at ninety. So somewhere they must have kept the spool of wire, never played again, with that voice from forty years ago locked up on it.

Van Leunen gets the machine started. A voice booms out from it. "Is it running?" As if the machine itself were asking Tom and van Leunen.

A second voice, van Leunen's. "Yes. See?"

"Uh-huh." The sound is distorted, and half drowned out by the decadent air conditioner. Tom must lean closer to make it out.

"I think you had better start by saying your name."

"Do we really need to —" Tom cannot identify the voice. Which member of the study group is it? He just cannot place the voice squawking out of that primitive machine.

"What is your name, please."

"James Stivers."

TEN

THE BOY IS WATCHING a program on which men in blazers with network insignia show scenes from football games and then discuss them. The film clips are in slow motion, so I can at least see where the ball is, as I never could when Tom would drag me off to Memorial Field on a frigid Saturday afternoon, rationing the whiskey from his flask as if we were crossing the Sahara. I would watch two gangs of boys, in the leather helmets and light padding they used to wear — so they were shaped like humans, not mobile homes with legs — running into each other, again and again.

I'd be shivering from the cold and wanting to pee, while everyone around me would cheer or groan each time the boys collided and fell to the ground. Tom loudest of all, shouting, clapping me on the back while I tried to figure out where the ball was. I never could, and accordingly the gangs' halting progress to one end of the field or the other seemed arbitrary and foreordained. At halftime I'd insist I had to study, and I'd head straight to the library, to the men's room over by the classics stacks.

After each clip the men in blazers gravely appraise the prowess of whichever walking house trailer starred in the episode. Their critical lexicon is limited: the players are big, yet surprisingly fast on their feet, they hit hard, they throw or catch well or poorly. How do men watch this stuff, year after year, the endless repetition, the ritual monotony as punishing as Wagner? The boy is taking it in with grim attention, though he'd rather be watching cartoons. He and the men in blazers, with their forced joviality, own the world. They can do whatever they want and declare it normal by simple force of numbers, and they spend their power making one another watch this dreary ballet. With one eye on the next fellow, to make sure they're all having fun. Oh, and perhaps they are, perhaps the boy honestly likes this as much as Howard and I like old Barbara Stanwyck movies. I just don't want him to, I want him to be a boy watching cartoons, unformed. Not a finished man doing the brutal and tedious things men do.

I haven't looked at any of the new mail Howard brought. I peek into the plain brown envelope. It is a catalogue of clothing for men with perfect bodies. I don't have to take it out to know what's inside. The shirts are little strips of synthetic that the models stretch across their pectorals like bunting. In the center pages are a hundred varieties of underwear; stitched together, all one hundred could not cover my midriff. Who are the men who wear these outlandish things, and where do they hang out? It doesn't matter: wherever they are, they have taken over completely, our parodic answer to the football players. My generation all wanted to be Noël Coward; our successors dream only of being able to wear those shirts.

I seal the metal clasp on the envelope and move on to the rest of my mail. Bills, a couple of sweepstakes entries. *The New Republic*. Can it be that they have devoted another entire issue to fretting about Israeli politics? The alumni magazine. I didn't see it for years, but they tracked me down somehow, like a mother finding the child she put up for adoption.

I glance at the stuff about '47, my undergraduate class, and of course it is like a knife: so much achievement, a senator here, a great physicist there, a flock of corporation presidents. I hardly knew them. Older than I, many of them, back from the war and finishing up. Most of them talk of grandchildren now, and a scattering are already in Florida. As for what lies ahead — for them, for me — I need only look back at '37, or '27, our advance legions on the march to the grave. They stagger forward (the hip fracture is mending nicely) and do not mention the brothers who fall by the wayside. At last there is a tiny fraternity of survivors, '14 and '17, men who never spoke in school sending one another the only words left to them: I am here, I am still here. As Tom would be, if he were.

I scan '53, looking for James Stivers, a mention, any tidbit. Nothing, of course. No one you want to know about shows up in the alumni magazine. Maybe he just dropped out, as I did, after Tom was gone. Maybe he couldn't finish either.

For a little while, the fall after Tom died, I went on with the charade of working for my degree. I'd been at it five years already. With my protector gone, Tom's colleagues laid down the law: I had to take my prelims that fall and get on to my dissertation, and they couldn't continue my assistantship just now. I'd been supported enough years, and there were men with wives and kids who needed the help. Even the Slater fellowship created by Tom's will: even that they awarded to someone else.

That part didn't matter; the little settlement I got from Tom's brother would have been enough to get along on until I finished, if I had lived austerely like a proper student. Still, I could tell I wasn't expected to finish. I'd done well enough before, handing in my clever papers more or less on time, like a performing seal. But they all assumed Tom had been helping me. I was an embarrassment, Tom's catamite probably, a reminder of the explosion they were trying to get over.

Without teaching or Tom or anything to structure my days, I began of course to drink. I'd get up late, read a couple of hours — things I was supposed to have read years before and used to lie to Tom about — then go to a little Italian restaurant just off campus and have three manhattans. Pretty soon they would see me coming, and the first would be on my table before I'd even settled in my chair. I took that as a sign of respect or even affection. When I had eaten and paid up I would step out into the hectic daylight and hurry back to my rooms at Winthrop House by a side way, so I wouldn't run into anyone. After my nap, I would go to the library and try to read again. But pretty soon I'd head over to Ollie's and buy a pint of scotch. I'd drink it with tap water in my rooms, from an old coffee cup — my days were so full I never found the time to buy a proper glass.

I'd have the radio playing, and I would thumb through old bound volumes of *The New Yorker* that I'd borrowed from the library. The very issues I used to read in Winslow when I was dreaming of escape. Once in a while a student would knock on my door, seeking the resident advice that was still the price of my rooms. I would pretend not to be there, as if I'd gone out and just happened to have left the radio on. At ten or so I would venture out for a burger and then, still thirsty, I would wander down to the Garland. Or sometimes to the bar at East Station, which was only somewhat gay and where a pickup was that much more gratifying, because of the extra layer or two of ambiguity you had to work through. Strangers drank with me on Tom's money, and once in a while I would sneak one back to my suite. But, with a pint or more of whiskey coursing through me, I was seldom able to bring things to a satisfactory conclusion. No one ever visited a second time that fall.

In December another graduate student and I sat in an overheated room and contemplated the written part of our prelims. We can't have had the same exam. Mine was too plainly aimed at me, tauntingly demanding the very things I knew least about and concluding with a question — the committee must have laughed as they made it up — about George Herbert. My colleague was busy scratching away, nonstop, as though he were just taking dictation from the muse of examinations. I couldn't hear her. By Christmas I was gone, having drunk up half my little residue of Tom's fortune.

A few times that fall I would run into Jimmy, in the library or on the quad. We didn't usually speak; we had never been friends. I would just look at him, Tom's widower. He looked splendid — if anything, healthier and more alive now that he was out of the shadow of Tom. Graver, too, perhaps, but not grieving. As if Tom had given him, in place of the bequest I had already cravenly surrendered, his own high seriousness.

Once we did talk, just for a minute, over near the hilarious monument to the college's Civil War dead. He asked me how I was doing, and I said not well, I was probably on my way out.

He looked up at the statue, the emancipated slave kneeling gratefully before the dead collegian, who was held upright, and half obscured, by an angel with an upraised sword. He said, "It sure isn't the same here without Mr. Slater."

I waited for something more, but that banality was apparently going to be it. "No," I said. We just stood there for a minute. I asked him if he wanted to go get a beer. I suppose I wanted to pump him; even then I suspected he knew more than anyone about what had happened to Tom.

He said, in a voice meant to be gentle, "I'm not really interested." The way straight men say it when they want to be tolerant about it but wish to leave you with no misunderstanding.

"I wasn't thinking about that," I said. If I hadn't been, his preemptive rejection made me think about it. Only for an instant: the picture of my hands wandering where Tom's had once sojourned seemed to crash against some taboo I hadn't known about.

"It's okay, I could understand your thinking . . . but I'm not sure I even am. I don't think I am." The unmating call of the Wheaties eater.

"I wasn't asking."

"I — most people wouldn't understand this, but maybe I can say it to you — I kind of loved Tom." I thought what a shame it was we'd already put Tom's marker up. It could have read, *He was kind of loved.* "But I need to cut it out. I mean I'm going to, I met a girl this summer and . . . I'm pretty sure I'm going to."

"That's good," I said. I had, by then, given up thinking I would ever cut it out. But I still thought it was good, enviable. Meeting a girl and cutting it out made him a pledge of the grand fraternity that I was never asked to join and that runs the world.

"Tom would want me to, don't you think?" he said. Solemnly, needing my agreement. "That was the point."

"The point of what?"

"I mean, he knew I wanted to help him. He would have wanted me to go on and live a . . . you know, a normal life."

"I'm sure he would have," I said. What were we talking about? I felt the way I used to in Tom's seminar, when I was the only one who hadn't done the reading. But I also felt, just looking at him, that whatever sort of life he led would define the normal.

I must have shown my confusion. "Or maybe you'd understand this less than anybody," he said.

I have tried, once or twice, to look deep inside myself and identify whatever hole it was he thought he'd seen in me. I can't. I have any number of flaws, God knows; I just can't find that one. Maybe he meant that a run-of-the-mill fairy couldn't comprehend the chaste and manly passion he and Tom had shared, the one that was kind of like love. Or maybe he was just straining to be dramatic, in a flippant and collegiate way. Still, he has left me for a lifetime with this hole I cannot find and cannot fill in. Like the blemish in Tom's photograph, the one I cannot remember but that must have been there, under the spot they retouched.

"I don't think I want to have a beer," he said. "I'll see you around."

For all I know he's dead. Korea, maybe he went to Korea. Died young, like the other Wheaties eaters. No, there wouldn't have been time; it was over by the next spring. Anyway, killing him off is too easy: can't imagine a life for him, do him in after the first act. But if he had lived any second act, I should have heard of him. Anyone who began his career by throwing Tom to the lions ought to have reached the pinnacles of our society by now.

That is also too simple. Thinking that, if he toppled a giant, he should be a giant in turn. More likely he is just a gray old man like me. Gray and plump, sitting in his suburban family room and reading history, just a few pages of his Michener book before the after-dinner bourbon kicks in and he toddles off to bed. His wife, blue-haired and outwardly complacent, sits across from him, reading Barbara Pym. The children are all gone, grown and fled from Pittsburgh. Nights like this they sit and read, she looks up from time to time at his face.

Everything that could have gone wrong with his face has gone wrong. I can picture it, almost see what has to have happened to that face from forty years ago. The most minute miscalculations by the hand of time — a gob too much flesh here, the tiniest slackening of a muscle there — would have spoiled the balance utterly. With what delight the years must have taken that ephemeral beauty and turned him into the smug burgher of today, living his normal life in the family room. The lights have gone out. All that is left is the awful gravity he inherited from Tom. His wife dwells in his grayness and, only some nights, wonders idly about the secrets she knows he has, the small withholdings, the almost imperceptible drift of attention even on their wedding night.

Of course I want him to be gay. I want him — having done what he did to clear a place for himself, to build the normal life he thought Tom had bequeathed him — I want him, after some years of evasion, trying to cut it out, to have found his real place outside with Tom and me. But I want him still married, skulking in men's rooms and movie theaters, always afraid of discovery. Forty years worrying that someone would tell on him as he did on Tom. And his wife sitting across from him, feeling his secret and counting the years until it won't matter any more, not long from now. They'll move off to Florida with the rest of the class of '53, and it won't matter any more what kind of —— sexual he ever was.

No I don't, I don't want that. I want him, in that eternally credulous part of me where Santa Claus and even Jesus still hold some claim to my faith, in that part of me I want him to be happy because beauty was meant to be happy. I shall never outgrow this. Underneath the part that wants beauty to suffer because I am not beautiful is the part that wants all happiness to flow to him. Because, if I had been beautiful, all happiness would have flowed to me. I want him to have been that perfect me.

Perfect in his selfishness and calculation? Yes: the unimpaired I, moving from second to second with confident alertness, without malice or misgiving rising to the demands each moment put before him. Pure and amoral. Reaching out to Tom, when that moment came at the lodge, because it wasn't wrong. Then, just as naturally, cutting Tom loose, getting on the train to Pittsburgh and leaving the wire behind as he would leave the scene of an accident.

Like some animal, sleek and blamelessly violent. What a life I could have had, if I could have been that creature. The other night I might have raised a paw and, with one casual swipe, scarred my assailant for life, as he has done to me. Then strode away in all my muscular grace. But no, I had to be a platypus, an afterthought of nature, stumbling on afterthoughts as I waddle along with my webbed feet. One enormous compunction.

The boy makes a tour of the channels, a cop show, a situation comedy, a William Holden movie. He pauses. What is this movie? *Sabrina*, I think. Yes, there's Audrey Hepburn, it's *Sabrina*, I haven't seen this in ages. If I concentrate hard enough, maybe I can send a thought to lodge in the boy's otherwise untenanted skull: don't change the channel, don't change the channel.

My powers are insufficient. He returns to the men in blazers and their dreary film clips. An improbably large man, but fast on his feet, makes a touchdown. In the end zone he does an elaborate dance, wiggling his butt like one of the go-go boys at the old Mardi Gras, before it burned down.

Where is the line, I wonder? How outsized and brutal do you have to be before you can wiggle your fanny with impunity? Maybe just big enough that no one will wish to discuss it with you. But I am sure I never saw such a thing at the games Tom dragged me off to. What has changed? Did they all want to wiggle their fannies, Tom's Wheaties eaters, but simply didn't dare? No, I think they didn't have fannies, merely a sort of vagueness at the fundament of their bodies, unacknowledged or actively denied.

Their unseen butts, the wretched stepsisters of their bodies, sat upon, spoken of disdainfully, knowingly exhibited only as a gesture of contempt: here is the greatest insult I can give you, to show you my ass. The very seat of shame, never a Prince Charming to tell it that it's beautiful, it languishes unobserved until its very existence becomes tenuous and contingent.

I want so much for them to have no shame anywhere, my saints. I have gone through life with an inside that most of humanity despises and an outside that fools no one, a pathetic facsimile of Tom's manly armor. That the boy the other night punched right through and that I may never put back together again, despite the body's gift for improvisation. I want my saints to be of one substance, all the way to their hearts, like blocks of marble: all the same, no matter how far you cut into them. But inside them is shame and terror and doubt, that makes them want to *cut it out*, makes them sing on the wire makes them — as they kneel over me — raise their fists and strike.

The men in blazers have given way at last to the actual game of which they were the harbingers. The boy watches with perfect satisfaction. He is as if transported, doing here exactly what he would be doing at home. Unhappy only that none of his buddies is with him, slugging down a few beers and watching this incomprehensible spectacle. He is lonesome, my saint, caged here with a fairy who has no comfort to offer him.

We are on two desert islands, marooned together but separately on our parallel, proximate beds. I go back to the alumni magazine. Someone has just given the money for a new gymnasium the size of Cleveland. It will have multiple Nautilus stations. Here it is again, bodies, bodies. Everything else kids have to worry about, growing up, and now they must do this, an entire generation obliged to sculpt itself to look like the creatures in the soft-porn clothing catalogue. I see obvious bookworms, latter day versions of me, walking around with muscles of the kind that used to earn one the nickname Moose. The honest, sunken-chested fairy, with his turtleneck sweater and his volume of Firbank, is as extinct as the passenger pigeon. To whom, then, shall I give my resident advice in the giant Y to which Howard has consigned me? What would we talk about, their deltoids?

Michael the night nurse comes in. "You boys want anything?" he says. "Some juice or anything?" We boys shake our heads.

He comes to me with a fresh tube of ointment. "Got to keep you from drying out."

"Too late."

He smiles, but as he begins rubbing the ointment into my wounds he is merely businesslike. Almost cursory, not like last night.

"How did this happen, anyway?" he says. So it's not in the chart. Of course it wouldn't be: my wounds are just present facts, a run-of-the-mill 801. They might have appeared as spontaneously as stigmata for all the hospital cares.

The boy appears to be fully absorbed in his game. I lower my voice. "It was a trick."

"Oh, oh, that almost happened to me once." He pulls back involuntarily, as if being beaten up were contagious. "That's awful. I hope you're going to be more careful."

"To the point of atrophy."

"Not judging from last night." He waves the tube of ointment. "Got to keep better track of this tonight," he says.

"I'll be good."

"Oh, don't. You're an example to us all. Just do be more careful." He caps the tube, puts it in his pocket, and goes out.

In the lobby, I sat behind the counter with the receptionist while we waited for the ambulance. Stephen, the nice boy on the seventh floor, came in the front door alone — having, I assume, struck out at whatever nice boys' club he goes to. So it was only closing time. My nemesis and I had acted out our whole drama while everyone else was still circling in the bars.

Stephen saw me and said, "Oh. Oh, God." He stayed on the other side of the counter, as if he felt, like Michael, that it was catching somehow.

The receptionist said, "He walked right by me. He came out of that elevator not ten minutes ago. He was smiling. He waved at me and he smiled." (That means, come to think of it, that he didn't take with him anything he couldn't stuff in his pockets. As I don't have any diamond bracelets, too garish, he didn't get much.) He was smiling: it was nothing to him.

He knelt above me. He looked down at me, not smiling just then, frowning and thoughtful. He still had his dungarees on, so I couldn't be certain, but I was pretty sure he wasn't hard. That should have alarmed me, I guess, but I wasn't so awfully astonished that someone could look down at me and fail to be aroused.

It was nothing to him. I wonder if he had ever done it before. He might have: for all I know he was the one who tied up poor Walter last year and — but I don't think so. I think he was making up his mind even as he knelt above me. I was pinned under him as I used to be by one or another of the bullies in the schoolyard, the ones who wouldn't let you up until you gave them what they wanted. Sometimes just the standard code of submission, *Uncle*, which meant the same thing my late schnauzer used to mean when he'd sit looking up at me and raise one forepaw: yes, you're top dog. Sometimes I had to utter a more specific formula that had reference to my sexual preferences or my mother's prostitution, an especially laughable concept. It didn't matter; it was always Uncle.

Anyway, there he was above me, not hard but thinking hard. Before we got on the bed, before he got me into or I just assumed that classic posture of submission, he had said, "We can't . . . you know, the way things are, there's things I don't do." And again, "I mean, I only do safe stuff." Of course these remarks might have been mere stratagems, to lull me a little longer into thinking we were just going to carry out our contract. Still, they seem gratuitous: if all he had in mind was to wait until he had me at the best angle for the first strike, why was he declaring these limits we would never even approach? He must originally have thought we were going to do something. Something first, to get his rocks off, then down to business? Or was the business itself an afterthought, a sudden inspiration?

Perhaps, as he looked down, he was making himself despise me. That can't have been hard: an old man with too much money who thought I could buy him. Or maybe it wasn't that way at all, not that he had to make himself feel something, but make himself not feel — look straight past me at the object, at whatever he thought he was going to get. That must have been a feat, to make the dumpy mass of me simply disappear. So that hitting me was just like pushing at a door or passing through a turnstile to whatever treasure he thought lay beyond it.

That is how it's done, that is how Jimmy must have done it, just pushed his way through. Here he had taken an innocent detour on the way to whatever life he had planned — if he even had plans, if he didn't just figure everything would fall into place sooner or later. Just a detour, a few months exploring an out-of-the-way world he was always bound to return from.

Now summer was coming on, he was ready to go home to Pittsburgh, to a summer job in his father's factory or store, to parties with the friends he'd grown up with, ready to find a girl and let her lead him into the normal life. Blocking his way was Tom, looming before him, threatening to spirit him off to Paris and exile. Jimmy simply had to push by him, put him out of mind, or he would be trapped forever, never able to get back to the main road, the common world.

He finds his exit through the doorway labeled MARTIN VAN LEUNEN. Van Leunen's office has the sleek grandeur of a corporate executive suite, forcibly thrust into an ivied corner of quaint old College Hall. Paneled in blond wood, the color of Tom's last chairs, but with matched grains. The desk about the size of Jimmy's dorm room; on it, three telephones and a gray metal box Jimmy takes to be a Dictaphone. In a corner, an enormous globe, as if van Leunen ruled vaster domains than one somnolent campus. On the wall over the moderne, mantel-less fireplace, a portrait of van Leunen himself; the man spends his days looking at himself.

Just as I once stepped into Tom's suite at Winthrop

House and saw my future, so Jimmy looks around at the sterile lavishness of van Leunen's office and knows that this is what he is meant for. Not a college presidency, of course, but an office on the fortieth floor of some commercial ziggurat in Pittsburgh. This is the course he has set himself, from fresh-faced collegian to gray-flanneled junior executive and on up, floor by floor. The self-service elevator of his life was headed straight for this, until it veered so perversely off course.

Van Leunen is awesome enough, throned in a leather chair of almost parodic grandeur; he does not rise when Jimmy comes in. Yet whatever trepidation Jimmy feels in the face of this near-mythological figure is tempered by the sense that they are of the same species, he and van Leunen. He looks at van Leunen as a boy might watch his father shaving.

Van Leunen gestures to the chair across the desk from him, and Jimmy starts to sit. "No, wait," van Leunen says. "Why don't we sit over here." He leads Jimmy to the pair of club chairs by the fireplace. They sit facing one another, and for a minute van Leunen looks Jimmy over as if scanning a memorandum.

It is the end of May, examination period. Jimmy is an apparition in a summer suit, crisp blue cord, and he has already taken on a little summer color. He looks like a recruiting poster for the Ivy League, just the type whose picture van Leunen might have put in the catalogue. Not what van Leunen would have expected from Fuzzy's narrative: not like one of us.

Van Leunen says, "I'm awfully sorry to have to take your time, Mr. Stivers. I know you must be very busy studying."

"No big deal," Jimmy says, flattered that the great man should worry about wasting *his* time. "I've only got one more exam, and that's a breeze."

"That's great. You must be looking forward to the summer."

"Kind of. I've got to work, till August anyway."

"Well, at least you'll get a little time away. That can be important, you know, just to get away. Problems that seem like the end of the world here turn out to be very small if you just get away for a little while."

Perhaps he hopes this insipid homily will prompt Jimmy to spit out any small problems he may be having. But Jimmy just stares at him. Van Leunen says abruptly, "I thought that we had better talk about you and Mr. Slater."

"Sir?"

Jimmy affects a look of honest perplexity, the very expression my roommate wears half his waking hours. Perhaps he is convincing enough that van Leunen hesitates: what if Walgreen was deluded, or just nearsighted? To keep things rolling while he ponders this, van Leunen recites a line he had prepared before the boy came in. "My greatest concern is that an impressionable student not be injured at the very start of his career by an innocent mistake into which he might have been led."

"Are you talking about me, sir? I don't know about any big mistakes I'm supposed to have made."

Van Leunen looks up at his own portrait. "I think your mistake," he says carefully, "would be to persist in protecting Mr. Slater to the point at which people would have to conclude that you were . . . not an unwilling participant."

"I don't follow you, sir. About participating. We never spoke much about politics, Mr. Slater and me."

"You know I didn't ask you up here to talk about politics."

Jimmy gets up and just wanders for a minute, arriving finally at the desk, where he scrutinizes the object he has taken for a Dictaphone. It is some sort of recording device, anyway. He isn't sure at first how to tell when the thing is running, but satisfies himself that it is not.

He turns toward van Leunen and says, almost inaudibly, "Then what are we talking about? That Tom and I might have fooled around?"

Van Leunen stares at Jimmy's calm face and broad shoulders, the picture of American youth and virility. This isn't what we look like. And the phrase, "fooled around," said so lightly. He feels, not revulsion, but a moment's perplexity. As if he has stumbled on an accidental glimpse of Tom's city, or at least its suburbs. He cannot make it out, whatever he sees. He shakes the vision off.

As for Jimmy: Jimmy is remembering every indiscretion, every time Tom stood too close, every time he rounded a corner and happened on some friends, smirking at a joke he hadn't heard and refusing to repeat it. Fuzzy's statement is almost superfluous. Still, van Leunen goes to his desk drawer and pulls out the sheets covered with Fuzzy's monastic penmanship.

"What is this?" Jimmy says.

"Some observations by a Mr. Walgreen."

Jimmy reads. He registers at once the key point, that he is in unimaginable trouble. But he cannot focus on that: the words themselves are mesmerizing, the entomological account of his nights with Tom. Did they do those things? Well, he knows they did. But they seem so alien, laid out on that paper with all the feeling drained from them. He stares at the words, disoriented; he hardly even remembers that van Leunen's there.

Van Leunen doesn't notice his confusion; he wants to hurry on now. "You understand, I don't care what you did. But it's out now, people know. So I'm going to have to do something about it."

The boy is scarcely listening. Van Leunen says, "I need a statement."

Jimmy shakes his head violently, as if waking himself up. "You've got the whole story, what do you need me for?"

"It isn't enough. Uncorroborated, it isn't enough."

Jimmy takes a minute to grasp this: not enough. Perhaps he even imagines for a second that he isn't really in peril. "Well, then it isn't. I mean, if I don't say anything, then —"

"Oh, it's enough to ruin your life," van Leunen says, as casually as if he ruined lives every day. "It just isn't enough for me to act on. So I need your statement too."

Perhaps Jimmy feels, as I did the other night while staring up at the knife, an eerie calm. He says, reasonably: "You've got me anyway, why would I give you anything more?"

"You? I'm not after you." Van Leunen has moved too quickly, overestimated the boy. "You're the innocent one, you were just . . . misled, that's all, and you feel bad about it. So you had to come forward. You're a smart kid, you can see that. You're the innocent one, that's the way it's got to be. And besides, it's true, isn't it?"

Van Leunen still wants to believe it, just because Jimmy looks the way he does — that it was all a one-sided thing, as if Tom were a blot that had somehow spread itself over Jimmy's crisp blue trousers and that Jimmy should happily join in eradicating.

What do I want from Jimmy? To storm out, to raise the banner of resistance there in van Leunen's office, so many years ago? No, the most he can muster is a faint protest. "I like Mr. Slater," Jimmy says, simply and forlornly as a child. "He never did anything wrong to me."

"And I don't want to do anything to Mr. Slater. If I can just get him to cooperate this whole thing will be over."

"What?"

"He renounces his errors, and names the names and whatever the hell else they want and it's over. We forget the whole thing. Or you can make me go ahead with this and take him down with you."

Jimmy looks over at van Leunen, trying hard to show nothing. He is in such danger, even Tom would understand, wouldn't expect him to throw away his whole life when that wouldn't do any good. If he could save Tom by telling, well, that would be fine. But even if he couldn't, could only cover himself: why should both of them go to hell?

Van Leunen risks a paternal smile. "You'd almost be helping him, can you understand? You would be. If I can just get him to go along, this whole affair will be over, just forgotten, in no time."

"I've told him that," Jimmy murmurs. "I've told him that a million times."

Jimmy looks around at the office, his future. Does he even half believe it, that he is saving Tom from Tom? Do I want him to be a fool or a monster? Which is the perfect me: innocent Jimmy signing on to the plan, or knowing Jimmy cutting Tom loose to save himself? Or, most like the imperfect me: Jimmy making himself believe that he is do- ing the best thing, talking himself into it, closeting away the little kernel of self-knowledge that forces itself into the light only when Tom is gone or maybe never, not to this day.

Jimmy says, "I was going to cut it out, anyway. I mean I'm going home this summer and . . . I'm pretty sure I'm going to cut it out."

"Of course you are," van Leunen says. "Listen, I know a lot of boys here must go through this phase. These things happen; it's hardly even a question of right or wrong."

What does he mean, what do they ever mean, the people who say such easy things? Does he believe that he himself, given the right man on the right evening, might have done the same thing at Jimmy's age? Well, of course not: van Leunen cannot really think, looking over at Jimmy, that this is just a minor error, an everyday collegiate infraction, in a league with throwing up on the quad or high-spirited vandalism. No, this clean, startled, sparkling boy has eaten shit, under whatever compulsion or persuasion. Like a woman who has been raped, Jimmy may be a victim but he is not a virgin. Now van Leunen does feel, perhaps, a little revulsion.

But he makes himself say: "This is just something that happened. It doesn't have to screw up your life. I'm sure even Mr. Slater doesn't want you to give up your life."

"No."

Van Leunen turns on the machine. "Is it running?" Jimmy says.

"Yes. See?"

"Uh-huh."

"I think you had better start by saying your name."

*E*LEVEN

TOM SITS IN van Leunen's office, watching the reel spin. He is expressionless, his face the stern mask of his dust jacket photo.

Jimmy's voice is in midsentence. ". . . and then around the end of October he invited me to go on a fishing trip. He has this lodge he owns with some other people, it's kind of a club. Up at Hamilton Lake. So we went up there on a Saturday and, you know, fished all day."

"Were there other persons present at this lodge?"

"No. I mean, it sleeps a lot of people, but that time of year, I guess the fishing really isn't too good."

"So you were alone at this lodge."

"We were by ourselves, yeah. And that night, we had dinner and all. We had to go out and buy stuff, because we hadn't caught a damned thing. And then we were sitting around drinking whiskey."

"He gave you whiskey?"

"I think it was my whiskey. And, I don't know, we got drunk, or at least I got drunk and we . . . went to bed."

"Together."

"That's right."

"And what did Mr. Slater do then?"

"What did he do?"

"You were in bed together. You were drunk and Mr. Slater got into bed with you."

"Right, we — I mean, do you have to hear every last thing we did? I don't even remember. We had sex."

Tom shows nothing. I can picture alternatives, Tom crumpling in pain or gaping in astonishment or, even, smiling a little — smiling ironically at his own recklessness. Truly did make a fool of himself this time. But I want to believe that Tom sat there in his white suit and gave up nothing.

And of course van Leunen expects to see nothing. As it is inconceivable that anything he would call love has played a part in the situation, why should he be surprised that Tom sits there apparently unmoved? Tom might be any ordinary criminal, a bank robber, say, trapped by his accomplice's confession. Would a bank robber cry, or cry out?

Van Leunen turns off the machine. "There is a little more. But I should think you have the substance of it."

"I suppose I do. Some boy or other telling tales."

"Some boy or other? Are there a lot of boys around who could have told this story?"

"Any number could invent it." Tom stands and walks over to van Leunen's window, hands in his coat pockets, just as he would get up in the middle of his seminar when he had dropped a provocative remark and was waiting for one of us to manage an answer. The window is closed, because of the air conditioning. It is strange to Tom, to look out through a closed window at a summer's day. He feels as though he's at St. Martin's again, trapped in geometry class on a May morning.

"There is some corroboration. Mr. Walgreen —"

"Fuzzy? Fuzzy came to you?" Perhaps this hurts nearly

as much as hearing Jimmy's voice. Maybe more: it is as if his leather club chair or one of the portraits of dead deans had turned on him.

"Fuzzy, is that what they call him? You've been astonishingly indiscreet: I could have gone ahead just on what Walgreen could see from his window. But now that I have the recording . . . well, I think your options have narrowed some."

"Actually, I had settled on an option," Tom says. "I'm going away next month."

"Going away? Where?"

"Paris. For a while, at any rate. I'm not sure I want to die in Paris."

"I can't just let you go to Paris."

"How do you propose to stop me?"

"I've got contacts. I could get your passport pulled. Security risk. Too dangerous to travel." This is not a threat; he is merely improvising.

"I suppose you could. But that won't get you what you want."

"No, of course not. But I've got the recording. So the situation's pretty elementary. If you don't do what I want I'll play it. If you go along I won't. I hate to be as bald as that, but here we are. You just cooperate with the committee — it doesn't even have to be a public hearing, we can work something out, just an affidavit or something. Then we get rid of this damn thing and off you go to Paris." Other, less temperate destinations for Tom may occur to him.

Tom is still at the window, as if it were his own office. Through it he looks out at the deserted quad, van Leunen's little fiefdom. "I am afraid, you know, that you put rather too much stock in your ugly recording. Do you think there's anything on it that people haven't guessed? It would be, at the moment of its release, as tired as last year's song."

"I'm not sure everyone would find it quite so worn out."

"It is, though. It may have some residual value as entertainment, but as a weapon . . ." He takes out the platinum case. "Would you care for a cigarette?"

"No, I'm trying to stop. It looks bad. You go ahead."

"You mean in photographs, at your public appearances?" Tom sits across from van Leunen and lights his cigarette from a table lighter in the shape of the university mascot. What were we, anyway? Lions? Goats? "Yes, I can see that," Tom says. "That a cigarette might be a touch too epicene."

"You were saying, about the recording."

"Yes. I am leaving. You may, I suppose, prevent me from going abroad. I believe our republic has come to that. But I can go very far away. And leave you here with your precious spool of wire."

"Which I will play."

"Which you will play. Some tedious fabrications about a retired professor no one has ever heard of. Then you will simply have precipitated an additional scandal, and not a name to show for it. I can almost envision the headlines in the popular press."

Van Leunen can too, the tabloids: HOMO LOVE NEST IN THE IVORY TOWER. Tom continues. "I shall be reviled in absentia and you will be a former college president. No, it is quite useless to you." Now would be the time for Tom to sit back and fold his arms in triumph. But instead he cannot resist asking: "How did you persuade the boy to talk?"

"It wasn't hard. All I had to do was show him Walgreen's notes, and —"

"The notes, ah. Did Fuzzy come to you or did you —"

"I found him."

"Poor Fuzzy, to have been found by you. Why in the world do you suppose he agreed to help you?"

"How should I know? He did get your apartment . . ."

"Old unworldly Fuzzy. Do you think he'd turn on his oldest colleague for that, for a nicer suite of rooms? After a quarter of a century of breakfasting together at the Faculty Club?"

"Maybe he was doing me a favor," van Leunen says. He has the notes and the wire, it wouldn't matter if a pigeon had brought them. He is trying to think of what there is left to do with them.

"I can assure you that no one on this campus is much disposed to do you favors. I suppose he must think I'm rather wicked."

"Weak, I think he said."

Tom flushes at this. "I assume you agree."

"I'm not much given to judging people."

"Oh, come. I am sure you judge their utility." He stubs out his cigarette. "And, as I am no further use to you, I have won, I think. So you might, just as a matter of sportsmanship, let me go."

By now van Leunen has taken up the post at the window that Tom abandoned. He looks out over the quad with an air not proprietary but imprisoned. He may own what he sees before him, but it will never be the White House lawn. He hazards: "There's the boy."

"What?"

It isn't a new line of attack so much as a reconnaissance mission. "The boy. If I have to release the recording, people are going to know about him too. And he can't just fly off to Paris."

"Why should I care about him?" Tom says.

A splendid question. "I don't know."

"He made the wire. Let him be strung on it, if you like."

"Well, you're right. You don't owe him anything." Does he feel the least bit sullied, van Leunen, to be reduced to this gambit, to exploit in private the very tendencies he would denounce in public? Probably not: probably he is pleased with himself for having hit on it. "It just seems like a shame. He's a kid, confused, didn't know what he was getting into. And I pushed him. I mean I had to."

"Had to."

"Thanks to you. I had to, and he had to. I didn't leave him any choice. You can think what you want to about me. But he's just starting out. This could wreck his whole life."

He stops there and glances at Tom to see if he has made any headway. He can't tell, Tom just looks thoughtful. So he is at least thinking about it. Maybe softening a little. Van Leunen still doesn't imagine that the chord he is playing on has anything to do with love. But they do seem to stick together, these homos, in between turning on one another. Just like women.

"I think . . ." Tom says. "I think I should like to hear the rest of the recording."

Is that a good idea? Van Leunen can't remember what else might be on the wire. Something unforgivable, something that might make Slater decide to just let the boy hang? "I'm not sure there's much point in that."

"I should like to."

Van Leunen, uncertain but reluctant to make an issue of it, rewinds the wire an inch or two and starts the recorder.

"I mean, do you have to hear every last thing we did?" Jimmy says. "I don't even remember. We had sex."

Now van Leunen's voice: "I am trying to establish how Mr. Slater initiated this."

"I don't know who initiated what. I was drunk."

"Okay. Was there ever any recurrence of this episode?"

"What?"

"Was there any other occasion on which you and Mr. Slater . . . had intimate contact?"

"Huh." Jimmy snorts at the expression. "Well, sure. I mean, the very next morning we —"

"How did that occur?"

"I don't remember."

"Did Mr. Slater suggest that you . . . repeat your activities?"

There is a silence. The reel spins forth a foot or more of silver wire before Jimmy speaks again. "Yes. Yes, he did."

Tom's face shows something at last, a flicker that van Leunen notices but cannot interpret.

"And you agreed."

"I didn't know what to do. I was confused about it. I mean, I didn't think it was right, but I liked Mr. Slater. And so we — he wanted to keep on doing it and I . . . I let him."

It is halftime. The boy turns the channel, then looks over at me inquiringly, as if for the first time it has occurred to him that I might care about what we watch. I shrug: I can't force *Sabrina* on him, so I don't much care. But I am startled and touched, all out of proportion, by this gesture. As if we were some sort of friends. No, nothing so strong. All over this hospital roommates must be consulting over the channel, as a matter of simple courtesy. That is all: he has concluded that he owes even a fairy, however alien, this favor.

The boy can't find anything else on. He returns to the men in blazers, but after a minute they give way to some dreary halftime festivities. A band playing a dreadful thudding version of some popular song while goose-stepping. The boy gets up, goes into the bathroom. I hear the faucet running. Is he being discreet in the manner of Tom, relieving himself hygienically? But he is out in a minute. On the way back to bed he looks down for a moment at his cock, which is pushing visibly against the front of his gown, then up at me. Back in bed he lies as he did last night, exposed and ambiguously seductive. He is pretending to watch the band, which is now performing some intricate dance steps while playing Burt Bacharach. But he is keeping me in his peripheral vision.

He has washed himself, that must be it. He must think a cocksucker sucks cock the way a woodchuck would chuck wood, that it is automatic, nearly redundant. Of course all straight men think that. The homeliest of them imagines that he is in perpetual danger of unwelcome advances. Sturdier lads are less alarmed but no less persuaded that we are after all men at all times. No matter that I am bruised and scarred and still hooked up to an IV. If I were laid out in a funeral home and the boy were passing my open coffin, he would probably suppose that — if he whipped it out — my mouth would pop open. And why not? Why do I get to assume that he is all of a piece, his inside and his outside all one, and he not think the same of me?

What if he's gay? Or at least — what is the word old reptilian Cochran uses? — *educable*. Everyone always says that we can spot one another. Howard is constantly insisting that he knows, that he can tell in an instant, from the way someone walks or dresses or laughs. I have never had this gift. Everything about the boy says no: his evident interest in anything with skirts, even including Sharon the nurse. His corollary interest in the football game that has now resumed. The way he has balled up his bathrobe and thrown it into the visitor's chair. The way he is scratching himself, right now, under the gown. Howard would find some contrary sign: yes, but look how neat his nails are. Or, there's just something about his mouth. Through which he is now breathing.

He leans forward. Something momentous is apparently happening in the game; perhaps I will understand it when they show it again, in slow motion. He looks over at me, excited. If I were a buddy he would say, Hey, did you see that? I try to look excited, too, but he isn't fooled. He closes his mouth and turns back to the screen. There, they are showing it again, whatever happened, and now again from a different angle. I can't help it, it just looks like chaos to me, a bunch of house trailers in a terrible collision.

No, he is thunderingly straight. If he is really signaling what he seems to be — he is still posing, though the game has recaptured his attention — he is only hoping for a little relief. He would lie there motionless, with his eyes closed, like a hustler. He would let me do what I wanted, nothing more.

I let him do what he wanted, the wire said. *He wanted to keep on doing it and I let him.* Whack. I let him into the apartment and let him do what he wanted, thereby creating a disturbance. . . . They aren't exactly the same kind of untruth, the syntax is really not at all parallel. In the one case, the actor, Jimmy, claims to be the acted upon; in the second, I, the acted upon, become the instigator. But they are the same in effect: they turn a whole part of your life inside out. Now in memory I will never be the innocent victim of a calamity, but always the doting and contemptible old man who brought it on himself and then had the bad manners to make noise while it was happening. So for Tom those words — *I let him do what he wanted* — must have remade everything.

He steps out into the hall, from van Leunen's air-cooled domain into the heat, and he just stands for a minute, taking in the hot, natural air. Then he moves briskly, as he made himself do on the hottest days, toward the stairs.

Once he is outside, though, his bravado deserts him. On the portico of College Hall he rests against one of the white pillars and feels himself fading into it, an old man in white linen, an untenanted suit of armor. He breathes deeply and staggers on home. In his stifling living room, he sits and plays Jimmy's story over and over, as if he had the recording inside.

He tries to think of reasons. Some inconceivable force they exerted on Jimmy, until the tale just flew out of him like an exorcised devil. Or pushed its way out on its own: the little uneasiness and small refusals Tom has sometimes detected in bed — and felt on his own side — growing in Jimmy to outright rejection and denial. Or no feeling at all, no compulsion, just a cold-blooded calculation that turning on Tom was the practical thing to do. He weighs each theory in turn and discards them all, because they all make the boy seem foolish or cowardly or inadequate, an insufficient vessel for Tom to have poured his soul into.

If he cannot understand the Jimmy who could make the wire, then what does he understand? Jimmy is a stranger, and everything that ever happened between them is uncertain and obscure. So why couldn't it be true, what Jimmy says, all of it? He is that predatory Mr. Slater who made it all happen, what passed between them was never love. Jimmy just let him, for his whiskey and his conversation and his attentive ear.

All he has to go on is the memory of Jimmy's touch, and what does that prove? I have known hustlers who opened up to me like brides, and I have had lovers — or at least candidates on two-week free trial — who made me feel as though the money were on the dresser. Even I couldn't tell, just by touch, couldn't always tell for sure who was driving things, or what was behind the face pressed close to mine in the dark. Or the boy's face hovering above mine, three nights ago, with its thoughtful frown. How could Tom know, first time out?

* * *

How should I have known how to read that face? He did kiss me, the boy the other night did kiss me. Well, kisses are cheap. Still, it was an honest kiss, a kiss returned and not just suffered. He didn't just let me. Am I a child to suppose that a kiss was somehow inconsistent with what came afterward? Perhaps so. The kiss didn't come from inside him and it didn't reach inside, no farther than his nerve endings. He wasn't making any promises.

There was no inconsistency, he could kiss me and then rear back and strike me, seconds later. If instead, while kneeling over me, he had decided to go ahead and get his rocks off before proceeding with his business transaction: even that would have meant only a brief postponement. I can almost picture it. The boy having a companionable cigarette after the act, drowsing for a few minutes, then shaking himself awake, sitting up and — whack.

Once I would have found that intolerable. As if sex were no more than a cease-fire — like that awful story of the British and German troops drinking and singing together in No Man's Land on Christmas night, then returning to their trenches and their guns. I wouldn't have believed it, even a week ago I didn't live in a world where a kiss is the prelude to a skull fracture. But I have been in that world all along. Tom must have seen it, too: the revolution isn't ever coming, the city of friends is beyond the margins of the map. All you can do is wait for the intervals when the guns are silent and grab whatever you can.

I have been like the boy in the fairy tale who snatches the treasure from under the very nose of the sleeping giant. Every snippet in my erotic Rolodex was purloined, captured in an instant when the beast was drowsy or tipsy or just too lazy to raise its paw and strike. It was always bound to happen, one of them was bound to wake up. But what a lucky man I have been till now, lucky and clever:

how many trophies I have seized in the moments of cease-fire.

So tell me: is that a white flag waving from the next bed?

Tom's taxi turns into the alley next to Burton's department store, down the street from East Station. "You sure this is where you wanna go, mister?"

"Yes, down at that sign."

"Oh, that place," the driver says. "I forgot that place was down here." Tom looks at that place and very nearly tells the driver he was mistaken, this wasn't the right turn after all, go on. But he pays the fare, gets out, and stands before the neon cocktail glass.

The taxi driver says, through his open window, "This neighborhood can get pretty rough at night. I mean, trying to get a cab. You want I should come back?"

"Yes, would you?"

"Couple hours?"

"Yes, that should be long enough."

"Okay, you be right here, mister. Twelve-thirty. I ain't coming in for you."

"Right here."

Tom is rakishly got up in a blazer and white flannel pants. In his living room he sat with just the ceiling light on, in his modern chair next to the wall of unopened cartons, explaining to himself again why it was impossible, how there could be nothing for him at the Garland. He was still telling himself that as he knotted the red-and-blue-striped tie and decided against a handkerchief in his breast pocket. All the while feeling in his belly the rush of excitement and apprehension, the feeling that his will was in abeyance and he was going. What I felt, the other night when I sat at dinner and knew — didn't decide, but knew — I was going to the Corral. What I am feeling this minute.

He watches the taxi go on down the alley, turn and disappear. He panics for a moment. He can't go in, anyone could be there: students — well, not students, it's July — but a colleague maybe, or me. Imagine running into me. He can't go in, and he can't just stand there for two hours, waiting for the cab. He'll have to walk all the way down to East Station, at almost eleven. Not as scary back then as it would be now, but still not a casual promenade.

The door opens, a youngish man comes out; Tom gets a glimpse inside before the door swings shut. It is only a little bar, music coming from the jukebox, a few people sitting around quietly. The man gets partway down the alley, then turns to look at Tom. Tom looks back. In his mind he runs through the questions from my phrase book. Do you come here often? Do you live by yourself? The man walks away.

Tom goes in, finds a seat at the bar, orders a whiskey straight up, and draws a cigarette from his platinum case. As he tamps it on the case, he looks up at the mirror over the bar, scans the room as best he can. No one he knows is there. No one he wants to know is there. We didn't get many Wheaties eaters in the Garland.

The bartender brings his whiskey and lights his cigarette. He says, "I don't guess I've seen you here before. You from out of town?"

"Yes," Tom says. "I — I had a layover at the station, and I thought I'd get out and find a drink."

"Funny you should wind up at this hole in the wall."

"Somebody told me about it," Tom says, catching on with his usual speed. He will not, after all, require my phrase-book.

The bartender nods. "Well, it's pretty quiet tonight."

"I guess so." Tom gets up the nerve to turn and look around. At one end of the bar a man of his own age is talking very softly, but with sweeping gestures, to a very thin young man with his coat draped over his shoulders, so. At the other end is Millie, the owner, with her black cocktail dress and her broad hat. In the corner is a little bandstand with a chair on which sits, ominously, an accordion. A party of four or five at the one large table has been to the movies. What, that year? *Singin' in the Rain.* Or, better, *The Bad and the Beautiful,* the ghastly camp movie with Lana Turner drinking and Kirk Douglas foaming at the mouth. Someone at the table does Lana, in her cups. Tom looks away.

Well, yes, there they are. He is nothing like them. Still, he feels a gray exuberance. The bartender's coded welcome, the desultory glances from the other customers. Everyone here knows what he is. Or rather, they know one fact about him — one fact that, outside, beyond that door, would overshadow every other, his titled chair and his books and his money and his politics. Here that fact is a given, almost trivial, in this room to call him queer would be as redundant as the word COCKTAILS under the neon glass outside.

He turns back to the bar and finishes his whiskey too quickly. He orders his next with water, he has almost two hours to kill. As he sips it, he finds himself relaxing. This is a bar, he is sitting having a drink, an anonymous fairy no one thinks anything about. He might feel differently if there were anyone who interested him: then he would have to worry about the game of glances and formulaic questions and — if, impossibly, he could get through all that — whether he could manage with a certified queer the things he has done with Jimmy. The commonplace things they invented fresh, like the first men in the world.

No such challenge faces him, and he settles into his queerness as into his lost, familiar club chair at Winthrop House. If this will never be his world, it is a nearer miss than the world outside. He could sit here for two hours or a thousand. He crosses his legs. Not ankle on knee like a soldier, but more like Lana Turner. At some point it occurs to him that, while he recognizes no one, somebody could recognize him. He is not so modest as to be unaware of his own small celebrity. He scans the room again, but no one seems to be looking at him. And besides, he thinks, stumbling on an ancient law of the bars: if they see him here, they're here too. Outlaws together.

Tom is on his third or fourth whiskey when someone new walks in. A soldier, say, one of those Fort Devens boys who used to come down on a weekend pass and stumble into the Garland, possibly by accident. The whole place stirs, the pilot fish circling.

The soldier sits a couple of stools to Tom's left, takes off his overseas cap and tucks it in his belt. Tom uncrosses his legs. The boy is, perhaps, a little coarser than the standard issue Wheaties eater: his chin blue with stubble, his nose broken in a couple of places. He looks over toward Tom, and Tom realizes that he must have been staring. Tom looks down at the bar hastily, but the boy stares back for a moment, possibly because Tom is dressed for yachting.

The soldier gets a bottle of beer and feels in his blouse pocket for a cigarette. He finds none, and Tom without thinking offers him one from the platinum case. He flashes Tom a grin like the outbreak of peace and says, "Thanks, buddy. I could have sworn I had some on me."

"Of course," Tom says. He riffles through my phrase book, but nothing seems apropos. Perhaps he can improvise.

The boy lowers the volume a little. The game must be over; the men in blazers are back. He is posing urgently now, the gown up past his belly, his legs stretched straight out in front of him. How must he feel, making himself an object for me? Maybe he has done this for girls, strutting, cocky in its literal sense. But for an old man? I am tempted to make him go further. Make him ask for it, out loud. That would almost be fair: this once, he needs it more than I do. Or at least his needs are more likely to be met. He has narrowed them to the possible, washing away all his identity except his cock. He is not an angel but a penis. But still saintly, redundant: he needs what he is going to get, he is going to get what he needs.

I sit up, my legs dangling over the edge of the bed. To rationalize this I pour a cup of water from the pitcher on my nightstand. I am shaking so I can scarcely raise it to my lips. I drain the tiny cup in a second. Now I must pour another or lie back again.

I could be crazy, just hopelessly deluded. If there were some way to ask — but there is nothing in my phrase book for this, if I say anything he'll have to feign outrage. I just have to get up and march across No Man's Land.

I lock my eyes on the television, as if the men in blazers were about to disclose the secret of life. But they are interrupted after a minute by a commercial for razor blades, one of evident erotic content. The model has a towel over his shoulder, suggesting he has nothing on below the edge of the screen, the camera lingers on his chest as he picks up the razor. All this for only a teasing second or two, before a cartoon of the razor mowing down the enemy stubble. Just an instant of sex, a wink between the art director and his friends. Now the model is dressed, he and a woman are on the way out the door, she caresses his face, which is smooth as a light bulb. The men in blazers reappear.

The boy offers, at last, a sort of interrogative grunt. I turn away from the TV, just a little. All I can see are his feet. They are inscrutable. What is the worst that could happen? He wouldn't hit me, pathetic ruin that I am. All he could do is turn away in contempt. And what's a little shame more or less in my life? I'll never see him again after tonight, how could it matter? I'll never see him again, I'll never have another chance.

I look him in the eye for the first time. He is smiling. Not smirking or leering, but just smiling at me in a peaceable, patient way. It is going to happen, he is looking forward to it, aren't we both lucky. I am in Eden: his cock salutes me guilelessly as he mutes the television. Like a flag, sweetflag, a shoot of calamus.

I get up and, wheeling my IV with me, cross the tiny distance between our beds. I stand above him. Reflexively he closes his eyes, though he is still smiling. I sit on the edge of the bed and touch a hand to his thigh. His eyes open for a second, then he shuts them even more tightly, like Janice in the scary part at the movie.

Michael could come in any time. How would he take it? He's seen worse, surely, in a downtown hospital — addicts shooting up, whatever. Would he interrupt? Would he wonder how it happened, with what wiles or wheedling an old fart like me managed to snare this virginal hunk? Would he admire me, an example to us all?

What with my IV and my bandages it takes some maneuvering, but I lower my head and kiss his stomach. I stay there a long time, one hand on each of his hips, my lips wandering over the hillocks and valleys of the miraculous belly that is like an utterance of his soul. He puts a hand on my head and pushes, ever so lightly, to urge me lower.

It occurs to me, this late in the game, that I don't know where his thing has been. Well, in Janice of course. But he just might have been, years ago, one of those pocked skinny boys who leaned against the fence at McLellan Square. It would be a terrible irony if, having made it through the other night, I were to start my new life by — I am old, something will get me soon enough. I can't stop now.

I am not aroused. I am blowing the most beautiful man I will ever get, the picture of him as I look up will surely have pride of place in my Rolodex, but for the moment I am merely intent upon my work. I am giving him a gift. His eyes are closed, he will let me in no farther than his nerve endings. I am a pure sensation to him. While I would ordinarily be hurrying along now, wanting to end it before my jaw starts to hurt, I make myself slow down. I try to be as careful and attentive as Michael, when he was salving my wounds. I wish I could cure everything for this boy, with one perfect blow job fix his thumb, send him home to his Janice. Give him a future, in this tired country.

He moans happily. He is holding on to my head with both hands; his bandaged thumb hovers like a moon at the edge of my vision. If he keeps his hands there I can be sure he isn't going to hit me. But of course he isn't: his soft moans are so nearly continuous now, they are practically a song.

"Aw shit," he says, and he comes, not in jerks, but almost in an even flow, hot at the back of my throat. When it is over, I hold him in my mouth. This is when I would reach for myself to finish, if there were anything to reach for. After a minute he pushes me away. Not roughly. It's just over. His cock slips from my mouth, flops half-stiff onto his pale angelic belly, a last drop or two of come spilling out. Already he is pulling down his gown and reaching for the volume control. In the blue light of the television I stagger back to my bed, dragging my IV after me.

$\mathcal{T}$WELVE

MORNING. Tom sits in his living room, in his underwear. The place is suffocating. He ought to get a fan, or would that be too much like making himself at home? Perhaps he can see, through the bedroom doorway, a boy on the bed. I'm not sure. Maybe he just sat in the Garland until twelve-thirty and then stepped out to meet his waiting cab, having watched with bitter admiration as someone half his age swooped down on the soldier. Even if he got the soldier home, there are still so many possibilities: the boy drunk and unable, the boy sobering up and unwilling, Tom himself incapable of going through with it. Or Tom going through with it, discovering that he could indeed do this thing, that he had an aptitude for the everyday pleasures of ordinary men.

I can't picture it, try as I will. I can place Tom in a requisite posture, and I can put the soldier on top, or underneath, as the case may be. I can make the bed shake. But Tom's eyes are open and his mouth a narrow meditative line. I cannot make Tom pant or whimper or moan. I cannot even make his eyes close. It's as hard as imagining my own mother and father fucking. Except in that case I have at least the circumstantial evidence: myself, an ample and weighty body of proof.

But I am reminded too of something one of Tom's students said to me, that fall after Tom was gone. He said that, when he dwelt in the most serious part of himself, there was Tom looking over his shoulder. Tom embodied the serious, with his grave drab face. There was not one instant's lapse in the elevated attention he gave the world. Tom coming, Tom beside himself, is impossible, impossible as his mind wandering. Could he have felt the same way? Perhaps he stumbled forward — driven by his late awakening body into the new world Jimmy had opened for him — but still regretted the first lapse in a lifetime of unbroken consciousness.

He sits in his living room and realizes that he hasn't read anything in weeks, he hasn't written anything since he met Jimmy, he will never teach again. Everything he sank his energy into for thirty chaste years is gone.

The seminar above all, that famous seminar of his, that he first had the audacity to call "American Studies." Nowadays that means dissertations on "Gilligan's Island." But that wasn't what Tom meant at all. He never meant to study America, the whole shebang, in all its imbecile complexity. For him there were, perhaps, three hundred Americans in as many years. They dwelt together in a tiny village, Cambridge/Concord/Mannahatta, Puritans and Transcendentalists exchanging good mornings, and Walt Whitman peeping in the windows. A little Peyton Place of the mind, small enough that Tom could know every byway and every scandal. I am not certain that Tom, in his life, ever uttered words like "Idaho" or "Utah." Not unless there was a strike there.

He had made a little country of his own. In those first few years during and after the second war, America was what we talked about in Tom's overheated seminar room. Every week someone came into the room with a chance notion or an off reading destined to become holy writ for the generation that came after. As Jefferson thought it would take a millenium to settle the continent, so we thought it would take forever just to cut a few paths through the forest primeval of nineteenth-century letters. Now it's used up, all of it, from Massachusetts Bay to Calaveras County. But while it lasted: even I was excited some days, though I hadn't quite done all the reading and was there only because this was the life Tom had laid out for me. Even I felt, with Tom and his real students, like a conquistador, staking my claim on the imagined America that lived in that little room where it was so hot my glasses fogged up.

There was the real exile, maybe, when they shut the door of that seminar room in his face, cast Tom out from the land that wasn't just his birthright but to which he had given birth and a name. Now he is sailing away from it to the Garland, the outlaw life to which I have consigned him. With nothing left to him but his awakening body, the country he invented taken from him, where else can he go? Trapped in the country the rest of us live in, the adequate life he had planned for the rest of humanity, in his moderne cell.

Still, he has all the nerves in the usual places. He is equipped for ecstasy, like every man. He can do it, without love or transcendence or any other baggage, he has a body. The body of a forty-year-old, as the coroner would say, he could do this for years yet. He has a body and money and time for everything he has denied himself. He could go to Paris and do it night after night, a willing boy for each recalcitrant Wheaties eater who ever turned him away.

From where he sits he can, yes, see his sleeping soldier, stretched out on the sheets, his winsome butt naked to the morning light. Tom feels his cock stirring, the little dumb happy thing, and he forgives it. Strokes it lightly through his trousers. Welcomes it home, the prodigal, after its years of exile. What times they shall have. And let Jimmy hang.

The boy is sprawled face down on a tangle of sheets, his back glistening with sweat, his gown gaping open.

In the new light his limbs look like limbs, his back like a back. He is just an oversized boy who may lose his thumb, all the mystery of last night gone. But that is what mornings are for: in the night you stitch together a little glory and drape it around whatever body comes to hand; in the morning the boy shrugs it off as though it never fit. It is a great wonder that, after a thousand mornings like this, I can still find myself, come evening, tormented and amazed by the sight of a boy.

I sit up and look at him. A ponderous object with its massive, taciturn back, dotted with sweat, and stout, belligerent arms. The pale butt framed by the open gown, the twin moons that I have staked my life on, that I have spent the years nearsightedly mistaking for the divine.

Is it for this that I have thrown away my life? Signed away my patrimony? Lived out my days at the margins of the bureaucratic map, because it was safe hiding there. Scurried for cover at the sound of "Irish Eyes," suffered the withering stare from Dave the Patty. Is it for this that I buried my face in the filthy rags in the shadow of the looms? That I knelt in the bushes at Lowell Park, lingered in the men's room at the library, loitered at the train station, squandered ten thousand nights at the Garland and the Corral and all the bars in between? Was it for this that I was beaten?

He shifts a little, and his mouth is closed now, in the semblance of a quiet smile. Under the shut lids, his eyes are darting. He is dreaming: the revolution never came, so he needs to dream, even he. Carefully, even in his sleep, he shelters the tormented thumb they may yet pluck from him. Leaving him a useless paw, no way to work, no more life ahead than I have. His eyes are still now. Whatever dream vexed him has passed. I will never know what it was, I shall never get inside him. He lies peaceably smiling, a closed circle, as impenetrable as a saint. It has been for this.

Tom, a few nights into his post-Garland life, is sitting at home in his apartment, trying to read. He hasn't read any-thing in months. Oh, newspapers, mail, ketchup bottles, but he hasn't opened one of his cartons and taken out a real book. Even now he is skimming some trash he picked up at the bookstore down the street. *The Caine Mutiny*, something like that. The room is stifling. The little table fan he has finally bought pivots ineffectually back and forth. The din-ner dishes, and those from the night before, sit reproach-fully in the kitchen. Yesterday he saw a bug, he must try to keep house better, but it's hard after a lifetime of people cleaning up for him. All he knows how to do is make his bed, the way he had to at St. Martin's.

He tries again to focus on the book, watered-down Mel-ville. But he knows he's headed for the Garland. He gets up and goes to wash the dishes. It wouldn't do to have them just sitting there, if he should have a guest. And maybe he ought to move the fan to the bedroom, just in case.

He fills the sink and stands before it, looking down at the soapy water, not reaching for any dishes. If he should have a guest. How quickly this has come to seem natural, after just one time, a week or so ago. Will he really do this the rest of his life, charge out of this apartment or out of a flat in Paris and go shopping for the boy *du jour*? His heart or his gut tells him so, he can't locate the feeling exactly. Nothing could keep him from the Garland. Still he stands in front of the dishes. Everything he sank his energy into for thirty years is gone, and he is left only a body housing a schoolboy's libido.

He picks up a plate and begins halfheartedly dabbing at it with a sour rag. He will need to take a shower. And what to wear? Perhaps, thinking back, the yachting ensemble wasn't quite the thing for the Garland. The white suit? Worse, he would shine in that gloomy saloon like a fallen star. Oh, what to wear?

A knock. He thinks it's me, coming again to quiz him on his motives and his plans. He could simply not answer the door. But he has no curtains, no private life being led here, so he's afraid I might have seen him from outside. He will have to let me in. And, as I did with him so many times, he will try to make conversation while plotting an escape to the Garland. He dries his hands and starts for the door. Thinking suddenly, maybe it isn't me, maybe it's his soldier, back on another pass. He said, didn't he, "I'll be seeing you," that was the last thing he said, maybe it was a promise for once and not a farewell.

He throws the dishtowel over his shoulder and opens the door. Jimmy has a tan so profound that his eyes stare out as if caged in the deep, even sheen of it. His hair is as white as Tom's. He is wearing a Hawaiian shirt and he carries an incongruously tiny suitcase, such as a boy might carry on his way to an overnight at his best friend's, a night of board games and mischief after lights out. A bag for one night, not for a new life in Paris. Jimmy puts it down, steps forward and hugs Tom, tightly, before Tom has fully comprehended that it is he and he is really there.

Tom lets himself be held for a moment, then wriggles free and steps back. The ur-Tom is trying to compose the perfect thing to say, some finely turned aphoristic kiss-off that will blow the boy to smithereens, obliterate him, leaving no trace but a few tatters of Hawaiian print and a silly overnight bag. As he is polishing his remarks, his eyes wander to the open V of Jimmy's shirt. A golden lace of hair bedewed with sweat glimmers on a chestnut field.

"You're very dark," Tom says.

"Yeah, well, the job at my father's place didn't work out. I mean, business is slow, there wasn't anything for me to do and he didn't think I should just be hanging around there, it looked bad. So I've been going to the country club most days. You know, sitting around the pool."

"I see. And now?"

"Now?"

"Here you are. Rather lightly encumbered, so I take it we are not bound for Europe."

"Oh, that. I kind of figured that wasn't in the cards."

"Why?" Tom says. Wondering, if he pretends not to know, whether the boy will confess.

"Well, no reason, I just thought we'd left it up in the air. I — I kind of thought you might have gone by now."

"Did you? You've come all this way with your little valise thinking not to find me?"

Jimmy pretends not to notice the queenly tone of that. "No, I mean, I checked. I called the English office and they said you were still in and out, they didn't think you'd gone anywhere. So I came."

"You could have called me. You see, I have put in a telephone. Which has been silent, these many weeks."

"I wanted to surprise you."

"Well, you have done. I haven't any whiskey."

"That's okay. I could go get some at Ollie's, maybe."

"No, actually, I was on my way out. Let us just sit and talk for a few minutes." He sits in one of his severe new chairs and motions Jimmy to the other.

"Out where?" Jimmy says, as he sits. His, it turns out, is

the statistically correct body the chair is designed to embrace.

Tom hesitates. "To the Garland. I find that I am frequenting the Garland."

"That . . . that place Reeve used to go?"

"Yes."

Tom watches Jimmy digest this astonishing information. He is pleased to be able to astonish, feels a little of the outlaw exuberance he felt the other night, sitting on that barstool.

"Is that safe?" Jimmy says. Disappointingly accepting without question that Tom is of the species that frequents the Garland. But then he has already said as much, on the wire. "I mean, who knows who you might run into? Somebody could find out."

This Tom cannot resist. "It appears that a good many people have already found out the most extraordinary things about me."

"Oh."

"I am, however, gratified to find you suddenly so solicitous of my privacy."

"Oh," Jimmy says again. He sits for a minute, with his grave face like a parody of Tom's. "You got a cigarette?" he says.

"Certainly." A pair of ohs, then, are all he means to offer by way of confession. Tom extends the platinum case, Jimmy takes a cigarette, Tom lights it as smoothly as the bartender at the Garland. "Why did you come here?" Tom says.

The boy has prepared for this question. "I wanted to talk to you one more time, about what's happening. How you've got to go along, you can't keep protecting —"

"So you have told me, any number of times."

"But now you know you have to," Jimmy says. "That was the point."

"The point?"

"You weren't listening to me, you never listened. That's why I . . . you've got to just get it over with. And then beat it if you want to and start over someplace. You don't owe those people anything, your loyalty or anything else. I'd have done anything to make you see that."

"At the very least providing a spectacular example of disloyalty for me to emulate."

Jimmy doesn't respond to this. And it occurs to Tom that he doesn't want the boy to answer. As though, if they could leave it unspoken, it might never have happened.

"So that's why I came," Jimmy says. "I mean, I called, and I just couldn't believe it when they said you were still here. I thought you'd be gone. I thought you would have finished it and be gone by now."

Tom takes a cigarette for himself and settles back. "I am still here. And you are terrified that I am persisting in my obstinacy, and that consequently your name will be joined with mine in a scandal that is entirely of your making. That is what brought you here."

"Why would that happen? Why would you stay here and make that happen?"

"Make it? Make it happen? Oh, I had forgotten, I make everything happen. So I have heard, in your own voice."

"You've heard it?"

"Of course I've heard it."

"He played it. That shit, he said he wasn't going to —"

"Did he? Van Leunen said that?"

"He promised. He wasn't even going to play it to you, he was just going to tell you he had it and —"

"Then you might as well have left the spool blank, mightn't you?" Tom says. He wants to hear more, he would be satisfied now to learn that the boy was just phenomenally stupid.

But all Jimmy says is, "I didn't think he'd play it."

"Nevertheless, he did. And unless I cooperate he will play it for the world. What did you think? If I were to go to the farthest edges of the map, he would play it."

"Then you're going to have to. Cooperate."

"Why should I? I shall go, far away, as you are so eager to have me do. Why should I care what he plays or doesn't play?"

It takes a minute before Jimmy understands. Tom is gratified at last to see Jimmy's eyes open wide, brilliant against their field of even brown, as he grasps it, feels the wire tightening around him. Or perhaps not, after all, as gratified as he might have expected to be, only in the abstract way one is pleased when a syllogism reaches its conclusion.

"I was trying to help you," Jimmy says. In a high voice: not desperate but almost indignant, as if it were obvious. He was trying to help, and here Tom is leaving him to hang.

"Do you believe that?" Tom says. "How in the world can you have supposed it would help?"

Jimmy doesn't answer. Instead he says, "It's awfully hot in here."

"I put the fan in the bedroom. I could fetch it."

"No, let's go in there."

"To the bedroom? Whatever for, old times' sake?"

"I don't know, I'm just hot, all of a sudden."

"Go in, then. I'll bring you some water. But I keep forgetting to fill the ice trays."

In the kitchen, Tom turns the faucet on and dumbly watches the water stream out into the sink. He leans with both hands on the edge of the sink and watches the water. Trying to help, what a bizarre and pathetic excuse. But what else is left, what other explanation that doesn't turn love into just a momentary cease-fire? And Tom is, undeniably, still in love: the new life he has so bravely embarked on curves back to this. If only he hadn't laid eyes on him again, if I had been the one at the door. But it was Jimmy, it is Jimmy now lying on his bed, with his dark skin and his golden hair. Blocking Tom's way to Paris, yet seeming once again to hold in his hands the tickets to that other city. They are invalid, long since expired; some part of Tom must know this. But he cannot imagine any other destination.

While I lay in the ambulance — a long time, they were getting permission to bring me here out of rotation because they were afraid about my eye and this is the place for eyes — the police came back. I had already told them my humiliating story, I didn't know what they could want, why they didn't just let me go. "Can he sit up?" one of the policemen said.

"Why?" the driver said.

"We got this guy we want him to look at."

"I don't know. I guess." Then, to me: "Can you sit up?"

I said, "You want me to look at somebody?"

"Yeah, listen," the cop said. "We think we may have the guy. You think you could try to identify him?"

"I don't know."

"Let's try." The cop called out, "Jerry, come on." His partner appeared in the doorway of the ambulance. Beside him, arms evidently bound, was a boy.

I was half-raised on my elbows, no glasses and one eye swollen shut. The boy was silhouetted against the swirling lights of the police car behind him. I could make out that he wore a T-shirt and blue jeans, like my assailant, and his hair might have been right. Close on the sides, fuller at the top, as in the magazines. His face I could not make out at all, but it might have been he. "I'm not sure," I said.

"There wasn't nothing on him," Jerry said. "Did the guy get anything, do you know?"

"I don't know."

The boy stood still, hands fastened behind him like Saint Sebastian, awaiting my judgment. Perhaps in part I was already thinking — as later, in the ER, when they asked if I'd come look at their mug shots — about the newspapers, if there should be a trial. But I also felt sorry for him. This pinioned boy who, if it was even he, had kissed me for a second and walked away with nothing. I didn't forgive him, I don't. If I were strong enough, if anything could ever make me strong enough I would hunt him down myself. And what? Shake my fist at him, call him names? Utter the aphoristic kiss-off that would blow him to smithereens? I can't picture hitting him, I've never hit anyone, not since I was a little child.

Even if I could, that would be a different thing from watching him in the hands of the cops, who probably raided the Piazza twenty years ago and only now, after reeducation, were supposed to be on my side. No doubt they would joke later over coffee about how I had it coming. This was — it sounds silly, something out of a Western — between me and the boy. Nothing they could do in their courts or their prisons would give back to me what I lost when he looked down at me, so thoughtfully, and raised his hand. The picture of him in prison, stretched out under some enormous hirsute convict, his little ass bleeding, could not give it back to me. Maybe if we had our own courts, for all we do to one another. But this didn't belong to them.

It was cold, the cold that sneaks up on you on an early fall night. I was shaking, maybe starting into shock, and the boy was too, shivering in his white T-shirt. Roughly they pushed him closer to me, hoping I would see him better. I couldn't: I felt it had to be he, but I wasn't positive.

I said, positively, "No. No, this isn't the guy."

As he took the handcuffs off, the cop said, "Sorry. You

matched the description, we had to check it out. Sorry. We appreciate your cooperation." The boy smiled, whether at the absurdity of that last remark or from simple relief. Even I could see he was smiling, his straight teeth gleaming. Then he disappeared from view.

Tom pulls himself together and fills a glass with water. He goes into the bedroom.

Jimmy is lying on Tom's bed with all his clothes on. The electric fan makes his Hawaiian shirt billow a little. "Take your shoes off, please," Tom says. The boy sits up to do so; when he is done, Tom hands him the glass and sits untying his own shoes. Then they lie side by side, fully clothed, not touching, on Tom's perfectly made bed. Above them the ceiling light shines hard in its glass sunburst.

Tom lectures. "Your mistake, my dear, has been to imagine that there is some distinction between the use they will make of you and the used-up you they will cast behind them. You have tried to think it out, haven't you? Or they thought it out for you. They will treat you as the innocent victim of my seduction: they cannot conceive of mutuality. So I must have started it all."

"Well, you kind of did . . ."

"If you like."

"Anyhow, that's what they'd say, yeah."

"So you will get off with nothing. They'll let you stay, you'll finish up."

"I don't know that I can."

"I'm sure you can. You're a very strong boy." This said with no irony at all, as Tom lies not looking at him. "I shall expect to see you here in the fall."

"You mustn't be here by fall. Look, like you say, they'll let me off. You're the one who's got to do what has to be done, and then get out of here."

"I'm not going anywhere," Tom says. This is true, suddenly, not a resolution but a discovery. "I have been exiled again and again in my life, and I have no intention of going anywhere. This is the final stop. So don't flatter yourself that you've just bought me passage to Paris. We must finish this act, you and I."

"That's crazy. You could live fine somewhere."

"Would you join me?"

Jimmy smiles involuntarily. The idea that he would go with this old man and put an ocean between himself and the future he still hopes for.

Tom doesn't see the smile. He is looking straight up at the ceiling light, listening to the silence that answers his question. "At any rate," he says. "Your mistake, I was speaking of your mistake. You think that your official exoneration will make an end of it. But no one will believe it. Of course they must cast you as the innocent prey, but not even van Leunen will believe his own story. Everyone will always know that you're a . . ."

"I'm not sure I even am. I don't think I am."

"Maybe not. I hope not, who would want to be? But it's what everyone will suppose, and it will follow you always."

"Shit, I've known guys who screwed around a little in school. They live it down pretty soon."

"You're not a schoolboy screwing around. You're a near grown-up who went to bed with an old man, probably for some gain or other. In the eyes of the world, you might as well be Reeve."

The boy is quiet a long time. Finally he says, "I really fucked up, didn't I?"

"I'm afraid so."

Jimmy swallows. "Then maybe I'd better go with you after all."

Tom sees Paris for a second, the two of them together.

"And give up Pittsburgh? Start a new life, different from anything you ever got ready for?"

"I could handle it. I mean, if you and me stuck together —"

"And if I tired of you? There you'd be, a million miles from here and all alone, everything you ever meant to be left behind you, in a country where you'll never even learn the language." And penniless, too, without Tom; he doesn't need to mention that.

"Would you get tired of me?"

"I think I should." Yes, yes he would. It tires him just to think of their life together. Stuck together in that city for lovers. Tom trapped in the memory of the lodge, the boy long since ceasing to remember but shackled to him in desperation. "In any case you had better not count on me."

"Jesus." The boy starts — how could Tom not have expected this? — sniffling. This is what Tom wanted, isn't it, to let him hang from the wire? Not wanted, but was prepared to let happen, while Tom went on into his new life.

Tom is still looking up at the ceiling. "I told you this was hard, too hard for you."

The boy raises himself up on one elbow and says, "Why can't you just go along? With them, what they want, what would it cost you?" His voice high as a child's, nearly sobbing. "Maybe it wouldn't have to be public, maybe you could just give them what they want in private somehow."

"Their very suggestion. How uncannily like them you sound."

"I don't know what I'm going to do," the child bawls. The bed is shaking.

Tom is appalled. He sits up in bed and looks down at the vessel into which he has poured his soul. The slender body heaving, the eyes red against their field of flat, even sunbrown, glistening now with selfish tears. Disgusting, how can it be that he still feels anything for this chaotic heap of bone and flesh? Has it been for this?

The boy reaches an arm around him, heavy on his chest like the arm of the sleeping trick you wish you'd never brought home. Now the boy buries his damp face in the expanse of Tom's starched shirtfront. "I'm sorry," he whispers. "I'm so sorry I did this to you."

When I was little and my parents were angry with me I learned early to watch for the moment when they, for whatever reason, were in separate rooms. I would wait for that instant and go to my mother and whisper, "I'm sorry." Whether I was or not, whether I even knew what I was supposed to have done or failed to do, it almost always worked. Not if she was angry with me and we were all by ourselves, then she was never fooled. But if he was there, in the next room, and I made her pick sides; she always sided with me. Tiny as I was, I had discovered this stratagem.

She would go to wherever he was, I would hear murmuring, then he would come and look down at me contemptuously, look down from his great height and announce whatever moderate punishment she had negotiated, confinement to my room or forgone supper. Punishments not at all unlike being in hospital. So I was never spanked, not by him. But if he had lived, if he hadn't died when I was so very young, that would always have been between us, the way I ran to her and, with my little unfelt word, vanquished him.

Can that tiny word be enough? And does he mean it: is Jimmy sorry, will he ever be? Or is it only a stratagem, the first and best one spoiled children learn, and brought out now to save himself a spanking? Let it be real, let him feel some honest contrition, one great I'm sorry for everything we have done to one another. Let me add my own, because it wasn't me there that night, lying beside Tom under the glass sunburst.

It doesn't matter. If Tom believes it or not, it doesn't matter, he must pick sides. He is running his fingers through Jimmy's hair and feeling the damp face buried in his chest. "Don't worry," Tom hears himself saying. He closes his eyes to shut out the ceiling light and the sight of Jimmy. "I shall take care of it."

"You'll . . . you mean you're going to tell them?"

Tom is so absorbed in what he has just said that he scarcely hears this ugly question. He opens his eyes, looks down at Jimmy, and says again, slowly and with wonder, as if reading it somewhere on that golden head: "I shall take care of it."

He lets the boy lie heavily on his chest for a minute or two, then disengages himself and goes out into the living room. After a while the boy follows, in his stocking feet.

"I think you had better not stay the night," Tom says.

"I was going to."

"I think not. You can stay at the University House." He pulls out his wallet. "I can't remember how much their rooms are."

"That's okay, I've got money."

"All right." Tom puts the wallet down on his desk.

"Are you still going out?" Jimmy says. "To that place?"

"I may," Tom says, though of course he isn't. "You had better get your shoes on."

Jimmy goes into the bedroom and puts his shoes on while Tom stands in the hot living room, foolishly staring at Jimmy's tiny valise.

When he comes back out, Jimmy says, "Am I going to see you back here, in the fall?" The shoes are white bucks; Tom looks at them.

"I shouldn't think so. You were right, it's best to leave."

"Well, that's good. I mean, I'm going to miss you, but —"

Perhaps it occurs to him to ask exactly how Tom is going to

take care of everything on his way out, but instead he says, "Where are you going to go?"

"Paris," Tom says, with a hint of exasperation. "I said I was going to Paris. I have the tickets."

Jimmy ignores the plural. "That's good." He steps closer, but keeps his arms at his sides. He will make no motion, Tom will have to decide how they're going to say good-bye.

Tom says, "Wait, I want to give you something." Jimmy thinks he means something in particular, but instead Tom starts rooting around in his wall of cardboard cartons. Jimmy is afraid he's going to get some book or other, something awful he'll never read, a lifetime homework assignment he'll never hand in. But after a minute Tom is just standing in the middle of the room, looking lost, nothing left to give away.

He goes into the bedroom and comes back with the cigarette case. He opens it and takes all the cigarettes out, lays them on the desk, all but one or two. "I'm almost out," he says. "I left you a couple."

"I can't take this," Jimmy says, and in fact he doesn't want it, imagine walking around Pittsburgh with a platinum cigarette case.

"I insist," Tom says. "If you should ever come to grief, you will always have something to hock."

Jimmy smiles. "Okay." Thinking he will never come to grief.

Now they are very close. Jimmy raises his arms a tiny bit and tenses his shoulders. He expects to be hugged. Tom hesitates. Not because he doesn't want to, but because he knows he will hold on too long and the boy will shake himself loose: worse than not touching at all. Jimmy waits, uncomprehending, and finally picks up his valise. With his right hand; in the other he holds the cigarette case. So they can't even shake hands as Tom opens the door for him and he goes out into the hall. In the hallway he turns and says, "I'll be seeing you." But Tom is already closing the door.

My doctor appears. Saturday morning at six-thirty, what hours they must keep. I almost don't begrudge them the money. "Hey, you're awake," he says.

"Just now."

"I want to take a look at that eye. Then if everything checks out we'll shoot you on out of here."

"Great."

"You want the tape off fast or slow?" he says. This is perhaps a joke.

"Slow. I want to get every second I'm paying for."

Fee jokes are not to his taste. He mumbles, "This is free. Postsurgical care is bundled with the . . ." Then, louder, "Okay, you ready?" The boy in the next bed stirs. "Keep your eye closed now."

As if to make sure I get my money's worth he takes his time. And about half my eyebrow.

"That's great, you look terrific," he says. Those words were last addressed to me some time in the Nixon administration. But he is only admiring his own handiwork. "Now open your eye very slowly."

I am binocular. That is, at least light seems to be coming in the right eye. I reach for my glasses, but of course we've broken off the right hand side. "You see," he says. "I told you you shouldn't have done that. It'd probably be a little foggy for a while even if you had a lens. I mean, just a couple hours. Nothing really happened to it. But I want you to go see an ophthalmologist as soon as you're getting around, just to be sure."

He picks up my chart as I wave my hand in front of my eye. Yes, that's a hand, my consort. I open and close my eyes a few times. "The lid feels thick," I say.

"Yeah, a couple of little nerves were cut. What have you got, a little numbness?"

"Uh-huh. Up into my forehead."

"Well, that might go away. Or you'll get used to it, just stop noticing."

Sometimes I think I've spent my whole life hearing people tell me I'd get used to things, ever since the first Canuck whispered in my ear that it would stop hurting in a minute. They are always right.

"Anyway, you look fine. You're going to have a tiny little scar no one will even notice. Now, aren't you glad I talked you into going ahead?"

Ordinarily I wouldn't give him the satisfaction. I grant him a slight nod.

"Anyway, you should be able to go home this morning. Dr. Harris will be in to take out that heparin shunt, clean you up a little, stuff like that. I can't remember, are you married?"

"No."

"Oh, no, no you aren't," he says, looking down at my chart as if I required corroboration. I still cannot shake the fear that everything about my episode is on the chart, ready to be sent on to Blue Cross and thence to Mr. Pollen. "Do you have anyone to take care of you?"

"Um." If I say no they may keep me here. I cannot possibly spend another night with my roommate, the cease fire could end any minute. "Yes, I'm going to stay with a friend for a few days."

"That guy who was in here?"

"Uh-huh." This should be a splendid surprise for Howard.

"Good. You need to take it easy for at least a week. I'd keep you here, but admitting's already putting the heat on me. Your insurance company called yesterday, they've decided you're better. We need to put in ejector beds."

"Oh, I'm ready."

"I don't think so. Anyway, we'll call you in a couple of weeks for a follow-up. I want to see you again."

"Me, too." This joke is also not to his taste; I cover. "I need all kinds of other plastic surgery."

"I don't do that kind of stuff," he says. "I'm a reconstructive surgeon."

"Too bad. You could retire, just on me."

"Oh, guys my age, I don't think they'll ever let us retire. You know, the boomers, who the hell's going to support us in 2020?"

"Don't look at me. I've only got a couple months to go."

"Yeah? Till retirement? What are you going to do?"

"I don't know. I was just going to keep on working for a while. But after this, I don't know."

"Now, you should be able to get back to work. A week or so, like I say. Oh, that's right, do you need me to sign anything? For your job?"

"No, I'm on vacation."

"You need to change travel agents."

"Anyway, I don't mean I can't work. I'm wondering if I still want to."

He sighs and sits down; now he has to be the patient healer again. This is off the meter, postsurgical care. And for all I know he's been up the whole night. He says, in the special soft voice he must save for these sessions, "You know, I thought when I saw you down in the ER that you weren't reacting enough. Like it hadn't really happened. Now it's just the opposite; you're, I don't know, compensating or something. You'll feel a lot better in a few days, get right back into things."

"I don't want to get right back into things. I want to do all new things."

"Oh, oh, that's what you meant. Well, that's good, too," he says. He gets up at once, relieved that he doesn't have to deal with nonplastic problems. "Keep your head elevated."

"Yes, sir."

He goes out, leaving me with my new life ahead of me. I glance over at the boy. He has contrived somehow to wrap himself entirely in the sheets. Only his feet stick out, callused and ungainly, attached to an anonymous heap of linen that rises and falls with the uncertain rhythm of his snores. I want to do all new things, I said. And I have started out with the unprecedented activity of falling for an empty-headed straight boy and trying to tell myself that he's somehow different. Educable. Well, no slower a learner than I. Some lessons I can't get after sixty years. My new life.

Jimmy has gone, Tom is alone with the life that is left to him. There are four, no, five cigarettes on the table, strewn in a pattern some augur might have interpreted. Had he already made up his mind, when he spoke the promise there was only one way of carrying out, only one way to take care of it? Was it when he handed over the cigarette case that had nestled near his breast all his grown-up years, the next to last thing he had left to give away? Or is it just now, looking at the austerely finite pile of cigarettes and thinking, I shall smoke these, and then I shall be done?

He goes to the wall of cardboard cartons and drags down the one marked MEMORABILIA. He fishes through the junk he has carted from home to home, through each station on the way to this terminus: the picture of himself in the pony cart, the key from his senior society, the diplomas, the card marked P.P.C. and the engraved invitation to Mr. Slater's wedding, indefinitely postponed. He doesn't look at any of it, just feels blindly until he comes upon his AEF officer's revolver. And further, rattling around near the bottom, a couple of rounds of ammunition. Thirty years old or more, are they still good? He only needs the one.

Tom sits at his desk, pulls out his shirttail, and starts to clean the gun. After a while just absentmindedly buffing it, over and over, in a single spot, making it shine as if there were to be inspection tomorrow. He is drowsy, and he lights one of the cigarettes automatically, trying to stay awake. How can he sleep — as if rehearsing — with the little time he has? But he has all the time in the world, time is his now, the tireless rounding of the second hand on his new electric clock will go on as long as he wants, no longer. So he snuffs out the cigarette — four left — and goes into the bedroom. Once again he lies down fully clothed, no matter the heat; it will be for only a minute. Where Jimmy was, there lingers a little scent of his hair oil. Tom buries his face there and sleeps untroubled through the night.

When he opens his eyes it is like any other morning. It takes an instant to orient himself. Yes, he is on Marsden Steet, that must be the garbage truck he hears in the alley, a cuff link is digging into his cheek, he has gone to bed dressed for some reason. Right, this is the day. Somewhere in his mind a little resistance flickers, a tiny provincial uprising that burns itself out before the news has even reached the capital. Now he really ought to just get up and do it, why live through any more of this morning like any other morning? But *ought* has lost its power, he cannot even be bothered to move his arm; he feels the cuff link graving a faint S into his face.

Hunger moves him at last. He gets up quickly, the way at St. Martin's he and the other boys, having dozed through the first bell, would leap up at the second and magically dress in time for assembly. That's how Tom got up every day of his life, including the last one. He heads automatically for the bathroom but, in a decisive break with routine, does not shower. He runs his two brushes through his clipped hair and looks at his face for the last time without especial interest, certainly without valediction. He tucks in his shirttail, grimy from cleaning the gun.

Appetite has got him up, but why should he bother to eat? The plaint of his stomach will be stilled soon enough. He goes to the living room for one of his little hoard of cigarettes. Three left after this one. He has to finish them. This is a religious conviction, formed as quickly and as bindingly as his devotion to the Party or his compulsion to start up stairs with his left foot. So he will be around a couple more hours, anyway, and he will have to eat.

There is nothing in the icebox. He reconsiders. He had not meant to go out into the world again, and now he faces an expedition to the corner grocery. Perhaps it would be better to get on with things. But the hunger, the innocent demand of a body that knows nothing of his plans for it and is surprised at his indifference, pushes him out the door. Without a necktie, in the shirt and trousers he has slept and sweated in, he drifts down Marsden Street like a sleep-walker.

His friend — what's-his-name from physical geography, the one he used to go fishing with — sees him from across the street and steps over to say good morning. Tom answers with difficulty, as if struggling to remember the formulas for greeting in a foreign language.

The geographer plunges on. "Brown says the trout are good at Hamilton Lake." Tom just nods. "We ought to get out there, maybe in a week or two, if you're not going anywhere. Somebody said you might be going to France."

That exit, the route he must have considered a hundred times in his last weeks, beckons one last time. He conjures up the picture of himself, the ruined voluptuary at a sidewalk table with nothing ahead but the next brandy and the next boy, and turns away from it again. "No, not France," he says.

"Well, then we'll go up," the geographer says, without enthusiasm. He wants to show that he isn't turning away from Tom like everyone else. But with all he's heard and can no longer brush away, he isn't really eager to share the lodge again.

"I'm rather busy," Tom says.

The geographer is miffed. Even if he hasn't any intention to go play in the woods with the old pansy, the very suggestion is a fine act. Tom should be grateful. "Okay," he says. "Maybe in the fall. I'll call you." He starts away. "Oh, you've moved, haven't you? Do I have your new number?"

"I don't know," Tom says. He turns to look longingly toward the grocery store.

"Well, what is it?" The geographer searches for a pen.

"I don't know," Tom says, and he starts down the street.

The geographer mutters, "Son of a bitch," half hoping Tom can hear him.

In the grocery Tom picks up a half dozen eggs, a half loaf of bread in a cellophane wrapper, a half pound of packaged bacon, and one potato. At the register he grabs a newspaper and, not thinking, just from habit, asks for a fresh pack of Chesterfields. He feels for his wallet, but it isn't there. He remembers now, how he left it on the desk after Jimmy wouldn't take any money.

"I'm sorry," he says. "I've forgotten my wallet."

The woman behind the counter looks him over. An old man who has slept in his clothes and doesn't have $1.39.

"I'm sorry," he says again. He must look desolate, thinking of the terrible journey back to his flat and out once more.

She makes up her mind about him. "That's all right, Professor," she says. Not a daring guess in that neighborhood. "You can come back with the money."

"Oh, I can't," he says.

"It's all right."

"Well, just for a few minutes. I'll be right back."

"That's okay," she says. "Next time you come in."

He scurries out the door with his bag, like a thief. He is almost home when he realizes that he has bought the Chesterfields. He looks into the bag and there is the pack, twenty cigarettes sealed with their blue tax stamp. Twenty cigarettes are, at Tom's usual rate, almost a day's worth. With the three at home they might carry him through to tomorrow morning. They are like a pointer to the future, a deed to a little parcel of tomorrow. Then he could buy another pack, and so stretch out his life, a smoke at a time in a chain with no foreseeable end. He takes the pack from the bag and, decisively, sets it on top of a police call box. The blue tax stamp, De Witt Clinton, facing out so that some passing bum will be able to see it's a full pack.

At home, the crackle of the potato in the frying pan brings back to him the morning when he stood at the wood stove making breakfast for Jimmy. That morning when, having tasted at last and — as far as he could see — just for once the quotidian ecstasies of ordinary men, he saw ahead of him only life as it had always been and sadly stirred his potatoes. Until the pale figure summoned him back to bed and to the start of his short life. That breakfast they had never eaten. Now he will have it, close the brackets he has dwelt in since that weekend at the lodge.

He starts the bacon, then opens the carton of eggs and

tries to decide how he wants them. There they are, the last eggs in the world. He can't have them fried today and scrambled tomorrow, he can have them only the one absolutely right and final way. He stands paralyzed before this insuperable problem. How did God ever decide how many laws of thermodynamics there ought to be? More easily than Tom picking a way to have the very last eggs.

He will have to flip a coin, yes. He feels in his pockets. There is a lot of change, he could have paid for his groceries, he hadn't thought about it when he missed his wallet. Why, there is even a fifty-cent piece. He takes it out, looks at the date as if expecting it to be an important one. It is a 1934. He can't think of anything that happened in 1934. Was it Matthew that year, or Harry, the one who played lacrosse? And was that the year of the Popular Front, or was it '35?

No, of course he can't flip a coin. It feels heavy in his hand, as if something in him would let more ride on the toss than how he will have his eggs. He thrusts it back in his pocket. The potatoes are starting to burn. He cracks the eggs into the pan with them, one, two, three, four, leaving two to spoil. Five and six, then. He will crumble the bacon in, too, a new dish, something he's never tried.

He puts the bread in the aerodynamic toaster and gives a final stir to his eggs. As he sits down at the little linoleum-topped table, facing enough breakfast for three men, he murmurs grace as he has always done. He reads the paper as he eats — talk of drafting Governor Stevenson, or possibly Pogo, more dreary news from Korea and, at home, news of the terror, other Toms facing other van Leunens. The revolution has never seemed farther away.

He takes his coffee to the living room and sits down at the desk. He lights a cigarette, two left now, and thinks about writing a note. To whom?

To Jimmy:

I am doing this to vouchsafe you a future, so I will in passing eclipse it by leaving you this note.

To van Leunen:

I am doing this because you have won, so I will squander my last minutes composing an appeal to the conscience you do not possess.

To the world at large:

I am doing this to keep a secret, so I thought I would reveal it here.

The last is the most absurd. Maybe some suicides are trying to say something; that, at least, is what people always claim, especially about the ones who fail. But Tom is getting ready to inaugurate a silence, the long silence where I've dwelt for forty years without hearing his high, insinuating voice, the silence of the unplayable useless spool of wire.

No note, then, not even to me, just the indecipherable message of his will. He takes it out near the last. He places it neatly in front of him on the desk, just where the policemen would find it, lights absentmindedly the penultimate cigarette, and reads it over. The scholarship named after his father. The legacy to Martha, now Fuzzy Walgreen's housekeeper. The trust left to me, making me for a little while the absentee lord of Winslow. All this done years before, in '47 or '48. Perhaps now he actually does think about a codicil. A last minute bequest to Jimmy, so he can live his guilty future in style. A disinheritance of me, as punishment for not having been to see him in these final weeks, for not having been the one who rang his doorbell last night. As if my intervention, that night or ever, could have stopped him.

What different legacies for Jimmy and me. I got the trust fund, a sort of endowed chair from which to profess the outlaw life Tom never got to. Jimmy got his future, the wire rendered useless, impotent — in those days people weren't quite so hungry for gossip about dead men. My inheritance I had to give back. Jimmy still has his, if he lives, Tom's awful gift. No one would think of taking it from him. Oh, and the cigarette case, he got the cigarette case.

There is only one cigarette left. Tom could wait, if he is timing his life by cigarettes in this silly, superstitious way he really ought to just sit and wait till his body asks for the nicotine, asks in its perfect innocence, not knowing the price of it. But what would he do with those minutes? Finish the goddamn *Caine Mutiny*? Reminisce? Masturbate? Just sit and think? He doesn't want to think ever again. His life has been one endless drone of thought, broken only for a few minutes — seconds, really — by Jimmy on perhaps a dozen nights and once by a soldier, there, on the bed he can see from where he sits.

He lights the cigarette and reaches for his service revolver, brilliant in the morning sun from his curtainless windows. As he loads it he keeps the cigarette in his mouth, until the smoke burns his eyes and, irritated, he snuffs the thing out. As he raises the pistol and opens his mouth like a cocksucker, he thinks of the clerk behind the counter at the grocery store, trustingly waiting for her $1.39. Waiting behind the counter like Pauline at the altar. He feels a wave of remorse and self-hatred, all the shame of his life fixed in the image of that one forsaken woman. He despises himself utterly as his lips close over the muzzle and he pulls the trigger.

* * *

The phone rings. I get it as fast as I can, afraid of waking the boy. "Your wake-up call, madam," Howard says.

"Oh, I'm up. They're going to let me out as soon as the doctor gets here."

"Why are you whispering? Oh, your little roommate. Are you going to feel up to apartment shopping?"

"I don't know. I certainly feel up to lunch."

"I bet."

"In fact, you'd better keep your distance or I'll eat you."

"Such a flirt. I wish I'd had time to get someone into your place. I hate for you to just walk back into that mess."

"Yeah, well, we need to talk about that."

"What for?"

"Well, I . . . I was afraid they'd keep me here, so I said I was going home with you."

"With me? I don't even have a sleep sofa."

"I don't have to stay with you, I'll be okay. It was just so they wouldn't keep me in any longer. I'll go home, send out for Chinese and stuff. I'll get along fine."

"I won't hear of it. You're coming straight home with me."

"How can I?"

"Oh, it'll be fun. I have a queen bed, we can share that. It'll be like a week-long pajama party."

"Remember, I'm not supposed to tire myself out."

"I didn't mean anything funny, we tried that when dinosaurs ruled the earth. Anyway, I'll be down in a couple of hours, we'll talk about it."

"That long? They'll probably charge me for another day. Can't you come right away?"

"Not lately. I'm not even dressed, I'll be as quick as I can."

"Yes, do."

I look over at the boy. He is no longer shrouded. He

is on his back, the sheets in a knot beneath him, the coverlet down near his feet. Snoring cheerfully and offering a display that is likely to startle the woman who brings breakfast, if she ever gets here. Three days, and I am already reduced to counting the minutes until I get my puddle of scrambled eggs. I could just leave him as he is; I have seen worse sights in the morning, and so I suppose has the breakfast lady. But I get up and go to his side, wheeling my IV with me.

As I pull the cover up over his naked belly, his eyes open. He, for his part, may not have seen many worse sights before breakfast. "I'm sorry," I say. "You were . . . I was just afraid somebody might . . ." I turn away, hurrying back to my bed, and get tangled up in my tubes. I fall to my knees, my back to him, trying to disembroil myself without pulling the damn tubes out. He must be thinking I hobbled over to molest him while he slept. "I'm sorry," I say again.

He jumps up, I can feel him hovering over my shoulder like a thunderhead. I raise one hand to fend him off: this time I will at least raise a hand. But he wraps his own great arm under mine and starts to lift me. Now he has both his arms around me and is raising me to my feet, effortlessly as the angel in the Civil War monument held up the dead collegian. As he helps me back to my bed, holding on to me with one arm and steering the IV with the other, I feel his hip against my hip. A thousand times more intimate than anything that happened last night. He sets me down on the bed, delicately, as if I weighed nothing. Then he pulls the cover over me as I have just done for him. He stands for a second and I look up at him, my chevalier. I say thank you and consider resuming my explanation, how he was uncovered and I only meant to — but I just look up at his broad, mute face.

The boy goes back to his bed and turns on the television,

hunting for cartoons. He pauses only for a second at the news — something about East Germany is just finishing, Hungary is starting, everything breaking up — and settles on an exercise program featuring a trio of Amazons. It is not clear to me what exactly they are exercising, but it is evidently clear to the boy. He watches with the light smile of a connoisseur.

I pick up Tom's book. A week cooped up with Howard, maybe I will actually read it. From the beginning:

In the year 1855, while the young men of Europe were butchering one another beneath the walls of Sebastopol and the settlers of Kansas were staging their bloody rehearsal of the impending conflagration, two reporters for the New York dailies — one in Brooklyn, the other a correspondent in London — were issuing the first dispatches from a new city, one to which the rest of the world is only now finding its way. Together Walt Whitman and Karl Marx . . .

I close the book. I will never finish it, any more than I'll get through *Daniel Deronda*. "I'm saving them for my old age," I used to joke, Eliot and Proust and Slater. As if giving myself lifetime homework assignments, as if old age were the time for completing every incomplete course. When really all I want to do is loaf around with Howard all week and rent old Barbara Stanwyck movies. Or maybe fast-forward through his countless videos of acrobatic youth. Anything but drown in this travel guide to a fanciful place the world never did find its way to.

The boy jumps up and heads to the bathroom. He leaves the door open; under the relentless chanting of the exercise maidens, I hear him piss in a steady stream, one more thing for me to envy, then the voracious flush of the toilet. He doesn't come out for a minute. From where I lie, I can just see the mirror over the sink, and a slice of his reflection in it. He is looking at himself. Pushing the matted hair off his forehead, then just gazing at his own wide, innocent face with neutral wonderment.

He has caught me staring. His eyes meet mine in the vortex of the mirror. I look away, then back; at last I hazard a wink. His usual look of bafflement marks his brow for an instant, then he smiles and shakes his head in amused reproach. He shuts the door, slowly, still smiling. I scarcely hear the click of the lock, the portal of the city closes so gently.